Called Home

Two Hearts Answer

Gloria Schumann

Savant Books
Honolulu, HI, USA
2010

Published in the USA by Savant Books and Publications
2630 Kapiolani Blvd #1601
Honolulu, HI 96826
http://www.savantbooksandpublications.com

Printed in the USA

Edited by Tara Dine
Cover Photos and Design by Daniel S. Janik
Title Page Illustration by Gary Knippa

10 digit ISBN:0-9841175-7-1
13-digit ISBN: 978-0-9841175-7-4

To God for guidance and providing

me with the best support system ever—my family.

Thank you all. I couldn't have done it without

your encouragement.

Called Home

Chapter 1

It felt like home and yet it didn't. The farmhouse Emma stood in now was the one she grew up in and was still the same, with the exception of some sorely needed repairs, yet it seemed different. Emma couldn't decide whether it was like she'd been tossed back in time or thrust forward. Either way it had an odd feel. She thought she would be out on her own, making her own way at this point in her life, but circumstances had called her home.

"You have to let him go, Mama. We can't afford his help." Emma tossed her auburn, just-past-the-shoulder-length hair behind her shoulders in frustration. "I know that you don't want to make things difficult for the boy, but there are farms as far as the eye can see around here. I think he'll be able to find someone that needs a hand."

Nancy's bewildered expression remained as she lowered into the turquoise speckled, vinyl-padded chair at the kitchen table. "I suppose you're right. I guess part of me just doesn't want it to be true."

"I'll tell him if you'd like." Emma pulled out the chair across the shiny white table from her mother and sat with a plop. "It has to be done—and the sooner the better. We can't afford to keep paying him when we barely have enough to get by."

"I know, I know. I'll be the one to tell him. I hired him and I'll be the one to send him on his way. I hope that his mother won't be cross with me. We see each other every week at church."

"She understands the farming life. The last thing she would want you to do is hurt yourself just to keep him on here. You know that. The whole community is always on the lookout for one another. If one of us is down, the next thing you know, a neighbor is on your porch asking how they can help."

"Yes. I know, you're absolutely right. It's just a hard thing to do. And you know me. I never want to put anyone out. It's my problem, I'll figure out how to handle it."

"You're not alone anymore, Mama. That's what I'm here for—to lean on and give advice. And you know how I love to do that."

"Ah yes, how well I do know."

"Very funny." Emma rose with a scrape of the chair and went to the sink to start washing the dinner dishes. As she reached for the dish soap sitting on the window ledge that overlooked the kitchen sink, she realized that it was almost completely dark outside. It was only six-thirty in the evening on an early spring day and the full light of day should have been shining.

"Mama, look! It looks like midnight." She directed her mother's attention to the black just beyond the sky-blue, filmy curtain in the window.

Nancy stood at the counter leaning toward the window in an attempt to see anything. Only shadows of swaying trees and shrubs flitted through her vision. With the flash of lightning, she jumped, causing her daughter to follow suit. She let out a breath and placed her hand on her chest. "Sorry. That one surprised me. It felt like it took aim at me."

"That's okay. It was awfully loud and bright." Emma turned to the left and reached out to push the button on the television. "Maybe we should see if we could find out how bad . . ."

"Ahhh!" The flash of light and the scream were virtually simultaneous.

Before Emma could reach her, Nancy had turned pale. "What is it? Did the lightning surprise you again?"

Nancy shook her head slowly, raised her arm and pointed out the window. "No." The word was barely audible and she just kept staring.

Emma got right in her mother's face and forced her to focus on her. "You need to tell me why you screamed."

Nancy snapped out of the daze. "Oh, I'm sure it was nothing. I'm just seeing things."

"What sort of things, Mama?" She took her mother's shoulders and held firmly. "Remember, we take care of things together now."

"Really, it's nothing. My emotions are all churned up right now, because of having to let the Landis boy go. My eyes are playing tricks—"

A loud banging on the back door cut through the relative quiet. Both women jumped as they clung to one another, trying to wish the knocking away. Instead of vanishing, the knocking became more insistent.

"I know there's someone in there," a deep voice boomed.

The women looked at each other with the look of terror etched on their faces. Emma took the lead and headed toward the back porch. "That's great, but we're not opening the door to a stranger who doesn't have the sense to stay out of weather like this."

"That's why I'm knocking on your door—the weather. And I'm not a stranger, I went to school with you, Emma."

"Well, do you have a name or am I supposed to take your word for it?" She stood with her hands on her hips, glaring at the door as though he could see her.

"David. David Schlosser. Come on, let me in where it's warm and dry. I'm soaked through."

"Since you're already all wet, one more question won't do any further harm."

"If I'm not struck down by lightning first." As if on cue, the sky lit up like stage lights switched on all at once.

"Answer quickly then. Where's your family farm?"

4

"Over on Highway N just past the railroad tracks. Now let me in, before the next bolt decides to strike me dead." The doorknob twisted under his insistence.

Emma unlocked the door and before she could pull it open, David came bursting through, along with what seemed like half the rain. The door skimmed narrowly by his heels as she slammed it closed. "Don't just stand there dripping all over the place, get your jacket off while I get a towel—maybe two."

Before she could leave the enclosed back porch, he grabbed her arm. Stunned, she looked him straight in the eye and opened her mouth to speak, but David cut the stream of assuredly pointed comments before its inception. "We need to go to the cellar directly."

"Unhand me. You don't come in here and start ordering me around in my own house!"

"First of all, I believe it's your mother's house." He nodded his head at Nancy. "Hello, ma'am." He returned his attention to Emma and continued, "And second of all, I thought you might want to be in a safe place if the tornado decides to head this direction."

Emma's eyes went wide with concern. As she looked up, she was close enough to see the brown specks scattered throughout the green of his eyes. They were intense, bordering on the edge of wild. His wet, scrambled hair and the disheveled clothes that hung on his thin but sturdy frame contributed to the look. His rugged, narrow features hardened his image, although she was sure he'd caused more than one woman to look twice in his direction. Neither homely nor handsome, there was something that drew Emma in and held on.

"We need to get to your cellar now." David gave the last word its due emphasis.

She gestured for her mother to go ahead and said, "Follow my mom. I'll be right down." Luckily for them, there was access to the cellar from both the inside and the outside of the house. Many of the farms were set up with only an outside entry. They were old and never remodeled, but kept, for the most part, in immaculate condition. It was part of the personality of this little corner of civilization.

As Nancy led David down the stone cellar stairs, Emma plucked a pitcher from the refrigerator. She set it on the counter and lifted three small glasses from the cabinet. She held the glasses between her arm and her body, in order to have the other hand free to cart the lemonade.

When she showed up below, David exploded. "Oh that's right, I forgot we had to get the lemonade first. What are you thinking? You're worried about getting refreshments when the tornado could come through at any moment! Are you completely insane?" His arms flew around as he spoke and his feet wore a path in the dirt floor of the cellar as he paced its twelve-foot length.

She watched with a mixture of amusement and irritation, having to smother the grin that threatened to bloom on her lips. "I knew I had time. The wind was still whipping through the trees. It hadn't become calm yet. So why don't you stop pacing and take one of these glasses, before I drop them all on the dirt floor and we have to drink from the pitcher. I don't think that's proper etiquette when entertaining company." Her head tilted as she gave him an innocent, but challenging look.

He took two glasses, held them out for her to fill and glanced over his shoulder at Nancy. "I don't know how you live with the attitude on this one."

Playing along, Nancy shrugged. "Well, you know. You get used to it."

"Oh. very funny. I see how the teams are going to line up." Emma nodded her head knowingly.

"Shh!" David held his index finger up to his lips. "Do you hear that?" He tilted his left ear toward the ceiling, straining to listen.

"I'm afraid I do." It sounded like a train rumbling in the distance. She knew it was a tornado close enough to hear.

Moments later, Emma labored to hear, wondering if she was still hearing the rumble or if it was just the memory of the sound caught inside her head. "Can you still hear it? 'Cause I'm not sure if I actually hear something or it's my imagination."

Nancy's gaze shifted to the stairs. "I feel like you do. I'm not sure of what is real and what I'm afraid to admit is real."

"If it's that hard to hear then we're fine. We should hang our hats on that fact." Holding out his glass to Emma, he attempted a lighter tone. "How about some more of that delicious lemonade?"

The glass now full, Emma sat on the wooden barrel in the corner, crossed one ankle over the other and looked to David. "So what were you doing out in this storm anyway?"

"I was heading to my parent's house when I realized I was also heading into a nasty storm. About a mile from your house I spied the funnel cloud hanging low and didn't want to chance it." He leaned against the shelves facing her, putting his weight on one leg.

He was a bit too close for her comfort. There was plenty of personal space between them but for some reason Emma was feeling trapped. "So, you remembered where we lived and just popped in?"

"Yeah, that's pretty much it."

"When was the last time you were home? I mean, how did you know that we still lived here? A total stranger could have answered the door and left you stranded in the storm." She looked up at him towering over her, which turned out to be a mistake. His gaze latched onto hers, making it impossible for her to break the spell he held unknowingly over her. It only added to her discomfort.

"Unless you took off from here extremely recently, I knew you were still the owners of this fine farm."

"You seem awfully sure of yourself." She studied her lemonade rather than the fascinating green eyes of her guest.

"I usually am quite certain of myself. Besides, my mother would have told me if a dog moved out of the area, so I was confident in the fact that I would have been informed of such a major change as this farm being sold.

There is nothing that escapes the contents of the letters I receive from home." The humor showed on his slightly tanned face.

"Ah, I see what you mean. I've gotten many a letter like those." She turned to grin at her mother. "Haven't I, Mama?"

"I do believe you have."

David returned his attention to Emma. "By the way, to answer your first question—I haven't been here in seven years."

It was evident that he wasn't about to expound on the answer. Now was not the appropriate time to press the issue so Emma filed the information, hoping to acquire additional details in the future. "So, do you think it's safe to go back upstairs?"

"I'll go up and check. You two stay put." David pushed off the wall and headed for the tiny cellar stairs.

"Yes, sir." Emma added a salute for good measure.

"Be my guest." His arm swept across the room to the stairs. "If you'd prefer, I'll stay put so you can have all the fun." Grinning on the inside he thought, two can play this game.

"No, that's okay. I just wanted to make it clear that I don't do anything I don't want to do. And I certainly am not about to take orders from you." She elevated her chin.

Nancy was a calm, no-nonsense kind of person who naturally stayed out of other people's business. But her daughter was being entirely too rude for her tastes. "That's enough, Emma." She turned to David. "I'm sorry. I'd be very grateful if you would check out the storm

9

conditions."

He placed a comforting hand on Nancy's arm and spoke calmly. "I'd be happy to, ma'am. And there's no need to apologize. Believe me, I've taken a lot worse." He locked gazes with Emma as he spoke the latter, then headed up the stairs.

Emma knew her mother's look without having to see it with her own eyes. "I know, I know. I'm sorry, Mama. He just seems to get me riled up. We're doing him the favor by letting him in and all he does is boss me around. Like I can't handle it myself. I've navigated many things on my own before his rude arrival. "

Emma headed for the stairs and ascended, deciding she should make nice. She took her time going up the narrow steps.

"What's the word?" Emma asked when she reached the kitchen.

David was peering out the window above the sink, straining to see anything. "I can't really see much. It seems pretty calm at the moment."

It was still pitch dark but as Emma crossed the room, she noticed the stillness of the trees. The bottom fell out of her stomach.

She grabbed his arm and attempted to drag him to the stairs. He wouldn't budge. It was like trying to pull a hay wagon with a bicycle.

"Have you been gone that long? Don't you remember? That's the step before the tornado goes ripping through! You know: the calm before the storm. There's a reason they say that. And this is it!"

In the quiet seconds after her mini-lecture, they suddenly heard the rumble. David quickly looked to the window as the rumble became a roar. His head whipped in Emma's direction and saw that she was stunned frozen. Not willing to wait to gauge how far off it was, he picked her up like she was no heavier than a pillow and made a dash for the stairs.

She was stunned by the sudden move and flung her arms around his neck and held on. What took no more than three seconds played in slow motion from her perspective. His face was mere inches from hers. Suddenly, she was quite aware of his lean, hard body and firm, strong arms against her. A sensation, like fireflies lit with electricity, shot from her chest to her toes.

He navigated the small cellar stairs with amazing ease considering the precious bundle in his arms. As he negotiated the last step, Emma pushed on his chest in an attempt to be freed. "Let me down."

"Okay, okay. Let me finish getting down to the cellar. Unless you want to risk being dropped?"

"We wouldn't be doing this if you hadn't grabbed me up there. What possessed you to snatch up someone you hardly know and take off with them in your arms, like they were a baby or a dog that didn't know any better?"

He gently set her feet on the floor. "Because you weren't moving. And I thought you might prefer being carried off than possibly flattened by a tornado." He walked to the other corner of the cellar to put some space between them. "Sorry if I miscalculated your wishes."

"Sorry." It was difficult to say. "I don't like being manhandled like—"

Nancy broke into the inane conversation. "I don't mean to be rude, but what on earth is going on out there?" Her lovely face wrinkled in worry.

"Oh, sorry, Mama. When we were upstairs, the sound grew louder by the time we reached the door to the cellar. Figuring we'd better get our butts down here, we didn't take the time to see if we could locate it or what direction it might be headed. So all we know is that it was close." She rested on the barrel once again.

The sound intensified and the occupants of the cellar were monk-quiet. Even breathing ceased for a moment. With Nancy's hand over her gaping mouth, she didn't move a muscle. Emma's fingers turned white as they clung to the edge of the barrel and David watched the color drain from her face. As fast as the worst of the noise barged in, it was gone. Just like that. It was like a bad visitor. It came uninvited, did its damage and then left without a word.

Silently, after waiting to see that it wasn't going to double back, the three of them went up to the kitchen and straight to the window. They leaned as one, looking at the branches strewn around the yard.

Emma saw that the sky was brightening and spun to go out the back door. "I'm going to check on the barn and the cows and everything."

David put his hand on her back and began to walk with her. "I'll go with you."

"I'm perfectly capable of doing it myself. I would

have had to, if you hadn't so kindly dropped in." She raised her eyebrows in his direction.

"Are we going to go through this again? Can't you just let someone help you or is it against your fundamental beliefs?"

"Well, you don't have to be huffy about it." Emma was behaving like David was the one being difficult. Her general rule was to do it yourself and don't rely on anyone else.

"I don't believe anyone has ever called me huffy before."

They reached the door and she faced him. "Well now, there's a first time for everything." She strode off ahead of him.

Her attention was focused on the branches about the yard, wondering how long it would take her to clean it all up. After her survey of the personal garden her mother tended, taking note that the damage was scattered and spotty, she turned her sights straight ahead to the barn. At first glimpse, her eyes widened and her jaw dropped. She managed a step or two before she fell to her knees and brought her hands to her face. The sting of tears pushed at the back of her eyes as she fought to keep them at bay.

David had seen it an instant before her. He came to her side, put his hands on her shoulders and knelt down with her. He concluded that there were no words that would comfort and remained as a silent support beside her, connected.

She gathered her emotions and tucked them away. Rising to her feet, she started to run toward the barn. A storm would not defeat her. There were other things in her life she considered worse that she refused to let take her down. This would not either.

Partly in preparation and partly to catch her breath from running, she took a deep breath and entered through the door that had been sucked open by the power of the whirling storm. The cows and various barn cats appeared to be accounted for and in good condition. She was unsure as to how, but grateful. Emma offered a silent prayer of thanks.

It could have been worse, she reminded herself. Although that thought was hard to latch onto when the majority of the barn roof was missing.

David leaned against the doorjamb, trying not to crowd her, but insisted on staying close by. It was a lot for anyone to absorb. The work and money that it would take to return the place to its former standing would be daunting for the average farmer, but especially to a woman and her mother on their own. He vowed then and there to do whatever he could, or whatever she would let him do, to help.

Emma passed by each stall in order to see with her own eyes that each of the cows made it through the storm unharmed. At the end of the row of stalls on the opposite side, she found herself directly in front of David. "Well, I guess you can be on your way now. The storm did what it came to do and seems to be done with us."

"You really are a stubborn woman." He watched a flicker of incredulous expression cross her face.

"I'll take that as a compliment."

"It's not always meant as one. Anyway, I'll leave for now." He turned on his heels, heading in the direction of his car.

"What is that supposed to be, some kind of threat?"

"No, only an intention to help in whatever way I can." He waved over his shoulder. "See you around."

"Wanna bet?" she mumbled. She stared after him as he left the driveway. The whole encounter was bordering on the surreal. The storm, David and his odd appearance out of nowhere, it was weird. You couldn't make this stuff up, she thought.

The gaping hole where the roof should have been was the one detail that slapped her in the face with reality. At least it was spring. The cows were not in danger of getting too cold any time soon—another fact for which Emma was incredibly grateful.

On her way back to the house, she once again inspected the grounds, noting a passel of branches, some verging on enormous, littering the yard. This is going to take a good deal of work and time to get this cleared, she thought.

Resolving to start the cleanup tomorrow, her thoughts went to her neighbors. They often did around here — everyone looked out for one another in Brooks, Wisconsin. She hoped that no one had been hurt during the harsh weather and that property damage was kept to a bare minimum.

Called Home

Chapter 2

In the morning the sky was as blue as it could be, without even the wisp of a cloud in sight. The weather was generally spectacular after a storm and Emma was appreciative of the beautiful spring day. It would give her the opportunity to begin the widespread cleanup necessary to restore the farm to its former status.

With the early morning chores done, she was firm in her conviction to spend every waking hour, outside of the daily chores of a dairy farm, returning it to pre-storm condition. In order to start on the barn roof she had to have supplies. The first order of business was to get them.

Emma plucked her keys from the hook by the door. "I'm going into town. You need anything while I'm there?"

"No. I just went the other day, remember?" Nancy hollered from the front of the house.

"Okay. Well, I won't be any longer than I have to

be. I want to check on materials for the roof." Stepping onto the back porch she yelled, "Bye!"

Once in Brooks, about a five-mile drive, Emma headed straight for the lumberyard on the edge of town. She hopped out of her little economy car, spied Jim helping Mr. Jenkins load up his truck, and waved. "Hey Jim. How's it going? Mr. Jenkins."

He nodded as Jim returned the wave. "Good. You?"

"Could be better. We lost the roof on the barn in the storm yesterday. That's why I'm here."

He finished with Mr. Jenkins' load and came beside her, putting his arm across her shoulders. "Oh, man! That stinks. I can help you if you need. I don't have a day off until next week though." He scratched his head, racking his brain for a solution to his scheduling problem.

"That's okay, Jim. I'm sure there'll be plenty of people willing to pitch in." She patted his arm and offered a smile.

It did nothing to alleviate his frustration, it only enhanced it. *He* wanted to be there. *He* wanted to be the one to assist Emma. Jim's feelings for her had been with him since grade school. Now that she was back in the area and they were both adults, his feelings were more intense than ever before.

Emma was aware of what she termed a small crush on his part. The thing was, she had never felt more than friendship for Jim. All along, she had hoped that it wouldn't get in the way of them being friends and thus far it hadn't. "So, is enough lumber available to all but replace the roof?"

"We're going to have to put in an order."

"How long is that going to take?"

"We should get it in by next week sometime."

"Great. Hope there's not another storm in the forecast or I'll be milking cows in the rain." She sighed heavily.

Jim faced her with excitement in his eyes. "Hey, why don't you forget your troubles and come out with me. I'll take you to dinner and we can find a dance somewhere. I'm sure we can. There's always one somewhere within driving distance. How about it?" He put his hands gently on her arms in hopeful anticipation.

"I don't think I would be very good company with all this on my mind. It's probably not a good idea."

"That's exactly why it's a *great* idea. C'mon, it'll be fun."

He was the same age as Emma, but gave the impression of being years younger.

"No. I'll be a drag. Really, you should find someone that's as excited by the notion as you are." She was resolute in her decision to let him down easy.

He pulled away at her refusal. "I don't want to go with anyone else. If you change your mind though, you know where to find me."

"Thanks for the invite. And don't forget to keep me posted on the order." She headed for her car. Calling over her shoulder she yelled, "Thanks again. Bye!"

Jim stood looking after her as she pulled out of the lumberyard. I'm going to wear her down eventually, he thought. And the sooner the better, I can't take much more of this.

Emma turned the car in the direction of the hardware store. It was in the middle of town, sandwiched between the shop with the turning barber pole in front and a clothing store displaying lumberjack shirts, work jackets, boots, gloves and a leather flight jacket in the window, enticing the passerby to come in and browse. The short block of storefronts was connected, yet each store was made distinct by various facings of wood, brick and stone. An overhang and a wooden boardwalk spanned the length of the businesses.

She had to stow the car on the street, since the hardware lot was busting at the seams around the back. She peered through the windshield, thinking it looked like she had gone to some kind of reunion. Everyone she knew from the community was there. I guess they're all here for the same thing—to get supplies to put back together what the storm tore apart, she thought. I hope George has what I need. I can't stand the thought of sitting around waiting on everything to eventually arrive. Stuff needs to be done. Never very good at waiting, her tendency was always that of action. In her mind, doing was invariably superior to waiting.

Emma located the aisle she needed and began to sift through the bins of hinges. "Well, I may have to wait for wood, but I can at least clean the yard and fix the hinges and latches that were busted," she said aloud.

"I beg your pardon?" The voice came from just down the aisle.

She turned sheepishly and saw David grinning at her. "Figures," she mumbled. "I was just happy that what I need is in stock. You always listen in on other people's conversations?"

"And who would you be having that conversation with?" He raised his eyebrows and looked up and down the aisle.

"I can talk to whomever I please." Emma turned her attention back to the hardware, chin up, locating just the right pieces. Suddenly, David was behind her, reaching in exactly the same box.

She stood statue-still, even her breathing ceased. The brush of his hand on hers lit a fuse of sparks in her fingertips. Her amber-toned hair fluttered from his breath and more lit at her ear. Meeting in her stomach, the fuses set off small explosions she immediately suppressed.

David didn't back off a bit. "Seems we need the same thing."

She could feel him watching her. She knew if she faced him she would get lost in the green pools so she kept her focus on the hardware. "It appears you couldn't wait your turn." The hinges all blended together at this point, so she grabbed several, hoping she had what she needed. She spun away from David and started to take off toward the checkout.

"I just thought we could be neighborly and do it together!" His stride made up the distance to Emma in mere seconds. "Why are you rushing off so quickly? You in a hurry?"

Not bothering to stop, she strode with efficiency

to the checkout. "I've got a lot to do. I don't have time to waste with idle chitchat." Emma stood in line and kept her focus ahead.

He lined up quietly behind her and she eventually turned around, eyes narrowed. "What are you doing? Are you stalking me or something?" She lifted her purse and nodded toward it. "I carry mace in here. And I know how to use it."

A slow curve of his mouth adorned his face. "I'm just here to get what I need and I'll be out of your hair." He leaned toward her, suddenly serious. "You wouldn't know it if I were stalking you."

A chill ran down the length of her as he pointed to the register. "It's your turn." He shot his best smile her way.

As she drove back through the countryside that had begun to green, she played over the encounter in the hardware store. Thinking of David brought on feelings of anger, distrust, maybe even fear. But the sensations he invoked by his sheer closeness were unprecedented in her experience. She knew she couldn't trust her physical reaction to him, she had to be objective. It wasn't like he was asking her out or making a pass at her, but he made her uneasy. A distance would have to be maintained. She would do her level best to keep herself out of range. Besides, she was in no way looking for the complications of a man. That was the last thing she was looking for during her time here, helping her mother. Nancy needed her and she would not let her down. She'd been caught off guard at other times in her life and only pain and heartache came from it. Not again, not ever again.

This was her chance for a new beginning. As she navigated the country road through the delicate spring colors, she likened this point in her life to the earth in springtime on the precipice of bursting to life. That's what she needed—a fresh start.

Back home, Emma scrounged around the cluttered utility room in search of the best tools for the job. At least she could replace the bent hinges and broken latches, which would go a long way to improving her attitude about the condition of the farm. If she was able to do any little task toward the desired outcome she felt she was in control, which was not only important but also crucial to her well being. She could not allow herself to be a pawn in the game of life. She refused to end up like her mother.

"I'm going out to repair what I can, with what little I was able to get my hands on," she yelled to her mom in the kitchen.

"Wait." Nancy moved near Emma. "I just got off the phone with your cousin. She's bringing Alan and Abby by in an hour."

"What! You don't have time for that any more than I do." She stood with her hands on her hips. "The nerve of some people. We've enough of our own work without having to entertain two, how should I put it —" Her hand cupped her chin as one finger covered her lips. " —little irritations."

Nancy gave her that expression that mothers often do when their child, no matter the age, is behaving poorly. "They had quite a bit of damage and it's going to take a lot of work on her and her husband's part to put back the pieces. We need to help our own. We're going to have to ask for some ourselves, soon enough."

Emma softened a bit. "I know, but I had my mind set to fix and straighten what I could around here today because I have to meet with the bank tomorrow." She went to the door. As it creaked open she said, "Well, I'd better get to what I can before the monsters show up." She grinned.

When she had finished replacing the hardware she was in no mood to head back to the house. She knew that if her mother really needed her, she'd find her. Through the back of the barn, she walked along the tractor path toward the woods. So much had happened since she arrived home. She had looked forward to the peace and quiet of the country and the comforting company of her mother. Her mind was in desperate need of a respite from the deception, hurt and betrayal of the last couple of years. She had been disillusioned about her future after the completion of college, and paid for it. The person closest to her managed to erase her image of the road ahead, which was paved with fulfilled dreams and a life that was satisfyingly her own. And she had allowed it. Never again, she promised.

Emma used the peaceful stroll to regain her perspective and order her thoughts. The walk through the ever-greening underbrush and the canopy of newly budding trees displaying a lacy, light green haze overhead brought her calm. A bird's song filled the air, along with the occasional rustle from a rabbit or squirrel scurrying away over the carpet of leaves still left from fall. Breathing in the clean, fresh air of the country the day after a storm provided cleansing for her soul and rejuvenation for her weary body. As she reached the edge of the woods, she felt certain she was ready to handle whatever life threw her way. Her determination was bolstered and her countenance refreshed.

A movement caught the corner of her vision. "What on earth is he doing here?" she muttered. Flight was her initial reaction, but then she thought better of it. Her pride wouldn't allow it. No, she would face David with her renewed confidence and in no way be swayed by him. Yes, she would go on the offensive rather than retreat like a scared rabbit being chased by a coyote.

He saw her walking with purpose directly toward him, seemingly on a mission. He waved and called out, "Hey, how's it going?"

"What do you think you're doing? Nobody invited you here." She stood with her hands on her hips awaiting the answer.

David replied calmly, "I thought you could use a hand cleaning up all these branches strewn about your yard and I figured you were busy elsewhere so I started in on it myself." He pointed to some tools lying on the ground. "You can use that saw and start wherever you like. There are plenty of branches to go around."

"If you think I'm taking orders from you then you need your head examined by old Doc Stevens." Her arms were folded across her chest.

"I think he retired," he said calmly with a smirk. He turned his attention back to sawing, not waiting for her inevitably curt reply.

She continued, "My mother and I have been running this place for years on our own. I'm quite positive we're still able to handle what needs to be done. So if you don't mind, I'll take over and you can go back to wherever you crawled out from and stay there indefinitely."

"I don't intend to take over here. I thought it would be nice to lend a neighborly hand, since you both were so kind to give me shelter in the storm. But I could either use some help or a very large cup of lemonade." He watched the emotions change in her eyes, softening from a defensive anger to consideration. "You pick. I'll be happy with whatever you choose." He blithely went back to the task at hand.

It was silly to reject an offer of help in this situation. Her pride had a way of backing her into corners that required much maneuvering to escape. "I won't have much time to help you out before I'm needed to assist with my cousin's kids." Swinging the saw around to a moderate-sized branch, she began to strip it of its twigs and prepare the perfect pieces for firewood. Nothing was wasted on a farm. "They had some damage at their place they need to fix up, without the help of the kids." She chuckled, acting as though she had never confronted him and accused him of thinking she was inept at managing the tasks of the farm. Apologizing was too much to ask, but she was capable of polite behavior.

The smile was good to see. He didn't think he'd seen one from her yet. It was stunning. She was stun— he cut his thought off mid-word. No, no, no, he thought. Dangerous territory, buddy. Focus, just focus on what you're doing. "Oh they were the little angels I saw being delivered, huh?"

"They're here?" She moved with purpose to the next part of the tree that could be taken care of with a handsaw. The rest would have to be handled with the chainsaw and she wasn't about to fire that up with the children running about.

"Yeah, they arrived a bit ago. They pretty much bounced from the car to the house. You think they have your mother tied up yet?"

Emma let out a full laugh, with the image of that scene playing in her head. "I'm thinking that we would have heard her scream for help by now," she said between chuckles. "Unless they gagged her too." The giggling continued.

Her laugh washed over him like a warm shower. It was good to hear her having fun, if only for a short time, after the hassle of the past day. But he was genuinely worried by the response his body had to her elation. "I suppose you're right. She raised you, so I guess she knows how to handle difficult children."

"How dare you refer to me that way!" She picked up a glove he had left on the ground and threw it at him.

His hands made it up just in time to deflect it from hitting his head. He looked at her from the top of his eyes with his head down and debated throwing it back, but thought better of it. "Tell me I'm wrong."

She turned her attention to the branch at her feet so she didn't have to look into his intense eyes. Those eyes held his secrets, and she suddenly had the strong desire to discover them. "You're wrong," she said as she sawed determinedly.

A wide grin appeared on David. "Should I ask your mother and see what she remembers? You think her answer might be a little different than yours?" He stood watching her, with more curiosity than he'd ever had about another woman. He thought, why am I so drawn to her? She's so independent and sure of herself. There's no room for anyone else in her world. So why am I so determined to be sure she makes room for me?

"You will not bother my mother with this nonsense. Get back to work. If you're going to hang out here annoying me, it'd better be for a good reason." The light mood held a smile on her face and softness in her heart. She was grateful for the reprieve from the chores and problems of everyday life. In particular, the break from the enormous issues that faced her and her mother.

"Yes ma'am." He continued with the branches. She could hold her own with the manual labor, he noticed. Growing up on a farm, especially without men, she would have had to learn a wide variety of tasks. She certainly didn't wait around for someone to bail her out of a fix. He found he was impressed with her competence and eager to learn more about Emma Benson — actually, everything. She intrigued him, she surprised him, she pulled at him in ways that were new to him. Not sure he cared for the feeling, he encouraged his mind to pursue more relevant lines of thought. The kind of place he wanted to live, his work, anything other than Emma.

They worked side by side for an hour. Emma decided a break was well deserved as trickles of sweat trailed down her back. "Hey, how about that lemonade now?"

David ceased his work, wiping his face with a bandanna from his jeans. "Sounds like an excellent idea to me. Lead the way."

She started for the house. "C'mon, let's cool off inside."

"Good plan." He followed her into the bright, homey kitchen.

Emma washed at the kitchen sink. "The washroom's just over there," she said, pointing to her right.

David, feeling refreshed after cleaning up, was greeted by a spread of homemade sugar cookies and a large glass of lemonade. "Ah, thanks." He grabbed a cookie as he lowered his body into the seat.

The lemonade went down well. It cooled her down after the energy exerted cutting firewood, but it did nothing for the hum of energy that ran just below the surface of her skin. What was wrong with her? It wasn't like she was totally inexperienced with men. She'd been in the company of more than one handsome, confident man. Her reaction was generally next to nonexistent. Why react to this one? She suppressed the thought with a shrug of her shoulders.

"Wasn't there enough to do at your parents' place to keep you busy?" She snagged a cookie. They looked far too delicious to leave them all to David.

He finished masticating the bite he had just stuffed into his mouth before washing it down with a giant swig of lemonade. Upon swallowing, he answered, "No, actually there wasn't. The farm escaped without so much as a branch being thrown from a tree. From what I've heard, the damage was confined to this area a bit west of town." His eyes dropped to the plate, which now contained only one lonely cookie, then rested on Emma to study the effect her pulled-back hair had on her face. He concluded that the manner it was arranged at the nape of the neck gave her a younger, more athletic appearance. As his eyes came to hers, they remained still, as did his entire expression.

She couldn't read him. It unnerved her. "I'm glad the farm came through unscathed. And I *do* appreciate the help." She stood, opting for a mindless task as an outlet, and took up her glass, reaching for the cookie plate. Suddenly his hand was around her wrist.

"Wait. You can't waste the last cookie." His gaze traveled from plate, up her arm, across her face to her eyes and held. His hand detected her radiant energy.

All she could do was stare into his eyes as he reached with his other hand toward the plate only to run his hand down her arm. The warmth from his grasp and the brush of his hand crept up the length of both arms and met in her head with a dazing effect. "You going to take that or not? I haven't got all day." The attempt at a casual retort did nothing to dampen the feeling growing within.

David held her in his grip until the cookie reached his mouth. As the cookie touched his lips, his gaze dropped to rest on her full mouth and he imagined the taste of sweetness he knew he would find. "Thank you." He released her reluctantly.

Emma was already at the sink rinsing and she uttered some sort of sound in reply. She turned to retrieve his glass and as she reached out to take it, two blurs came between her and the table, nearly knocking her over.

"Ah, they must be Alan and Abby." His eyes followed their trail through the kitchen and out again.

"You guessed it." She took up the glass and rinsed it. "I'd better give my mom a hand, before they tear the place apart. You can see yourself out, I assume." Emma didn't intend to wait for an answer and headed for the door after Alan and Abby.

Before she could extract herself from David's company, Nancy rushed into the kitchen. "Those two in here?" She looked harried as she surveyed the room.

"Well, I think they were, but I couldn't be entirely sure. The motion was such a blur. And there's no telling where they might be by now." Emma looked to David and back. "I'll give you a hand. I'm done with the work for now and David was just leaving. Weren't you?"

Nancy jumped in. "Oh, why don't you stay for lunch. We'd love to have your company, wouldn't we, Emma?"

A barely perceptible sneer formed on Emma's face as she, as if forced, answered, "Mmm-hmm."

He rose from the table, pushed in his chair and kept his gaze on Emma. "Thanks, but I've got some things I need to do." With a polite smile for Nancy he excused himself. His features transformed in a flash and thoroughly studied the full length of Emma without a word. Nancy was off in search of the little people.

Emma could no longer ignore the discomfort. As she turned to the sink to rinse dishes, a hard body abruptly greeted hers. His move was so smooth and quick that it had gone unnoticed, until contact was made.

Now she was in the middle of her own personal battle. Why was this so arduous for her? Everything within her was in conflict.

Before rational thought could take root, David brushed the stray hairs from her face, pulling out the band that held the rest in place, leaving his fingers to wade through the thick softness. Like lightning, his mouth was on hers. Emma was stunned by the move, but not so much as to not respond. As he pulled her closer, she slipped her arms around him because it just felt natural. She forgot the promise she had made as the intensity took over. A wave of heat washed through her body and infused her lips with a burning fire. Her head flitted with dizziness and, as quickly as it started, he backed away.

"Until next time, Emma." He spun on his heels and was out the door, leaving her staring at where he had just been.

Snapping out of it, she began to mutter. "Next time. We'll see about that." She wet the dishcloth and commenced wiping down everything in sight. It's not like she fought the advance, she thought, but then again he can't go around kissing people unaware. I was just in need of some comfort after the last day and a half. That's all. The storm and the damage put me through a lot and my defenses were down. It won't happen again. "I'll make sure of that," she mumbled. That kiss only heightened her conviction to reinforce her defenses. It will not happen in the future. There won't be a next time.

Called Home

Chapter 3

Gentle rolling hills of green dotted by houses and barns stretched out in front of him. Ribbons of blacktop formed a checkered pattern in the landscape. This corner of the country was the complete antithesis of living in the big city. From most vantage points in the city, he couldn't see more than a few blocks; from here, the miles seemed to expand infinitely around him. The blue sky was as endless as his imagination and the hills continued until they met the sky in its infinitude.

The change had already done him good, David thought. He didn't feel as rushed or harried. It was like being in the middle of a blender in New York. If he personally wasn't expected to be someplace or do something, then it was someone close enough to him for the urgency to rub off. There was a need for him to be there early on in his career, but now he could write anywhere. Success had come quickly for him and with it, financial security and recognition of his work. He would never have removed the experience from his life. It formed a significant portion of the person he was today, but by no means all.

Back to his roots — that's what he longed for at this point. He yearned for the grounding that coming home would provide for him and sometime, for a family. The simplicity of rural living in Wisconsin was the missing piece to his personal life puzzle. Not that there wasn't hard work involved in the life, but he never shied away from putting in a great deal of effort into what he wanted. This was precisely where he needed to be.

His plans for a new life did not include a stubborn, jumpy, ready-to-fight-at-any-second young woman. But then why did she keep wandering into his thoughts? Seeing her deep, blue eyes clearly in his mind's eye caused a spear of longing to pierce through his system. Encountering her charms again would undoubtedly pull him straight into the mess he was attempting to avoid.

He couldn't help but wonder about how he ended up in situations up to his neck with the threat of drowning while his back was turned. Then by the time he caught on to the true meaning and consequences of it all he was stuck too deeply in the quagmire to surface.

The only thing he was sure of was that he was certain to have more encounters with Emma.

David headed for town in search of some of the essentials of rural living. The main purpose of his quest was work boots — a bit of attire that had been missing from his wardrobe for many years. And instead of risking the demise of a perfectly worn-in pair of jeans, he thought he'd better go for the whole work clothes ensemble, including heavy-duty gloves.

He was like most men on a mission, systematically patronizing only the stores necessary to accomplish his goal. He made a beeline for only the items on his list. For all intents and purposes there was nothing else — the stores held no distractions for him. David advanced forward, spied the target, captured it and marched to the next mark.

The warm spring day was so gorgeous it refused to be ignored. After depositing the packages in his car, he strolled through town. He glanced at store windows and waved hello to every head nod, honk of the horn or arm out the window he encountered. The park on the edge of town was before him; he shrugged, wondering, why not? It was virtually deserted, except for two young people sitting across from each other at a picnic table, gazing at one another and holding hands. David remembered those days. It's not like he had a lot of girlfriends, but he did have the occasional one and knew exactly what they were experiencing. He tossed the thought aside with a knowing chuckle and wished them well, but only in thought.

He settled on a bench in the sun allowing it to lightly bake his skin. The warmth was nothing compared to that which Emma induced in him. A puzzled expression appeared with the thought — now where did that come from? Banishing it from his consciousness, he closed his eyes to dream of his own farm, complete with cows and horses, cats and dogs, maybe goats. Most especially, it would have horses. He missed them being a part of his life, as they had been when he was growing up. The image of him on a shiny black stallion galloping with abandon across the golden fields, feeling the wind rush his face, invaded his thoughts. Furthering the dream, the sound of hooves grew behind him. Turning toward the sound he saw Emma racing toward him, with her amber hair trailing out behind her and glinting in the sun's rays. The force of emotion nearly overwhelmed him.

Snapping to, he casually glanced around the park, afraid that someone might be completely aware of his mind's meanderings. He was convinced otherwise when he saw that the park was now empty. The best thing to do was to set his mind on practical matters. First in line: the quest for a farm he could call his own.

With pictures of how his place would look and what animals he would own flitting across the screen in his mind, he sauntered in the direction of his car. Once again, he made the appropriate gestures at the appropriate times. The ambiance of the town filled him with contentment. This was what he wanted, this was what he needed.

He passed the ice cream stand and caught sight of Emma with the kids in tow. He crossed the street and approached them. "Hey, long time no see."

She knew who it was before she looked up, and sighed. "You're everywhere, aren't you?" She handed the chocolate dipped cone to Abby and received the last one for herself.

He took a seat with them at one of the rainbow, umbrella-covered tables and said, "I guess you're just lucky, that's all."

"Lucky? That's what you call it. I believe I have a different opinion of it — cursed." The ice cream proceeded to get her undivided attention.

David eyed the children intently slurping on their ice cream. "So you decided they weren't hyped up enough, you thought they could use a bunch of sugar?"

"Ha-ha. No, I thought the drive into town would be something to do and then I could take them to the park to run off the energy." Emma licked a drip of ice cream before it reached her hand. "Can't waste this day stuck inside. It's too gorgeous. Besides, I get enough of the stuffy indoors during the winter." She stuffed the last bite of cone into her mouth.

His eyes went wide. "Don't choke on that. You wouldn't want me to have to resuscitate you."

She rose and headed straight for the napkins. Grabbing a good-sized gob of them, she returned and began the large-scale cleanup. "Good thing they have plenty of napkins," she said as she picked up another handful and moved on to wipe off Alan.

"Yeah. You know what I just realized. You didn't offer to share your ice cream with me." He posed, offering a sad little boy look.

"And why would I do that?" His expression was nearly irresistible, but her pride commanded her response. She gestured to the order window. "You can get your own anytime you want. Don't let us get in your way."

"I thought it might be the thing to do, since I slaved at your place this morning cutting branches until my hands were raw." David pretended to pout, which the kids thought was hilarious.

"Right. I already gave you cookies and lemonade. What more do you want?"

"I have a very good idea of what I want."

"I'll tell you what you can do with your idea."

"You might want to temper your remarks, with them within earshot." He indicated to Alan and Abby with his head.

"You're lucky you have a buffer." She narrowed her eyes and glared.

"I think you might want to rethink your position on that. I believe you might be the lucky one in this situation."

She caught his drift and counted herself so. "I'm taking them to the park." She motioned for Alan and Abby to follow. "Come on. Let's go get our wiggles out on the play equipment."

David jumped up. "Okay, I'm ready."

"What? See, I told you you were stalking me."

He bent over and whispered in her ear, "Remember what I told you in the hardware store."

A shiver ran the length of her, but not of fear. She rounded up the children and began the trek to the park. David fell in step. "I'm coming."

She marched away from the stand determinedly. "It's a free country." She was fully aware of his presence right beside her and it made her uneasy.

When they arrived at the park Emma announced, "Not it!" Alan and Abby followed suit in quick succession. She looked to David with satisfaction. "I guess that leaves you."

"Then I would think you'd all be far from here by now." Once he had counted, he started after Alan with his head down. David let him scuttle behind a tree and hide.

"Abby, I bet I know where you are." He peeked behind a large tree, on the other side of the bathroom building, around a trash can, playing the game to it's fullest. Before long, he sneaked up to the far side of the playscape and grabbed Abby's shoulders. "Gotcha. Now you get to help me." He whispered conspiratorially, "I saw Alan duck behind that tree over there." He directed her to the exact one. "You work on tagging him and I'll get Emma. Deal?" He held his hand out to shake on it.

Abby took his hand and shook. "You've got it. You can count on me." She ran with the responsibility given to her by David.

Emma held her position on the other side of the gazebo. Sitting on the ground in the shade, she enjoyed the light breeze carrying freshness that was only detected in spring. She could have sat there for some time without moving a muscle and was in no hurry to be found. Closing her eyes, she soaked up the warmth and willed her mind not to think of all the things there were to do.

A scream broke silence. Before she could react, she realized it was just Abby finding Alan. Abby's giggles of delight followed and filled Emma with happiness. Alan announced that the two of them were going to the swings and David said, "Okay, but don't go any farther."

Emma heard their simultaneous reply. "We won't."

She picked a clover and held it up to study. He's never going to find me, she thought. At least if he does, it'll take him forever. The gazebo was on the other side of the park. Songs kept playing in her head as she watched a squirrel run back and forth and up one tree, down, and then up another. Contentment reigned.

Without warning, David's voice sounded behind and to the side of her. "You know, it doesn't do very well to hide and then proceed to hum. It kind of gives your position away." He sat down beside her.

"I was not."

"Mmm-hmm. I just followed the lovely little tune and here you are." He took her hand. "What have you got there?"

She tried to subtly remove her hand from his, but his grip tightened slightly. "Just a clover. I had a lot of time on my hands, waiting for you to find me." Turning to him was a mistake. When she did, his face was only inches from hers. His olive green eyes were intent on her, studying. Locked in his gaze, she could not move, she could not free herself. She wasn't sure she wanted to be free. But of course you do, she chided. Remember the last time you were sucked into a relationship?

Before she could break the spell, David was on his feet pulling her up. "The little charmers are on the swings." He kept one of her hands in his, leading the way.

It was a natural move and in no way awkward.

She let it stand as she walked quickly to keep up with his long strides. His hand had a firm grasp of hers and his profile outlined his strong features. Between the contact of his hand and the statuesque image, Emma's heart pumped with fervor. This is ridiculous, she thought, snap out of it, Emma. "Hey, why don't I really remember you much from years ago?" They reached Alan and Abby.

He let go of her hand and directed. "You push Abby and I'll send Alan here over the bar." He gave Alan a big push that had him screaming 'no' in jest.

"Well, to answer your question. It's probably because I was a few years ahead of you. By the time you were entering high school, I was already gone."

"You took off in a big hurry, didn't you?"

"Higher!" Abby yelled.

"I'll give you higher. Here you go flying into the air." Emma gave her an underdog and sent her flying.

David carried on the conversation. "Yeah, I couldn't wait to get away from here back then. I thought this was the last place in the world I wanted to be. In my opinion, nothing of any importance went on around here. So I fled to New York. My plan was to be discovered for my brilliant writing and everything else would fall in line. I thought it couldn't help but do so, if that happened." He paused to reflect on his attitude in the past. Shaking his head, he almost couldn't comprehend it.

"So you left with your lofty ideas and then what?" Directing her attention to the kids for a moment, she asked, "You guys sick of swinging yet?" She received a resounding "no!" in response. "Okay, but let us know if you do."

"My lofty ideas, as you so succinctly put it, got me far enough. I'm not sure how far they would have gotten me, had I not been relatively lucky. The articles I wrote on current events at the time were sent from newspaper to newspaper and from magazine to magazine, until it landed in the right person's lap. After a few of my articles were published in various newspapers and magazines, it became a more regular thing. I did that alone for about two years, until I got the bug to attempt something a bit longer—a novel."

She looked at him in astonishment. "You wrote a novel?"

"If I'm that believable to you, I'm amazed I've sold as many as I have. And actually I've written four novels and many, many articles."

Suddenly a snap of clarity came to Emma and it showed on her face. "Oh, yeah, I didn't put the two together. I have seen your name in the bookstores. I guess I just didn't know you well enough to think of it being you. Well, I'm in the presence of a real celebrity."

"Right. That's me the celebrity d'jour. It'll pass." He stopped pushing Alan and received no protest.

"I doubt it. Two of your books have been best sellers." Abby jumped from the swing. The two scurried off to the play equipment.

David and Emma trailed behind and found a picnic table nearby. "I became disillusioned with the whole lifestyle in a fairly short period of time. It's hard to know whom you can trust, because so many people come

44

out of the woodwork when you become a name. They hang around hoping they'll become famous through their first class associations. I got tired of being forced to hang out with people that only wanted to use me. So here I am." He watched her struggle with what she thought would be the correct response. Watching her was becoming a habit of his. One that he rather enjoyed.

"But is your career going to suffer, because you've removed yourself from the party circuit?" She seemed to truly be concerned.

"It might have early in my career, but now I could probably become a complete recluse and it wouldn't take too much of a hit. Anyway, enough about me. What have you been up to the last several years? Well, I mean after the high school years."

Emma stood. "I don't think we have time for all that at the moment. I've got to get them back, before their parents show up and wonder what we did with them." She hollered to Alan and Abby, "Come on. It's time to head back so you don't miss dinner." Turning to David, she thought of apologizing and then thought better of it. She had to go and there was nothing else to it. Therefore, there was nothing to say she was sorry about. "See ya." Gathering the kids, she steered them uptown to the car.

David was left to contemplate the encounter alone. The time he spent with Emma, working or hanging out at the park, it didn't matter, he discovered was time well spent. There was some kind of pull she had on him and he wasn't certain he cared for it—although it was becoming more and more difficult to ignore. No one had ever held any type of hold on him that he didn't allow. The problem was foreign to him. And what was up with that abrupt departure? She obviously did not want to discuss her past with him. That was abundantly clear. But why? Did she have some dark secret?

Upon arriving home, Emma spotted her cousin's vehicle in the driveway. "Uh oh, I hope your mom hasn't been waiting long."

Abby spoke up. "She won't care. She loves to talk." The innocence of youth came through in the simple statement, making Emma grin at the overt honesty.

"Well, let's go see if you're right."

The burst of noise filled the kitchen instantly as the two scurried to their mother and threw their bodies at her. "Mommy, Mommy! We just came from the park!" Abby said.

Alan offered his own information. "Before that, we had ice cream!"

They both wore big wide grins. In unison they chimed, "Can we do it again? Please, please!"

Crystal looked to Emma. "Well, I guess the day was a big hit. I really appreciate it. We got quite a bit done."

The two little urchins tugged at their mother's shirt. "We want to stay and play!"

"No, no. Aunt Nancy and Emma have things to do. Maybe we can make a play date for another time." Crystal winked at Emma.

"For tomorrow?" asked Abby.

"Maybe a little later than that. Let's go." She

turned to Emma and Nancy. "Thank you so much. Just let us know when you work on the roof and Jeff and I will be here. Bye." She hustled the kids out the back door, before they settled in and became even more difficult to extract.

* * * * *

Birds sang cheerfully just before the dawn. Emma scooted to the curtains, still drowsy, and pulled them aside. A giant red ball began to peek over the horizon. As she stood to watch the sunrise, she hoped that the cheery start to the morning was a good omen that would carry throughout the entire day. She could use one today. The meeting with the bank was scheduled and she was not looking forward to it. She had to convince them to give her, actually her mother, additional time to catch up on payments on the second mortgage. It had become increasingly difficult in recent years for Nancy to make the payments and now she was well behind. Continuing to pay what she could and occasionally the whole payment had kept the bank at bay for some time, but the situation had come to a head and was now Emma's affair to handle.

She had already made up her mind to write a check for what was left in her checking account, but it wasn't enough to bring them up to date. She hoped and prayed that reason and good will would prevail. They were all one community here, but she wasn't oblivious to the realities of the situation. It was a business. And no matter how much anyone at the bank might want to be courteous and neighborly, she knew that it was likely not his or her choice. They would be bound by the constraints

47

of the policies set forth by that particular institution. She sighed at the thought of what lay ahead, hoping that an amenable resolution could be reached.

"Well, it's not going to go away. I'd better get dressed so I don't add tardiness to the list of negative characteristics they may very well use to describe their delinquent customer." Emma had a habit of talking out loud, especially when there was an issue to work through. It made her feel that she was really giving it a good shot at wading through a specific topic, aiming for a solution. Whether or not it actually made a difference was highly debatable, but it made her feel better, so what did it matter to anyone else.

She slipped into her interview suit skirt. It was charcoal gray in a plain, straight-to-the-knees style. Opting to forgo the jacket, she pulled on a silk ivory blouse that was feminine, yet all business. The part she was dressing for was an extremely important one — one in which she yearned to be flawless. She had to be. Her singular goal was to convince the bank that she and her mother were willing and able to pay back the loan. She could not fail.

A couple of hours later, Emma came out of Mr. Collins office with as much of a reprieve as she could expect, yet the overwhelming feeling of doom hung over her. The openness of the lobby of the bank felt larger than its reality because of the sheer enormity of the meeting and the consequences it held. Standing in the middle of the room, with its high ceiling and row of windows, did nothing for the oppressiveness she experienced in the aftermath of the encounter with the bank officers. She should feel good in one way, and she did, but the gauntlet still hung overhead.

They would not foreclose immediately, but the time frame allowed was next to impossible. Where were they to get that kind of money running a small dairy farm? She could get a job teaching but that wouldn't help. Summer was almost at hand. Also, if she did, they would have to hire someone to help on the farm, defeating the purpose of her being there and sending more money out the door. Maybe it was still hopeless. The short deferment of the ax falling was likely only helpful in drawing out the process.

Her head hung low, allowing her to wallow in the darkness briefly before she made for the front door and the relief of escaping the suffocating building. She had made it about ten feet before she ran into a hard chest. Opening her mouth to apologize, she closed it just as quickly as she looked into David's face. "What are you doing here?"

"Well, that's a fine how do you do, after running into me like that. Just doing some business." He could read her face like a neon sign. Something was seriously wrong. Assuming she had enough of reality for the time being, he attempted to lighten the mood. "So you deliver the two wiggle ridden beings to their mother yesterday okay?" He watched the gravity drain slightly from her delicate features.

"Yeah, they had so much fun they wanted to stay. I guess we did all right with them. They promised they'd come back soon." Now, she was able to sport a small smile. "They insisted that we invite you along next time too."

"Ah, good little kids. I like them more already." They walked out the large glass doors, pausing on the other side. "How about a bite to eat?"

"No. I've got to get back and get something done. A lot to do and no one but mainly me to do it." She spun quickly toward her car.

Before she could take a step, David's hand was around her wrist, spinning her back to him. "What happened in there? Maybe I can help."

The heat ran up her arm so quickly that all she could think to do was escape. "No, no one can help." I'm alone in this, she thought. She bit back the tears that were threatening to spill over and fixed her face with a determined expression. "I've got to get back," she said flatly as she looked down to the wrist he still held, in hopes he would take the hint and let go.

He started dragging her across the street to the diner. "Come on, let's go fill our stomachs. Besides, I'm starving and our brains will likely work more efficiently then."

She struggled to keep up the pace he set, determined not to make a scene that could be interpreted by the town folk in any number of ways and be dispersed throughout the residents by the end of the day. "Are you always this much of a bully? Don't you know when to quit?"

"No and no." He stopped on the sidewalk outside

the nearly full diner. "Are you always this stubborn when someone is trying to be kind?" He let go of her.

She raised her chin and narrowed her eyes. "I am when I'm being forced. It's not help when it's unwanted. Now if you'll excuse me, I have to be going. It was... *interesting* running into you." She flashed a put-on grin his direction and was off.

Calling after her he knew he had to let her go, but wished he didn't. "See you soon." He smiled, knowing the thought would spread like a virus in her. Even if her thoughts were of avoiding him and how to rid her life of his presence, she would still be thinking of him — he hoped. And that was a start. Besides, he knew she didn't really believe he should be banned from inhabiting a portion of her life. At least he didn't think so.

As he made his way to his car, the thought rolled around in his head. Bumping into her was becoming a habit — one he intended not to break anytime soon. He would make sure he saw her again. And he would make sure it was memorable and that he was irresistible. Somehow, Emma just had to conclude that he belonged in her life.

Called Home

Chapter 4

A week had gone by without her having to handle any unwanted encounters with David. If he wasn't around, she didn't have to be concerned with the response she had to him. It was unnerving and she didn't like it in the least. It was less tolerable that she couldn't seem to suppress it.

She insisted that she would never again be out of control of her actions or anything that happened to her. That's the whole reason she was taking the bull by the horns and selling what she could do without from the farm and working an evening job at the only bookstore in the county, which happened to be located in Brooks.

It worked out perfectly. She could get all the chores done on the farm and then, after dinner, spend the evening at the bookstore. The work was easy and as far as Emma was concerned, as good a place as any to spend an evening. She loved to read — romance, mystery, thriller, fantasy, almost anything. If left to her own devices, she would hole up in her room and read with every spare tick of the clock.

She was stocking the latest shipment when she found herself looking back at those intense green eyes. His latest book hadn't been out long and, even in this country bookstore, it was already sold out of the original shipment.

The door jingled open and her attention to the book and picture in it did not wane. He sure was manly looking, had rugged good looks and eyes that were rarely readable — unlike his books.

The book drew her in, just as the man did when in his presence. She flipped to the first page and read several, sitting on the floor in the aisle under the guise of stocking the bottom shelf. The story had pulled her in already with sympathy and, at the same time, disgust for the main character. As she continued reading, she wondered how you could feel both, but she did. She credited it to the skill of the writer.

She heard someone clear his throat behind her. She scrambled to her feet and nearly fell.

He caught her by the arm and pulled her up. Being in very close proximity with David had her heart drumming hard and her blood racing through her system. She had dropped the book in the tangle of arms getting to her feet.

David looked to the floor at his book. "So that's what you think of my book? If that's the case, I'm in trouble." Although he enjoyed the sensation of holding her close to him, he let her go —after a very long hesitation that only sparked his nerves. The woman could accomplish that with a look, let alone being caught in the bold embrace of his arms. There wasn't a need to have physical contact to have a connection with Emma.

Raising her head she met his eyes, which she recognized as an immediate mistake. It was like being caught in a rip tide, being pulled away from the solid and the objective.

The curve of his mouth and ease of expression did not coincide with the depth of emotion held in his gaze. He had the ability to strip her bare or bolster her with what he kept there. Surely, his resolve and experience did the same for him.

"You just startled me." She leaned over to retrieve the book and place it in the proper spot on the shelf. "I was just stocking the new shipment of your latest contribution to the literary world. It must be tolerable. People seem to be buying it. We've already sold the first batch sent to us. And that was mere days ago."

"Don't you want to continue reading it?"

"I can't be sitting around reading while I'm working." She stocked more of the books. "And I can't be standing around in idle gossip either."

"I never gossip," he retorted. "You don't have to worry about me. I won't tell anyone. You could buy it, you know. Then you could take it home and read it when you wanted."

She glossed over the fact that she had no money to spend on frivolous items and said, "I don't have time to read. I'm busy running a farm and working in this wonderful bookstore." She gestured to his book and continued, "Reading that stuff is for people that don't have anything better to do with their time. That's not me."

"Speaking of working here, what are you doing working in this place?" He leaned on the counter at the register as she retreated behind it.

"I'm stocking shelves and taking paying customers money and — "

"Very funny. No, I mean, you have a farm to run. Isn't that enough for you? Do you have some kind of need to work in a bookstore or overwork yourself or something of the like?" He watched her stay busy. She was hiding something. Actually a great deal, he thought.

"It's none of your business. And I would very much appreciate your keeping your nose out of it, lest you find it in a place you'd rather it not be, like out of joint." Her deep blue eyes challenged him to continue.

He could have pressed, but decided it would be unwise. "So when do you close up shop?"

"The store rarely sees customers much past nine, but then I have a bunch of straightening to do and closing out the register. I'm generally out of here just after it closes at ten."

David slapped his hands on the counter. "Excellent. I'll be waiting outside at ten."

"What are you talking about? I close up by myself all the time. Crime is virtually nonexistent here."

"I'm not coming here to walk you to your car. We'll go for a drink after you're done." He stuffed his hands in pockets to keep from reaching out to touch her.

"I don't think so. For one thing, I've got to get up early. For another — "

"We pretty much all do around here. It won't take long to grab one drink. And it sounds like you deserve one."

"Secondly, I don't recall you asking. I prefer to go with someone who has the manners to ask. We aren't cave people grabbing what we want." The word *want* came out like a choked pig, as he firmly grasped her face in his strong hands and pulled her to him across the counter.

Smashing his lips to hers, he couldn't contain his need. Her warm pliant lips added fuel to the fire that already burned within him. She didn't struggle to free herself. They were two moths to the same flame and it would consume them if they weren't careful.

The sensation that took over her entire being was like sinking into a warm bath and not being able to surface, but in an exhilarating way. The objective side of her brain was no longer functioning. She had fallen into the liquid world of pleasure, not wanting to leave even if she could. His mouth was firm and commanding and found hers demanding right back. She was lost in a world of delight to an extent never before experienced.

As abruptly as she was pulled into the sensations running rampant, she was shoved back out. David had backed away, attempting to calm his own system. He took a long hard look at her, then turned and strode out without a word.

She leaned against the counter for stability and

stared at the door until her breathing and pulse began a normal rhythm. Astonished at her own participation, she admitted that she had never responded to anyone with such intensity. The power of it was nearly overwhelming. The excitement was intoxicating.

The ring of the bell brought her back to the present. There was no sense in pondering the events of the evening since she did not intend to encourage David any further. He was a distraction she couldn't afford. The cost of a relationship was too high. It endangered the ownership of the farm and her very well being. She was not willing to pay the price again. Never again.

Time passed with few interruptions. With each day she worked, her level of contentment grew for the time she spent in the old cramped bookstore. It offered a certain character that the chain stores lacked. It became a way to put her troubles at bay for at least a few short hours, but those hours became more and more precious, offering her a vacation of sorts from the physical strains of working a farm.

"Hello. You made it just in time, we'll be closing in about ten minutes." A patron walked in late, unusual. "Is there anything I can help you find?" She didn't recognize him but then again she'd been gone for several years. Things change.

"I'm just browsing. Thanks." The customer milled around the displays of the latest releases near the front.

Emma went back to stocking the remaining books she had left. She sighed as she finished and bent to retrieve the boxes strewn about the floor. With three boxes in one hand and two in the other, she straightened to take them to the stock room. Not much of one really—it was hardly bigger than a walk-in closet.

She brushed the curtain aside with the boxes and once through an arm came around her neck with force. The boxes hit the floor as her hands flew to the arm severely restricting her breathing. Fear flashed through her. Attempting to speak, the words came out with a gasp for air. "What do you want?"

The man traded his grip around her neck for a firm one on her hair. Emma gulped for oxygen. With his other hand, he poked a hard rounded object firmly to her back. "Move." He guided her direction with what she assumed was a gun at her back and the handful of hair that he used like reins on a horse.

Her mind was racing. This isn't happening. This sort of thing never happens in Brooks, Wisconsin. Why is it happening here? Why me?

Emma's legs felt like two rubber bands. Her movements gave her the sensation of not being hers. Certain she would fall into a heap on the floor soon, she mustered every bit of strength she had in order to follow his commands, for fear of being shot.

A picture of her mother flashed across her mental screen. She was alone in a cramped room, cluttered with furniture and remembrances from the farm. With her head held in her hands, Nancy's shoulders heaved jerkily with every ragged intake of air used to fuel the next sobbing breath.

The scenario sent fear racing through her already

spent body. She had to survive! Her mother was counting on her and her usual practical personality to see them and their farm through another year.

I must prevail, but how?

Hoping against hope that some last minute customer would come to her rescue, she glanced to the door.

Feeling the slight tug on his grip of hair, he squelched her hopes. "I locked the door so no one could disturb us." He jammed the gun with force into another spot on her back for emphasis.

Her hopes crashed to the floor, where she was certain she would be heading soon.

Leading her to the register, he said, "Do anything stupid and you die. Do exactly as I say and *maybe* you live."

Hanging on to the hope that he was being sincere, she did precisely what he said. She reached the portion of the counter that rises in order for one to pass behind it and heard a loud crack as the gun fired. The thief slumped over, half on her. She caught herself from being knocked over by clinging to the portion of counter she had raised and pulled herself away from him.

As she whirled around to thank her savior, she saw David standing there with a pipe wrench in his hand and a warrior look in his eyes. The wooziness took over during the spin and she slid to the floor, landing next to the burglar.

Stashing the gun in his waistband, David knelt down beside Emma. It was only then that the creeping edges of a pool of blood made its existence known to David. Panic rose rapidly and took the form of action. Locating the wound took a meticulous search of her limp body. No evidence of damage was found on the front of her so, in the process of rolling Emma toward him, he placed his hands on her side and felt the wetness of what he presumed to be blood. He yanked off his shirt and pressed it firmly to what appeared to be a surface wound. Or maybe it was more hope than reality. He would know more when he was able to stop the bleeding. He kept the pressure with one hand and reached for the phone on the counter with his other.

Now that the authorities and medical help for Emma were on their way, he had to insure that the assailant was restrained, for he was sure to wake soon. He took off his belt and used it to hold his shirt over her open flesh. That being done, he bound the thief's hands behind his back with duct tape and turned his attention back to Emma. As he stared down at her pale, motionless face, he realized that he never wanted to feel this way again. Intellectually, he knew that she would likely be fine physically in several days, but the fear that had clawed at his insides was unbearable. This intensely passionate feeling had always eluded him in the past. He was unsure of it ever being a real possibility in his life. Now that he found it, he was not about to lose it.

The guy on the floor a couple of feet away was lucky that David's full attention was on Emma. David's urge to strangle the life out of him was eclipsed only by his concern for Emma.

The sheriff pounded on the bookstore's front door. As he stood to let him in, David noticed that Emma let out a small squeak and began to slowly move like the gradual ascent of a roller coaster—click-by-click, inch-by-inch.

After David unlocked the door and let the stocky-built sheriff in, he pointed to the man on the floor and told the lawman flatly, "That's him." David was back beside Emma, brushing her hair lightly from her face, as her eyes, fluttering, made their way open. It was fairly obvious that she remained behind a foggy veil.

She squinted, trying to adjust her focus, and saw enough to know that David was with her, his eyes revealing concern and hinting at anger. The effort was too wearing and she let her lids droop. "What… happened?" Her voice raw and her body weak, each word came out in a spurt.

He brushed his fingers lightly over the side of her face. "You're going to be fine. Help just pulled up." She drifted back out again. He pressed his lips to her forehead as he said a silent prayer.

The paramedics rushed in to assess the patient as David did the only thing he could—he stood over her, watching and praying. With clean bandages on the wound, Emma was hoisted to a gurney and rolled to the waiting ambulance. He stuck to her like glue, not wanting to leave her for a second.

Loaded and ready to go, the rather large paramedic put a hand to David's chest and announced that he could meet them at the hospital. David, hyped up with adrenaline from the incident, shoved the guy back forcefully. Before either of them could react, there was a sheriff's deputy exerting a steel-like grip from behind his man. The one built like a body builder said, "Okay gentlemen, isn't the objective here to get that girl to the hospital? Now then, Bill you get in and be off. You," he pointed at David, "cool it and you'll be let go. If not, you can come with me to the jail house."

After the rig left with Emma en route to the hospital, the deputy lit a cigarette and leaned against his patrol car like he had all the time in the world. "Now, this can take a long time or a short time. And it can be complicated or simple. The choice is yours." He took a long drag on his cigarette, savoring every nuance of the experience before continuing. "What will it be?" He blew out a long stream of smoke.

David knew he'd been unreasonable, but that proved impotent in smoothing the edge about him. He knew the only way to get to Emma was to play the game, so he packed down his emotions and put up the veil of courtesy. "You're right, I'm sorry. I'm just concerned about Emma. May I go now?"

The deputy eyed him suspiciously as he brought his vice to his lips. "Sure. Drive carefully." Officer Schultz puffed twice deeply prior to discarding the butt on his saunter toward the crime scene and his partner inside.

Already to his car, David waved a hand and answered. "Got it." Jumping in, he started the car in one move. He threw the car into drive after backing out of the space and sent gravel into the air as he attempted a balance between speed and care so as not to invite the sheriff's deputies to impede his joining Emma. That was his sole intent. It was the only thing occupying his thoughts—Emma.

On the way there, his depth of feeling for Emma clearly crystallized. He would have never thought it possible for a person to become ingrained into his life in a matter of days, but she had. Now, the fear he felt at the thought of the remote chance of losing her was physically apparent, his head and stomach churned and his pulse raced. However irrational the thought of losing her at this point was, it didn't matter. It existed. So did the ache in the very core of his soul.

The next thing that Emma comprehended was waking up in a hospital room with David sitting beside her, with his head in his hands. She touched his arm with the lightest of fingers. He jumped. "I'm sorry. I didn't mean to startle you," she said with a voice like a little girl. She was weak from the injury and the medication.

He stood so he wouldn't touch her and walked to release excess energy. "No problem." He turned to her as he reached the window. "How do you feel?" He started pacing toward the door.

"A little out of it." She attempted to shift positions. "Oh wow. I'd better not use that arm for hefting myself." She settled back into position.

"Yeah, you'll be sore for awhile. Doc said you were lucky. It didn't hit any organs and you have just a mild concussion." He couldn't say out loud that she'd been shot. For some reason it made it seem even more real and more painful.

"It? What do you mean? What happened? I feel like I lost a chunk of time. Could you please fill in the blanks?" She looked at him with eyes as blue as he'd ever seen the sky and he dropped his gaze. He couldn't stare into them as he told her. It was too scary. It was too painful. It was too real.

"Do you remember the attempted robbery?" David crossed his arms attempting to build the frame of mind that he was just telling a story—like one of his novels. Keeping his emotions out of it was nearly impossible, but vital to his survival. He appeared cross.

Emma searched her memory banks and furrowed her eyebrows. "Vaguely." It was fuzzy. It was there, but not at all clear. It was remote, just out of reach and *almost* attainable.

"Well, to make a short story even shorter, as the would-be robber slumped to the floor the gun went off and you were hit by it."

Confusion ruled her expression and her thoughts. "Why would he crumble to a heap on the floor?"

"I hit him." He watched her process the information as he fought for detachment.

"You hit him. Why—I mean how did you come to do that?"

"I came back to convince you to at least get a friendly cup of coffee with me. That's when I saw him with his hand holding a fist full of your hair and a gun at your back. I wanted to bang on the window and stop it immediately, but I knew all I would do was aggravate him and who knows what kind of response that would have created. So, I went around back and came through the stock room. The pipe wrench I borrowed from the back knocked him out with ease." His smile was quick and fleeting.

He was back by her side, not able to keep the self-imposed distance.

"How can I ever thank you?" She took his strong hand in hers. "Thanks. It seems so inadequate." His eyes were unreadable as he searched her face with a seemingly emotionless expression.

David brushed his thumb over the back of her hand. "The only thanks I need is for you to recover fully and quickly." He let go of her and moved toward the door. "You need rest."

"Wait! Don't go. Will you take me home? I don't think I can drive just yet." Emma pushed back the covers to swing her legs to the floor.

"What do you think you're doing? You must have lost your faculties as a result of the stress of the whole thing." He lifted her legs back to the bed and covered her. "You're not going anywhere."

"I'm going home." The haze in her eyes was still quite evident.

"No, you are most definitely not. You've been shot." The words were close to a yell and hung in the air like a stinky fish. David's stance and expression were unrelenting in their sternness.

"You said I needed rest. I'll never get any here.

They've already patched me up and besides, my mother will worry if I'm not there."

"I called her and let her know what was going on and that she should stay there until I can come get her. Now be a good patient and lay your head down or I'll call the very mean-looking nurse in here." The look in his eye told her that he would do exactly as he said.

"Okay, let's get the doctor in here and if he says I can go will you take me?"

"I think it's a mistake, but if he puts his stamp of approval on it, then consider it done." He went to the call button and pushed.

A half hour later Emma was being released with a whole list of dos and don'ts and a slew of things to watch for, between her wound and her head. It was not what the doctor would have preferred, but he told David that in his experience a patient that was that insistent was better off at home. Being less agitated, the person would get more rest and recover quicker. The doctor told him that she would have to be watched carefully. Head injuries were unpredictable. David assured him that she would be well taken care of at home.

David pulled into the driveway at about three in the morning. As he did so, the light switched on. Nancy was out the door before he could lift Emma from the car.

"Oh, I was so worried." Nancy shut the door after David and Emma cleared it.

Emma felt completely ridiculous being carried like a child. "You can put me down. I'm sure I can get there myself." He carried her in through the front door as if she had said nothing.

In the kitchen he asked Nancy, "Where's her room?"

"It's up the stairs, first on the left. But you can just put her in my room here."

"That's all right. I've missed my workouts lately." He offered a friendly grin.

He went up the stairs without a noticeable strain. How strong he is, Emma thought as she felt the muscles in his chest become firm from hefting her weight. She felt safe in his arms. No, she scolded. You can't trust anyone but yourself. You know what happens when you do. They just let you down in the end. It's better not getting involved in the first place. Don't be an idiot.

She was gently laid in bed and tucked in when she put on a perfunctorily polite expression and proceeded to thank and dismiss David. "I appreciate it, but I'm home now and need to rest."

"No problem and I agree. So you close your eyes and do just that."

She was satisfied she had made her point, closed her eyes and fell asleep quickly.

She woke up to full sunlight pouring into her room, a song from a bird nearby her window and David in a chair beside the bed watching her.

He raised a coffee cup to her, "Morning. How we feeling?"

"What are you doing here in my bedroom?" Her forehead was wrinkled in concentration and irritation.

"You seem to be asking me that a lot lately. I'm

here to keep a watchful eye on you. Doctor's orders. Are you hungry? Your mother has cooked enough for twice as many. I guess she didn't want you to starve and I'd say that's not likely to happen if she has anything to say about it." A smile bloomed on his face, reaching his eyes. It was a relief to see some color back in Emma's face. He gulped down the remainder of his coffee as he stood to go.

Emma sat up and said, "I'll eat after I milk the cows. It's late and they're probably ready to explode."

David put a hand to her shoulder to keep her put. "It's already done. I did it first thing. So how about that breakfast?"

"Only if I can get out of this bed to have it." She stood too quickly and swayed.

He grabbed her firmly at the waist and lowered her back to the bed. "I don't think so, hot shot. Breakfast will be coming to you." He covered her with a blanket and headed for the door.

She ate in silence and felt extremely foolish having a baby sitter. "I'm done." She shoved the tray in his direction and he held it in place.

"That's only half of what's on your plate. Eat up or I'll tell your Mom you said it was unpalatable." A mischievous grin danced across his face.

"You wouldn't dare." She eyed him carefully. "You would, wouldn't you?" She obediently stuffed in several more bites, shoved the tray away and glared. "There. Satisfied?"

"It'll do." David retrieved the breakfast dishes from her lap.

"I don't think even a lumberjack could have eaten all she heaped on there. And when you take the tray down you can go home and get some rest yourself. You look terrible."

"Gee, thanks. I've always wanted to hear that." He set the load on the bureau. "Especially from a beautiful woman. I'll make you a deal. I'll leave you alone and make myself more presentable, if you take one of these and rest some more." He held out one of the pain pills and a glass of water.

"If that's the only way to get rid of you, I guess I have no choice." Reluctantly, she took the tablet.

"That's a girl." He took the cup from her, kissed her forehead and left without another word.

Chapter 5

Sleep was more elusive than it should have been. Her body was weary from the trauma and the medication most assuredly should have kicked in by now. It was his fault. He had to call me a beautiful woman, she thought. That's all her mind would keep replaying—over and over. Emma willed it to focus elsewhere and would invariably be dragged back to David's statement. Why did he have to say that? Why now, especially when I need rest? He can't just say something like that and leave, but he did. And now I am left to ponder what he meant and why he said it.

The big question was how she felt about it, about him. It depends on when you ask, she concluded. He did rescue her, which was, as a general rule, not necessary for her. But there was more than gratitude in her feelings for David. If she was being honest with herself, which she could do best when she was alone, there was exceedingly more to her feelings for him than being grateful.

He made her nervous. No one had ever achieved that level of response from her in the past. Emma was a confident woman who did what needed to be done without constant guidance from others and rarely showed any nerves whatsoever. It's just the situation in which I find myself, she thought. All the farm business, then the storm, the financial concerns and on top of it *he* comes around taking kisses when they're not offered.

That's all it is—just an overload of the system. A set objective and a plan of action are all that's needed to right the ship and get it back on course. She had to set her mind and focus on the goal. The most vital pieces of the puzzle were no distractions. And by distractions she meant David—the biggest one.

Once recovered, her sole purpose would be the running and maintenance of the farm. She would make it abundantly clear to David how unwanted his presence was and that he had better keep a significant distance from her.

Satisfied with her resolution to turn things around, she let the medication take over her will to stay awake. Sleep settled in before she could even form the next thought. The only thing was that her dreams seemed to be less controlled by her and led her in directions she cared not to go.

Caught in dreamland she saw David as a superhero. He wasn't sporting the usual spandex outfit, but wore worn-in jeans and a tight fitting tee shirt over expertly toned muscles. The villain bore a strange resemblance to her ex-boyfriend and gave off a high creep vibe. David swooped in to pluck him away from her just before the villain's knife connected with her flesh. When the bad guy had been dealt with, David was back to gather her in his arms and whisk her off to safety. She already felt safe in his strong, competent arms. Not a word was said, but all that needed to be was communicated to her through his eyes. There was so much there—care and concern, irritation and anger. Why was he angry if he cared so deeply? It left her more confused than ever.

She carried that confusion with her into the next dream. Chaos reigned. There was action all around her and yet she felt separate. Cars crashed, loved ones died, neighbors lost jobs, relationships crumbled. She was in the middle of it, yet remained untouched. As she stood baffled, the scene around her changed to people engaged in happy events—parties, weddings, cooing over babies, couples hand-in-hand on a quiet walk, graduations, a loud family dinner, a loving embrace. But once again, although she was there in the center of it, she remained unaffected by each situation. This time though, she wanted to be included. She wanted to be a part of the celebrations, the close connection with the people in her life, but was restrained from doing so. David came to her to explain that she could not be allowed to join in without first taking the "leap into life train." If she refused to accept all parts of life then she was only able to be a spectator and not a participant. The bad comes with the good and there was no way to separate the two. Many have tried, he said, with dire consequences. To keep the pain at arms length was to keep the joys of life there also.

Suddenly she was standing alone in the midst of a vast canyon. She called out. There was no answer except the echo of her own voice, calling again and again. This time she yelled and waited to no avail. No one was coming. No one was there. She was so alone she couldn't even remember any names to call. The emptiness became cavernous. It felt like she would drain into it and become nothing herself. She woke before the last flicker of her own light faded.

It was dark and she had trouble focusing. She thought there was a foreign form in her room. She groaned as she struggled to sit, when a hand swiftly grabbed her uninjured arm to help her up. She knew without seeing that it was David's. The size, the strength and the most telling heat that flowed into hers. "I thought I told you to go home."

"I know I haven't been around you very long, but you should know by now that I never listen to nonsense."

"Oh, nice. I just wake up and here you are to insult me immediately. How caring you are. Don't you have a home to go to, anyway?"

"No, actually not yet. I am working on it though."

"Well, if you're going to hang out here why don't you make yourself useful and turn on a light so we're not fumbling around in the dark."

"I think I might rather like fumbling around in the dark." She could picture the smirk on his face.

"Well, I don't. And it's my house, my room and

my injuries so if you don't mind I'd prefer some light to get to the bathroom."

"Fine, have it your way. I think you might be one of the only people who is actually more crabby after an all day sleep than more cheerful."

"I reserve it for you. Plus you seem to have a way of irritating me without effort. It must be a talent of yours." She stood, swaying a bit.

"I do have a great many talents." He grabbed her shoulders to help steady her.

"See. You're always handling me. I don't want to be handled." She unsuccessfully attempted to wrench her shoulder from his grasp.

"I'd be happy to if you would just heal already and stop being ready to topple over when you stand." He had succeeded in convincing her of her ridiculous behavior. "Now may I help you to the bathroom without risking retaliation?"

"I guess."

* * * * *

The coffee was hot, the eggs were fresh and the biscuits were homemade. Gail served a mighty fine breakfast at the local diner. Broad face and broad body, the stocky woman looked like she enjoyed her own cooking. She moved more quickly and much more smoothly than it appeared she could or would ever desire to. Efficient in her movements and more than competent in her profession, she handled the breakfast rush with ease. And there was plenty to handle this morning.

David lingered over a second cup of coffee when

Jim sat down across the table. "How's Emma doing?"

"As well as can be expected considering the trauma she's been through. You know her, always a brave front." He took a long sip of coffee as he peered at Jim over the mug. "You want a cup?"

"No. I was just picking up a breakfast sandwich. I got to get back to work. But that's why I wanted to talk to you in the first place. Emma's order is in at the lumberyard. We can deliver it anytime, but I didn't know if she wanted it staring her in the face while she's incapacitated." Jim folded his hands on the table, watching the gears of thought work in David's mind. "It can stay at the store as long as she needs."

"Can you have it there first thing tomorrow morning?"

"Yeah, sure we can. But do you really think—"

"Just do it." He tossed a ten-dollar bill on the table as he rose, then nodded to Jim. "Thanks."

"Jim, your order's ready." The waitress held up a bag at the counter.

As Jim marched out the door, he noticed David had moved over to another table and was huddled with three of the guys from town that he used to pal around with back in the day. He whistled his way back to the lumberyard, wondering when he should stop in to see Emma. He added buying flowers to his mental to-do list. He couldn't wait. He would be able to offer her the good news of her order being in and ready for delivery. If I don't go tonight, he thought, I won't be able to be the one to tell her. It was decided—he would go tonight after work.

David continued his impromptu meeting.
Spreading the word would be simple in a small town. A
couple of key people were needed—Gail, the owner and
operator of the original diner in the heart of main street,
and Stacy, the head cheerleader in school the same year
as David. Gail talked to just about every soul that walked
through the front door to her homey, yet unique, little
diner. Gossip—good, bad or indifferent—was the sugar
of life for Stacy. Between the pair, the town could be well
informed within an hour.

After work was finished, Jim bought a bouquet of
flowers, went home to clean up, change his clothes, and
was on his way.

Jim stood at the Benson's door, smoothed his
clothes, slicked his hand through his hair and held the
flowers in front of him in anticipation. Several loud
knocks later, no one had come to the door. Highly
determined, Jim tried again. The bolt was switched back
and the door swung wide open.

"Oh, hi, Jim."

"Hi, Ms. Benson. Can I see Emma?"

"She's resting right now. I'm sorry." His shoulders
dropped and his head hung. "Are those for Emma?"
Nancy indicated the flowers.

"Yes. Yes, they are."

"I can put them in a vase and give them to her for
you. Would you like me to do that, Jim?" She reached for
them even though he had yet to answer.

"Ah, sure." Disappointed, he handed them to her

and methodically turned and took each step as if in deep thought. At the bottom of the back steps, he stuffed his hands in his pockets in frustration and spun back around. "Tell her I hope she's up and running soon, will you, Ms. Benson?"

"You bet. And I'm sure she says a big thank you for the flowers and your thoughtfulness. Bye." She closed the door, intent on bringing Emma the flowers and checking in on her.

* * * * *

Instead of waking to the trill of a bird's morning song, Emma heard the distinct sound of hammering. It seemed as though it was just outside her window. Shaking off the thought as foolish, she got up to peer out the window. She'd never seen so many people working on the farm at one time. It was like ants crawling all over a mound—there were people, it seemed, on every inch of the barn. They hammered, they hauled, they brought drinks, and they removed scrap. Not one hand was idle.

Then she spotted David, standing tall and appearing very important. He was the one to whom they all lobbed their questions. Pointing, nodding, answering and directing, he looked so in command at the position of boss. His stride was strong and confident as he checked and rechecked the progress of each section. Satisfied, he started hammering himself.

Emma felt a pang of guilt as she watched so many neighbors, friends and family work on her mother's and her behalf. The need to be out with them was pulling hard on her. Emotion welled up at the caring of her fellow men. Tears to the brim, she put up the wall and decided to allow them to go no farther. With steely determination, she dressed gingerly and descended the stairs with difficulty, but her stubbornness outdid her pain and wooziness.

Intent on the work at hand, David didn't notice the movement in the yard until she was halfway across. He dropped everything at his feet, hustled over and slipped his arm around her. "What are you doing? Are you insane?" He attempted to turn her gently but she refused his suggestion and plowed straight ahead.

"All these people came to help us out. The least I can do is thank them. I want to be out here with them— hammering right beside them."

He impeded her progress by stepping in front of her. Brushing her hair to the side, he sympathized with her predicament. "I know you do, but the people here care about you enough to be here working hard. It would concern them too much for you to be out here. They might get distracted trying to keep an eye on you and hit their hand or fingers with the hammer." She was staring past him to the commotion of the work. David brought her gaze back to his with a gentle push of his fingers on her cheek. "You don't want to be responsible for that, do you?" He already knew how to get to her. It wouldn't be worrying about herself that would send her back to bed, but concern for the well-being of her friends and family.

Emma relented, knowing she wasn't going to win and admitting to herself that she really didn't belong out and about just yet, although she refused to say it out loud.

"Fine. If you think it's best for everyone involved then I'll return to the house. But you have to tell them how much I appreciate it and that I wish I were able to be wielding a hammer along side them."

His strong rough hands on each cheek, he couldn't resist her with the pout she sported. Kissing her forehead first, he made his way to her nose and finally to her soft lips. His hands slid into her sleek and silky hair as he kissed her full pouting lips with care and gentleness, invoking a response that was anything but gentle. He could detect it flowing just beneath the surface, making it even more consternating to him. Stuck between want, need and carefulness, he extended contact briefly before breaking away and swooping her into his arms.

Stunned by the kiss and mostly by her reaction to it, she was quiet. She decided it was best not to get into a conversation about it. It was just that she was feeling vulnerable in her current condition. She refused to be reminded that it was not just any old kiss, but her pulse pounded erratically and her head got lost in a fog that let nothing else invade. Her part in it had not been passive and certainly not just reactive, but voluntarily active.

David was here now and she would enjoy it. He was strong and dependable. He was hard working and loyal. He was challenging and real. He was everything she wanted and everything she was afraid of losing.

Nancy watched as her daughter was carried into the kitchen. David shrugged. She gave him a knowing look. "You seem to be doing a lot of heavy lifting lately."

"Your daughter escaped. I believe you'd better put

stronger locks on the doors and windows." He winked at Emma.

"I'll keep an eye on her. You can be sure of that after this little stunt." Nancy looked at her with a tsk-tsk expression.

"I'm right here, you know. And, by the way, I'm perfectly capable of taking care of myself. And while we're on it, I don't appreciate the heavy lifting comment either." She glared at her mother.

David turned his head to face her, ending up only inches away. He was slightly uncomfortable but he pressed on. "I'm not sure I'm buying the 'taking care of yourself' thing at the moment. Considering I found you outside wandering around in your condition, I don't think you have the common sense required to care for yourself. So, I leave you in the trustworthy hands of your mother."

Emma had enough of the two of them making fun at her expense and pushed on his chest. "Let me down." Not doing so immediately, she insisted, "I said let me down!"

He asked Nancy, "Here or in her bed?"

"Here is fine if she's up to it."

With a huff Emma answered, "Yes, I'm up to it. That's what I've been trying to tell you the whole time."

He would have liked to set her down with a plop, but he thought he should be a little more considerate of her injuries so he eased her to the floor, holding her until he was entirely sure of her steadiness.

"Well, work's awaitin'." He spun on his heels and was off.

Emma studied her mother and determined she would dive in headfirst. "So how come you didn't wait until I was well enough to be out there with them?"

Nancy wore a half smile along with her flowered apron. "Honey, I didn't know anything about this. I didn't know about it until I heard the construction noise myself."

Emma sat at the table. "So you weren't the one that set this up?"

"No. I didn't even know the supplies were in at the store. I think you know whom you have to thank for all the work being done."

She felt dumbfounded and stared at her mother. "Yeah, I guess I do." She rested her chin in her hands. "We're going to have to feed all these people."

Nancy put a hand to Emma's shoulder. "No. Before you get too panicked, he's taken care of that as well. Shortly after they started in on the construction he came to the door to reassure me that it was."

"How's he going to feed that many mouths?" She slapped her hands on the table startling her mother. "Sorry."

"He hired Gail to cater the whole thing. She'll be here in a little over an hour to set up. Outside no less, so as not to make a mess in here, David said." Nancy turned back to finishing with the blueberry pie she was baking for dinner. "He's so thoughtful."

"Yeah, thoughtful. That's not the word I had for it —more like meddling," she muttered under her breath. Unfortunately, it was loud enough for her mother to get the gist.

"Emma Rose. He is doing us a huge favor. The least you could do is be grateful and kind to the man." Her mother rarely got worked up, let alone angry. Emma knew that she'd better watch her step.

"Sorry. You're right. I'm just cranky from being stuck in bed and being treated like an invalid."

Rising from the table she announced, "I'm going up to my cave until I'm human enough to be around civilized people."

In her room now she could be honest with herself. She wasn't angry with David for interfering, she was just too used to having to do it all on her own. Handling someone more than willing to give unconditional help was a foreign experience to her—with the exception of her mother. She found it a bit unnerving. She didn't want to be beholden to anyone. She didn't want to owe anyone. The self-sufficient person she had always been felt threatened—and she didn't care for the feeling. As soon as she was able, she would pay him back and that would be that. Her obligation would be fulfilled.

After all the commotion of the last hour, she finally had to acknowledge her weariness. She gave into it and succumbed to the cloud of sleep that washed over her rapidly. She had rationalized the nap, which she considered a weakness, by telling herself that it was the quickest way to recovery, which led to her being in charge of her life once again. Almost any price was worth it if the end result was self-sufficiency. She couldn't wait until she was back to her routine.

* * * * *

The work lasted the better part of the day. At day's end, it was complete. The barn was as good as new. Well, actually parts of it were. Anyhow, as David looked back on it he admired the work that friends and family had done. He reveled in the sense of camaraderie felt by all who labored for one of the community.

He started to understand that this was part of what had been missing in the recent past of his life. People pitched in here because they truly cared for the person instead of what the person did for a living or what they could do for them. It was a pleasant change. One he intended to hang onto and build on. He was also beginning to see that he wanted Emma to become significant in his life. The trick was going to be convincing her it was right for them both. He grinned at recalling the stubbornness she displayed that morning. He would have to push without her catching on that she was being prodded in a certain direction. Not willing to be easily led, it would be a feat to accomplish, but one that contained very high stakes—and he would win. He had to win.

Back in his old room, the surroundings were like being in a time warp. All of the paraphernalia from his basketball days in high school still decorated the space. Trophies lined a shelf against the lake-blue wall. A school pennant was pinned to the curtains and ribbons bordered a cork-board on the opposite wall.

It was a weird feeling occupying the room. The room remained the same, but he hadn't. He had lived a part of his life diametrically opposed to the one he stood in now. His parents had never quite understood his need to leave or the life he'd been leading, but they were always supportive of him, although there was always the nonverbal wish for him to return home to the life they knew and loved. David had made it quite clear that he would not be coming home unless the call had been unmistakable to him. And here he was, called home by his own needs.

Called Home

Chapter 6

David sat on the bed after his shower in virtual darkness. His bones felt weary from the full day of work, but his mind ran wild with too many thoughts to organize. A feeling of restlessness enveloped his entire being. "Leave it to me to be bone tired and yet uneasy at the same time," he muttered.

Resolving to do something with the energy he possessed, he sat at his laptop and opened a new document. He would write. The story would take his mind off whatever was muddling it up. He sat in the creaky maple chair at the old maple desk, fingers perched on the keyboard, ready for action. The problem was, nothing came.

Thoughts of Emma began to encroach on the blankness. He could see her face cradled by his hands and feel the soft, silky-smooth texture of her skin. Her blue eyes pulled him to her without effort. Then the pool of blood beside her on the floor invaded his daydream and anger rushed into him. Pushing it away as being in the past, he pictured the stubborn expression set on her fair face when she tried to insist on helping, and had to smile. She was a feisty one, he thought.

After a half hour, he concluded that along with no sleep there would also be no writing tonight. The bottle of wine he had bought was in reserve for another time so he rooted around in the refrigerator in hopes of finding some beer. He had no luck in that regard and he stood in the middle of the dark kitchen watching the almost full moon stream light through the yellow curtained window. Bourbon—it burst into his mind and took hold. His father always kept some in the sideboard in the dining room. If that didn't calm his overactive brain he didn't know of anything else. Or did he?

That thought he couldn't allow, for there was no way to achieve the end at the moment. Emma was temporarily out of his reach. As he nursed his bourbon in the dark of the sitting room, he imagined her there beside him in the crook of his arm with her head resting on his shoulder. Only for now was the goal unattainable, but she'd better watch out when she fully recovered. I intend to make her see that we're meant for one another, he thought. He threw back the remainder of the drink and mounted the stairs, sure of his ability to sleep.

* * * * *

Emma trekked back from the barn after the morning milking. It was good to be back about the business of running the farm after being sidelined for a time. She was never very good at taking it easy. The morning suited her mood. It was warm and brimming with new life. The birds sang their cheery morning songs and the air was filled with the scent of newly blooming daffodils, tulips and crocus. She breathed in deeply, never tiring of the fresh smells of spring. Her energy was boundless and her mood soared.

It had been over a week since the barn was finished and not a sign of David the whole of it. She wondered just what went on in that brain of his. He comes to her rescue, organizes the rebuilding of the barn and then disappears. It's probably just as well. She didn't need him hanging around bothering her anyway. One less worry was fine with her. She had enough on her plate to handle, she didn't need to be dealing with him as well.

Why then, did the man continue to intrude on her thoughts and offer nothing but sleepless nights? He was a nuisance, whether present or not. Figuring she was too busy with the business of recovering to order her thoughts, she would write it off and start with the here and now and refuse to entertain dreams of David. Unpleasant or pleasant, they were all unwanted. And that was the point. It would stop.

Entering the cheery, homey kitchen Emma came to an abrupt halt with her mouth gaping half-open. The practical kitchen table was adorned with a dozen peach roses in a swirl cut crystal vase. Grinning on the other side of them was David. "Morning."

She moved to the coffee pot and mumbled, "Morning."

Nancy whisked into the room and gestured to the flowers on the table. "Aren't they beautiful? Sit. I'll dish up the breakfast for the two of you."

Glaring at David she replied, "I'm sure David can't stay for breakfast. He must have tons of things to do."

"No. I'm good." He talked to Nancy with pure syrup in his voice. "I would love some eggs, Ms. Benson. Thank you." He smiled at Emma, placed his napkin in his lap and picked up the fork.

"I figured with you being out of pocket for so long, that you would have better things to do with your time than coming over here begging breakfast off of us." Luckily, her mother had gone to the laundry room to deal with the bedding.

"I can't think of any place I'd rather be than right here with you, having a pleasant conversation over an excellent meal." His mischievous grin spread to greet his eyes. "The scenery is rather lovely, too, although, the expression on your face is somewhat souring that."

"I can think of a few dozen places *I'd* rather be. Like anyplace else." Her look challenged him to spar with her.

Not willing to take the bait, he pretended to be having a perfectly civil conversation. "Well, not me. I just got back from New York, I'm thrilled to be home."

"*This* isn't your home."

Knowing that she knew what he meant, he went on. "I came by to let you know that the guy they have in jail for attempting to rob the bookstore and attacking you is wanted in three other states for similar crimes. He thought the best way to finance his drug habit was to take from hard-working people evidently. I don't think he's going to have to look for a meal or a place to sleep for a very long time."

"You could have phoned with the information." She put the last forkful of eggs in her mouth.

"I came to see you also. I wanted to know how you were getting along after some decent recuperation time."

"Oh, it finally flitted through your brain to see about me?" She snatched up both sets of plates even though David still had a few bites of food left.

"You missed me, didn't you?"

"I most certainly did not. I don't know where you get that incredibly unlikely idea. Most people would be curious and courteous enough to check up on someone that had been shot before a week had gone by." She washed the dishes, clanged them around and plopped them down with the wrath that overflowed. It was considerably easier to display ire under the circumstances.

Suddenly he was behind her with his hands firmly on her shoulders and he turned her around. Pausing to see the anger attempting to cover the hurt in her eyes, he softened his features. "I told you I was in New York. It couldn't be helped. My agent forced me to come by threatening to come here. And talk about a fish out of water. No one would have wanted that." He let that sink in. "I couldn't think of anything but you and how you were doing. My mom let me know you were progressing, but I was about busting out of my skin with wanting to see for myself. And wanting to touch you, hold you and fortify you."

Held by his gentle words in the beginning, the spell was broken with the last of them. "*Fortify me? I don't need anyone to lean on or bolster my reserves. I'm my own person with plenty of my own strength to take care of myself and this farm.*" She pushed against his firm chest riddled with muscles in order to free herself.

He grabbed her hands with a quick, firm, confident move. His arms, swiftly moving with purpose and care, were around her, pulling her to him and him to her. Emma could feel her lips yearn to have his pressed to hers as he covered her forehead and cheeks with luxurious, long kisses. With each kiss, a spark was planted and each spark gathered to form glowing embers. When his mouth reached her lips she could barely contain the want and need within her. The painfully slow building of the passion fanned the embers into flames. With the heat came the melting of her limbs and clearing of her thoughts, save one—David.

He never entertained the thought that a woman could do this to him. Even with his imaginative streak and story telling, it didn't occur to him that he would ever be caught in a situation like this. He wanted to be with her. Although, if he were being truthful, it went beyond want and bled over into need. That was something that bothered him. Whereas he was always able to put a rein on his wants anytime he felt inclined in the past, he was beginning to become skeptical of the fact that he could do it under the spell of such need. Spell—that's what it was like. She had some kind of power over him that was unworldly. How did she do that? How could he do it to her?

Her lips were soft and hot on his. The initial hesitancy by Emma melted, paving the way for a giving that met David with some surprise. He reveled in it and gave more than he thought possible. The rhythm of it was lulling; the passion of it was lunacy. Hands roaming, lips searching, head spinning, he felt the whirl of it begin to take him. Like debris flinging out of a dust devil, David pulled back in search of his footing.

Emma braced herself against the counter. Unsure of words and how they would present themselves she faced the sink, picked up the dishcloth and methodically wiped down every square millimeter of the already clean counter and canisters within her reach.

David had put some space between them. He watched Emma expel her nervous energy as he leaned his shoulder on the door jamb separating the kitchen from the dining room. All it did was strengthen the urge to go back to her but, knowing her well enough, he kept his distance.

Somebody needed to say something, she thought. And he seemed perfectly content to stand there staring. She could feel it without looking. Hoping to sound casual, she said, "Thank you for the flowers. That was kind of you." Emma picked up the towel and began to dry the dishes to keep her idle hands busy and her attention distracted.

"Nothing kind about it. I want you to think of me

every time you see them, smell them. I want you to think of what's happening between us." He moved closer.

"There's nothing going on. Only in your imagination." She used the table as a barrier as she went to the other side, wiping the already clean surface.

"My imagination borrows heavily from reality." He headed for the back door. "The other reason I came by was to invite you and your mother to dinner tomorrow. I've been instructed by my mother not to take 'no' for an answer. So, you can come by about seven."

"I'll have to check with my mom. She may have something she can't miss." Emma was crossing her fingers and hoping that she would.

"She already said she'd love to, but I wanted to ask you myself." He opened the door and stepped through. "See you tomorrow at seven."

The bang of the door signaled Nancy's entrance. "Wasn't that nice of him to bring you flowers and check up on you? And now we've been invited for dinner. It's so exciting! I love meeting new people."

"If you're that thrilled by the prospect you can go for both of us. I don't particularly care for him coming around when he feels like it, disappearing without a word and then popping back into my life and ordering me around. He has another thing coming if he thinks he can do that." She had her hands on her hips and glared at the back door.

Nancy grinned at her daughter's reaction. "I think he's concerned about you and he explained his absence. It's a nice gesture for them to invite us to dinner. Now take it for what it is and be polite."

"Don't worry. I won't embarrass you, Mother."
Emma breezed out of the room to fume in the comfort of
her own room.

How dare he demand my presence like I was
being summoned to the king's court—insufferable man.
I'll go all right. I'll go and be as sweet to the rest of his
family as possible. As for him—he'd better beware.

The day went by as typical as it could after the
events of late. All she wanted for her and her mother right
now was a sense of normalcy—and security. That will be
a hard fought battle, Emma thought. One she was willing
to fight. One that she would not give up. One that she *had*
to win. There was no room for doubt or fear. And there
was no one to count on but herself.

The day was typical, with the exception that every
time she saw or smelled the roses she *did* think of that
moment in the kitchen with David. The flowers induced
the memory, but his touch, his smell, his eyes, his lips—
David—intruded on her thoughts all day long. She had
thought herself immune to superficial charms.

That was the problem though. She was beginning
to understand, much to her chagrin, that his charms ran
much deeper than the average Lothario. Although she
wished she could lump him into that rather standard
category and easily dismiss him, she had to admit that he
occupied a category unto himself. There would be no
easy handling of David. He was dangerous to her
stability. She had an unsettling feeling that he could
naturally insert himself into her life, without it registering

on the radar and then become indispensable. That could not happen—it would not.

She didn't want to hear promises that would not last and endure tenuous connections that soon would snap. There was no room in her life for games. Youth had brought her a lifetime full of them as far as she was concerned. Running headlong into a relationship was the last thing on her list of priorities. In fact, it was the first item on her list of things to avoid at all cost. Life had taught her that the pain was too real and the recovery endless. That act had been written, read, played, and the curtain closed. In her mind, she was better for it.

The day of the dinner was upon her and she was dreading every minute of it. On her way to the barn for the evening milking, she reminded herself that she was perfectly capable of handling a friendly dinner with neighbors. That was all it was and there was absolutely no reason to make any more out of it than was intended. It was simply a supportive gesture on the part of his family. She would take it as such and be on her way as soon as polite convention would allow.

In the barn was the sound of the milking machines doing their jobs and the subtle shifting of cows in their stalls. The job was no longer as time intensive as it once was when each cow received individual attention from milking by hand, but the process was much more efficient and the results higher yielding. Emma removed the machine from the cow's udders and emptied the contents into the large milk tank. By the time she attached it to the next cow in line, the second cow was finished giving up her milk. The steps were repeated until each of the massive animals were relieved of their burden and would be prepared to produce again in another twelve hours.

The majority of the herd was Holsteins with a few Jersey cows in the mix to make the milk richer. The black and whites were large producers and the beautiful brown cows gave an edge of quality to fetch a better price. There was a balance to maintain in order to command the most profit. The quality—fat content—of the milk had to be weighed with production levels.

Although she was a college graduate and had worked as a teacher, she took to this work with the ease of one who possessed it in the blood. She dreamed of one day being able to combine the two professions of her desire. The thought of hiring someone to run the farm while she was occupied and still having the luxury of having her hand in it up to a point of her choosing had her hoping. Hope, she thought. That was a sure way to fall face first into the cow pie of life.

She needed to keep her mind in reality. Her focus had to be the here and now. The pressing issues of the farm should be enough to order her mind and keep her thoughts out of the treacherous world of hopes and dreams.

As she cleaned and stored the last milking machine, she remembered what was in her immediate future. With a sigh she let the cows back out to pasture and headed for the house.

In her room, looking in the large dresser mirror, she was tempted to go in what she had on without showering. She didn't want to embarrass her mother or be rude to David's parents so she relented and stripped for her shower.

She studied her outfit, a pale blue, form-fitting, sleeveless blouse anchored by a full, Caribbean ocean-blue skirt, and felt certain that she achieved casualness. Satisfied with the wardrobe, she decided to leave her hair down and natural. The image that appeared in the mirror was still a bit too stark, so she adorned herself with earrings, no more than a simple silver hoop on each lobe.

At that moment, she heard her mother hollering for her. The voice came across as borderline frantic but, knowing her mother as well as she did, she attributed it to her nervous tendency to be perpetually early to everything she attended. "I'm coming, Mom. We've got time."

Emma entered the kitchen and Nancy took note and approved without a word. "Let's go. I don't want to be rude."

Emma took the time to pour a glass of water. "It's also not polite to show up too early." She swallowed several gulps without urgency. Finally, already knowing the answer, she asked, "So, you all ready to go?" She drank again, flipped on the faucet and thoroughly rinsed out the cup before placing it in the sink.

"You know I am. Can we go now?" Nancy went through the door without awaiting an answer.

"I guess we'd better since you seem to be halfway to the car already." With a competent pull, the door swung shut behind Emma. She didn't quite understand her mother's expectant mood toward the dinner. The Schlosser's were as unknown to her as they were to Emma. There was no anticipation bubbling over in her—more like impatience with the whole event.

On the drive over, Emma came to the conclusion that at the least she would have a good dinner that neither of them had to cook and, very likely, decent conversation. There was something to be said for the simple pleasure. She would ignore David as much as humanly possible and pour herself into being a model guest. The enjoyment she would get from closing him out would catapult her through the evening. She smiled at the thought.

After the introductions were made, she found herself in the living room of the old, immaculately kept farmhouse. In here, one would never guess of the dirt and smells that infiltrated a farm. She soaked in her surroundings as she sat in the antique wingback chair. The marble-flanked fireplace was the centerpiece of the room. It commanded your attention as the mantle clock drew you in with its steady tick of time and occasional chime of the quarter hour.

Carolyn, David's mother, announced, "We've time for a drink before the meal's ready so what will you have, Nancy?"

"Oh, ah, I'll have a glass of sherry." She nervously grasped her hands in her lap.

Emma continued to survey the room and its owners and her eyes happened upon David. As his gaze captured hers, she wondered how long he had been watching her. She was uncomfortable with the likely answer but refused to show it. She rose and went to offer her help to John, his father, as he deftly poured the drinks. "Oh, no, hon'. Thanks. I've got it. But you can deliver this to David for me." He handed her the sherry for herself and the scotch for David.

Great, I deliberately attempt distance only to get thrown to him anyway, she thought to herself. Well, that being the case, it will be handled with great confidence and little pleasure. She offered the drink to David with her head held high. "I was asked to deliver this. So here."

He couldn't help but smile at her ever so eloquent delivery—of both drink and statement. Taking the glass, he brushed his fingers over hers. He could feel the connection at the same time he saw Emma deny it. "Thank you."

She figured she had no choice but to engage in small talk with him. "Your parents have a very lovely home. Has it been in your family for a long time?" She sipped the sherry.

"Yes, actually for over a century it has been Schlosser land and I intend for it to stay that way for as long as I have something to say about it." The wish came with a determination in his eyes that told of his ability to make it happen. What she knew of David thus far more than suggested he would.

"Although the length of history isn't the same, I'm set on seeing to it that our farm stays just that also— ours."

He raised his glass to her. "Well then, to our family land." They touched their glasses and then she sipped her sherry and caught his stare as she lowered her drink.

David studied her without restraint and without excuse. He was comfortable in the act and unapologetic.

Almost immediately, Emma's uneasiness was evident. She refused to crumble under his scrutiny and with a straightening of her back and an iron will expression she returned his gaze. The drink she brought to her lips did not interrupt her stand as she took a hefty swig of the sherry.

David couldn't contain the grin that grew gradually as he watched her self-reliant countenance. His urge was to grab her, wrap his arms around her, hold her and never let go but, seeing as how they were in the company of their parents, he thought better of it. He wished he were in his own place having dinner with her —alone.

Just as Emma was about to make a snide comment, Carolyn announced that dinner was ready. She was slightly relieved at the fact that she was kept from making a scene for her mother's sake. Nancy would have been so ashamed and hurt. Emma could never do that. On the other hand, she wholeheartedly wished that she could have told David to take his grin and, well, toss it in the manure pile.

David put his arm across her shoulder to lead her into the dining area. Her shoulders shifted under him but, instead of obliging her, he only held her tighter. She was determined not to have a skirmish so she went to the table in his hold by his direction. It was only because of the circumstances in which she found herself.

It did not suit her—being led around like a puppy dog. She would set him straight the first moment she got the chance.

Chapter 7

The dinner was pleasant. All involved had a good time with good people and good food. Emma was thrilled that her mother seemed to be having such an enjoyable evening. It had been a long time since she had seen her that way—totally relaxed. Life had been difficult for her mother. There was no changing the past, but she could leave her mark on the future for the betterment of her mother's situation. And she would—with no interference from a guy who thinks he's a hotshot from the big city.

As David and Emma walked toward the barn, he swung his arm across her shoulders again. This time there was no buffer. She whirled out of his reach and stood with her hands on her hips and challenge in her eyes. "That has got to stop. I don't need some guy getting all chivalrous when all it ends up being is a big act."

He didn't say a word or act on his urge to grab her, for he could see real hurt in her eyes. She walked ahead of him, carrying herself with great dignity. As he followed in silence, he wondered who and what had wounded her, leaving her disillusioned. If he knew, he would like to impress something entirely different on them.

He decided to lighten the mood and caught up to her, meeting her pace. "So, you going to the rodeo this weekend?"

"I don't know. I completely forgot about it with all the *fun* of the last few weeks." Sighing, she was reminded of all he had done for her. "I wanted to thank you for all you did. Being there for me, the barn, and my mother loves the company." She looked to him with kindness and gratitude in her eyes. "I really appreciate it." Before he could say a word, she went on. "So, are *you* going to the rodeo?"

"Our family wouldn't miss it unless their blood stopped flowing. It's not only a privilege, it's a responsibility. They'll be taking a cow, various crafts and, if I'm not mistaken, a boat load of canned anything you can think of and baked goods my mother will spend the days leading up to the start of the rodeo making. She never misses an opportunity to bake and this is one of the biggest." He opened the barn door for Emma. "The other among them being Thanksgiving and Christmas. We never go hungry anywhere near those holidays." He laughed at the thought.

"Well, if you have trouble dispensing with all the goodies you know where I live." She entered the barn and froze.

David walked ahead to show the way, not realizing that she was stuck to the spot just inside the door. As he turned, he saw her standing still, holding her breath and staring straight in front of her. He followed her line of vision and it landed on the blonde mare with a white diamond on her muzzle. He walked the few steps back to her and held out his hand. "Come on. I'll introduce you to her."

Nearly motionless, she could only shake her head. When the feeling finally came back to her legs, she spun and ran out the door as quickly as she could. Her goal—the house—seemed to become more distant with each step. Forgoing her initial target, she plopped down on the grass and hung her head, holding her forehead in her hands. She let out several long sighs.

David, not knowing what he was dealing with, sat down beside her. Being fairly perceptive, he determined that she needed a bit of space and silence. He was certain she knew of his presence in the off chance that she would reach for him. His experience with her told him that she wouldn't even consider it.

Emma raised her head. The tears he expected to see were nonexistent. She whispered, "I'm sorry."

"Far as I can tell, you have nothing to be sorry for." He brushed her hair behind her ear.

"It was the horse." She felt compelled to explain. He had not tried to urge her toward being okay—no pat on the back or words of encouragement. She was grateful for the room he gave and the feeling of her reaction being in the realm of normal. Most people were too uncomfortable to give her the space she needed.

"You don't have to explain if you prefer not to." He wanted to touch her, but knew restraint was the wiser choice.

"I'm not afraid of horses *per se*." She folded her hands in her lap. "It's just that they're a reminder of an incident in my past." Breathing deeply, she sighed before proceeding. "My brother." David's eyebrows rose slightly at the mention of a brother and Emma swallowed, and then continued. "We were riding horses in the field with my dad. I was five and Mark was ten. I think the horses had as much fun as we did. Mark's horse was spooked by what we guessed was a snake. The horse stopped abruptly, and Mark was thrown over the its head."

She was quiet putting her head back in her hands. "He was so still. No visible signs of injury were evident. There was no blood, no limbs at odd angles. He looked as though he was sleeping in the field. His neck had been broken. I no longer had an older brother to be my playmate, to look out for me, to hassle me. I was lost and so were my parents."

David put his hand on hers. "I'm sorry."

She stood, shaking off his hand. "No. I don't need your sympathy. I'm just trying to get you to understand my reaction to the horse—especially that one. She looks almost exactly like the one Mark was riding. It took me aback. I've been fine around horses for years. The looks of her sent me right to that moment in time and I couldn't handle the force of it." She turned from him to watch the sun shoot its last rays over the horizon. "I'm fine now. We can just forget the whole thing."

He came up behind her and wrapped his arms around her in silence. Surprising even herself, she welcomed his presence and leaned against him. His lips pressed the top of her head slowly and tenderly. The imagination that he possessed was not good enough to pretend to understand how she felt. Thinking of his own family, he couldn't fathom losing one of them. They stood watching the sunset in silence as the brilliant reds deepened to purple and then to burgundy brush strokes that blended into the darkening sky.

Emma broke the embrace and turned for the barn. "Let's have you introduce me to that beautiful horse in there. I can't wait to meet her." She said it, in part, to convince herself. Her stride was confident, but her nerves were on alert.

He followed and said, "You don't have to do this."

"Yes. I believe I do. It's necessary for me." She stared at the door, hesitating.

"Here." He reached for the handle. "Allow me to be the gentleman." He held the door wide open.

She held her head high as she entered and strode to the horse's stall. It wasn't in Emma's character to back away from a challenge and she had set this one for herself. She was most definitely going to make it happen. The horse watched, slightly wary of this stranger, but mostly friendly.

Not quite sure of her next move, she watched the horse with appreciation of its strength and beauty. Her love of horses and watching them in fields as she whizzed down the road had not been relinquished she had just admired them from a distance. She always remembered the freedom she felt when riding through the open field. It had stayed with her from that tender age, but she hadn't mounted a horse since.

"Daisy, that's the horse, likes her muzzle rubbed." He wanted to encourage her without pushing. "Do you want to do the honors?"

Emma began to raise her hand and dropped it again.

David rubbed the mare between the ears and scratched behind them. "See? She loves it. She's the most gentle horse I've ever had the pleasure of knowing."

Taking a deep breath, she raised her hand and ran it the length of Daisy's muzzle. She did it again and again, enjoying each stroke more than the previous. It soothed her in a way she hadn't expected. Daisy decided she wanted more and nudged Emma in the shoulder. Emma took the hint and, lifting a brush from the hook, began the ritual of grooming. She had been only five, but she was taught to care for horses before she was granted the privilege of riding one.

"We have four other horses. I'll come back when you're done with them."

"Ha-ha. I forgot how special this time was spent grooming. It's a kind of therapy for whatever else is going on in your life."

She put the brush up on its hook and patted Daisy's shoulder. "There you go, girl. Feel better?"

"I think she would let you brush her all day long

or until she was rubbed raw anyway. Daisy is an attention sponge, one that can hold endless volumes of love."
David came into the stall on the other side of Daisy. "I could saddle her up if you're interested in a twilight ride."

"I don't know. My mom's probably waiting to go."

"I'm doubting that, the way she took to my parents and them to her. She was having a great time."

"Yeah, I guess you're right."

"Remember that," he said in a mock serious tone. "I bet you just don't want to risk losing a race to the master." He raised his brows in question.

"Master? I'm assuming you dubbed yourself that. I'm thinking of another name for you that might be far more appropriate."

"I'm guessing that I don't want to hear what it is." He rounded the front of the horse with his head slightly down and his eyes remained on Emma. "I believe you find yourself in a bit of a jam at the moment." He captured her shoulders in his grip and brought her closer.

"I believe I'll take you up on your challenge. You'd better be ready to lose, Schlosser."

"We'll see about that. But not before we get this out of the way." Before she could react, David possessively pressed his lips over hers and left subtlety behind. He found that he couldn't be in her presence for long without the almost suffocating need to touch her soft lips and experience the heat. It was more than just that though. The handle of his understanding on exactly what he felt was a slippery one. Just when he thought he had a good grip, it was greased with more emotion and he couldn't hold on.

Her need to push him away was smothered by the overpowering rise of the emotional tide. Each movement of his lips was another wave crashing at the rock of resistance she had set forth. She could feel herself sliding under as wave after wave washed over. Everything was cleared from her mind as David's tongue teased hers with mind numbing precision. Although her thoughts were wiped clean, her senses were heightened. Each flick of the tongue sent chills down her spine and heat racing back up her midsection to her heart, causing her pulse rate to hasten.

Disengaging was much more difficult than David had anticipated. He wanted to stay right where he was, doing what he was doing, but knew the danger. The thought that reinforced his will was that he would make certain they found their way back to this in the near future. With great effort, he stopped, spun around and swung the saddle from the stall wall without a word.

Being grateful for the chance to gather herself, Emma remained speechless as well. She leaned against the back of the stall, unsure of her stability, and shot for a casual stance. Her reaction to David baffled and annoyed her. She no more wanted to get tangled up with him than she was sure he did with her. The big city would probably entice him to return and she would be left watching his taillights. Nope, she couldn't let that happen. They could be friends, but that was all.

As he cinched the saddle tight, put the bit in Daisy's mouth and flipped the bridle over her head, he wondered about the power Emma held over him. She could send him into a tailspin within seconds. He had never looked for a lasting relationship in the past. Most of the women he went out with weren't in the market for a permanent situation either. They were just there to keep each other company and attend the necessary social functions of his trade. Until now, he wasn't even aware that he was capable of thinking past the next couple of months. Totally stunned, he had to accept the fact that he wanted more than the present and near future with Emma. He wanted a lot more. Trouble was ahead of him, he was sure of that much.

"Daisy looks ready to go. I'm not so sure about me," Emma said.

"Well, if you want to concede we can just take a walk instead." He knew she couldn't walk away from the challenge, especially since it came from him.

"If you don't get a horse saddled for yourself, it's going to be rather easy to win. And I don't want you complaining that it wasn't fair."

"Don't you worry, I'll be ready by the time you decide to hop in the saddle and take her out of the barn." He walked off toward the stall across from Daisy's.

Emma thought the time would be best spent getting further acquainted with Daisy. David had left the stall door open, knowing that Daisy wouldn't move unless led to do so and, considering that Emma was giving her such love and attention, the mare was not likely to wander from the soothing strokes. Emma caught a movement in her peripheral vision, looked up and saw

David leading a shiny black stallion out of the stall. "He's gorgeous."

"Yeah, he's a bit of a handful, but this way I'm positive I can win." He ran his hand down the sleek neck of his horse.

"Hah, you're a little cocky there, aren't you? I think we'd better actually run the race before you go off celebrating." The banter and her strong desire to put him in his place had bolstered her confidence. "Let's get a move on."

"In a hurry to lose, I see." He mounted the stallion and flashed a grin over his shoulder.

She watched him walk the horse out and didn't think twice before mounting Daisy. She tucked her skirt under her legs and tapped the mare into a walk. The horse felt strong underneath her and seemed to infuse her with its strength.

David waited on the other side of the barn doors. "Ready?"

"Yeah, I feel incredibly ready. I'm wondering now why I waited so long." She patted the mare's neck. "You lead the way, it's your place."

He walked them out of the yard and took his horse to a trot when he hit the tractor lane. His approach to gearing Emma up to run the horse was little by little, but not so slowly that the momentum was lost. Hitting the edge of the open field, he spurred Duke, the black stallion with short white boots, to pick up the pace. He could hear Emma and Daisy right behind him. Glancing over his shoulder, it appeared that Emma had not forgotten those early childhood riding lessons from her dad.

Luckily, the moon shone bright in an almost cloudless sky only days from being full, but he had to keep his concentration on the terrain so as not to run straight into a ditch. Lulled by the cadence of the horses hoof beats, he was momentarily puzzled when Daisy and Emma went galloping on by like he and Duke were standing still. He didn't even have to suggest that Duke get a move on, he was already in full run before David could consider the request.

Emma heard David call out, "You're not getting away from me that easily." She gave Daisy free reign and dug her heels in lightly to bring her to her optimum potential. Duke was gaining on them nonetheless and Emma put her mind to stopping while she was ahead. Pulling back on the reins, Daisy slowed to a walk as Duke and David flew on by them. It was a gorgeous picture.

David circled Duke around and trotted up beside Emma, sporting a wide grin. "You gave up rather quickly."

"Whatever do you mean? I won."

"I think you're under some kind of misconception, we haven't even begun the race. Besides, even if that had been it you cheated."

"I did not. I can't help it that you're slow on the trigger. Not my problem." She turned Daisy to the right and began a casual ride through the field.

Following suit, he and Duke caught up to them. "Oh, you're proud of yourself, aren't you?"

"Yeah, I rather am. I didn't even know if I could get up on a horse and here I beat you in a race in your own field."

"I'll give you this one, but—"

"You didn't *give* me anything, I took it."

"Fine. You took this one, but watch out next time."

"You're willing to subject yourself to another go? Well, if that's what you want I'd be willing to oblige you in your continued failure."

He raised his brows without a word of contradiction. It amazed him how happy it made him to see her completely enthused by the ride. If anything, at least he gave her that back. But he wanted so much more for himself—he wanted Emma. The clarity of the concept was so brilliant it could not be denied. He knew he couldn't stop until she was his. That statement sounded foreign to him, but the image of him and Emma together was as natural as breathing. She might have won the horse race, but he would win *her*.

They neared the woods. "Would you like to walk through the edge of the forest a bit? We can't go too far into it without flashlights, but we should be able to see enough to make it through the outer border." He dismounted Duke.

"Yeah, why not." She walked next to him, the horses trailing behind.

The evening had turned out to be so much more than she had dreamed possible. She let the cool of the night air invigorate her senses. The leather, the horses, the

earthy smell of the forest could not block out the scent of
David. She could detect the clean smell of his soap and
the leather that clung to him, giving him a manly scent
that Emma couldn't ignore. It put her nerves on full alert.

Emma jumped sideways at the sound of an animal
rooting around close by and landed right in David's arms.
Before she could straighten up and lift her head, he
turned her around and held her close. His lips were a
breath away and his eyes seared right through the wall
and saw more of her than she had allowed anyone to see
in a long time. It scrambled her thoughts and intensified
the already euphoric feeling she had from overcoming her
distrust of horses. She shivered, although not from the
cool spring night air blowing softly across her exposed
skin.

David gathered her close and wrapped his arms
around her bare ones, hoping to warm her up. It managed
to heat him. His fingertips felt the tickle of the ends of
her silky soft hair and could not be restrained from
venturing forth into the thick of it. Without a word
spoken, he understood. He wished he could remove the
hurt from her and replace it with the kind of trust she had
just rebuilt for horses. The obvious screamed to him—it
wouldn't be so easy. Refusing to acknowledge the near
impossibility of the task ahead, he savored the moment as
he let the feel of her arms around him burn into his
memory.

She had to snap out of it. This feeling, this stolen
time, this man was just a blip on the screen of life that
wouldn't last. Whatever feelings he had for her would die

—they always do. Whatever time he had here would end —he would go back to New York. The man in whose arms she stood would only break her heart if she let him —she would not. She pushed back gently, snatched up Daisy's reins and solemnly headed for the field.

David opted to be playful. Grabbing Duke by the reins, he said, "Oh, no you don't. You're not going to get a head start on me this time." He reached the boundary of the field and was on Duke in a flash. "Better get to it if you want to stay close enough to follow me back to the barn."

"Ha! Follow you, you must be dreaming." She kick-started Daisy and was to a full run in seconds.

He sighed and told Duke, "Time to catch the lady, my friend."

The mare was no match for the stallion, but he kept Duke from catching up until the last several yards leading to the barn. He turned at the entrance as if to wait impatiently for her. "That seems to be one apiece. Looks like we'll have to have a tie breaker another time so I can win."

"Yeah, only in your made up world of fiction are you going to win." Emma walked Daisy past him casually.

Chapter 8

Noises sounded from all around her. A bird chirping his happy call, a cottontail scurrying through the underbrush, leaves falling to the ground, trees rustling their leaves in the breeze, noise was everywhere in the woods but she couldn't detect the location of her aggressor. All manner of sound blared in her ears save the one she strained to hear—footsteps. If she heard his footfalls she at least knew where he was, how far he was, what kind of chance she had. She felt exposed without a clear picture of the situation. Her mind raced but got nowhere. She had to make a decision. She had to survive for . . .

"Hey there. Anybody here?" A female voice called out as the door closed with a thud.

Emma put down the book and came out front. She was slightly irritated at the disruption to her reading, but with a helpful clerk's smile she said, "Can I help you?"

The young lady had jet-black hair and fine narrow features on her pale face, which gave her the appearance of a china doll. "Where is your thriller section?"

"I'll show you." Emma expertly made her way without a wasted step to the section in question.

The woman kept up with her and rambled on. "I don't know why, but I'm drawn to these novels. They scare the hair right out of my head but I insist on reading them. Isn't that crazy?" Not leaving room for an answer she continued, "There must be something wrong with me."

At the head of the section, Emma faced the young woman. "Here you are. And I doubt there's anything the matter with you. There are plenty of people, including me, who get a kick out of a good thriller. In fact, I'm in the midst of one right now."

"Oh yeah, what is it? I'm sure it's just as good a pick as any other."

For some unknown reason she had the notion of not wanting to share the experience of David's book with anyone else. It made no sense whatsoever. She knew that millions would read his latest book. However irrational, it was just that being faced with it produced the reaction of wanting to keep his book—and him—all unto to her. Where on earth did that come from? I must be losing my mind, Emma thought.

"Here, I'll get it for you. It's up front. What I've read so far is fantastic. You won't be making a mistake by getting this one." She dismissed all previous thoughts and settled into her role as bookstore clerk.

After the woman bought David's book and left, Emma scolded herself for being such a schoolgirl. You have no claim on him. You don't even want to have one. What are you doing thinking this way? It will not be tolerated and it will not happen from here on out.

Breathing a heavy sigh, she cleared her thoughts of David and ventured forth into territory much more pertinent. She had to come up with a more long-term solution to the financial problems with the farm. The looming foreclosure and solutions to it had to be her sole focus. Given a reprieve by the bank was temporary and if she didn't come up with more than a part time job paying barely more than minimum wage, it would be lost. She couldn't let that happen. Everything in her power had to be done to ensure a positive outcome. She owed it to herself and to her mother. Life had been hard enough in so many ways. No more, she vowed.

She arrived home just after ten-thirty and the yard light welcomed her up the driveway and across the lawn to the back door. The back porch and kitchen were dark, leaving Emma there as well under the unusual circumstances. She continued her routine without giving further thought to its vague oddness. She peeked in on her mother and found her fast asleep after an evening of returning stray items to their proper places and cleaning the kitchen down to the last dirty fork in the house. Emma didn't need the light to know Nancy would not be peacefully sleeping without having done those specific chores—it wasn't in her nature.

Flicking off the lights, she mounted the stairs with

only one thing on her mind—a soak in a hot bath with no interruptions. Her physical and mental state would be all the better for having a pampered moment of a leisurely bath, even with having to forgo a portion of her sleep time. She refused to move from the tub for quite awhile and was rewarded by feeling her load lightened, even without the benefit of sleep.

She finally extracted herself from the luxury and combed her hair, hung the towel and threw on her pajamas before the warmth from the bath escaped her. The feeling of being surrounded by warm swaths of fleece enveloped her, giving her the determination to take it to bed and let it cuddle her as she floated off to the comfortable land of sleep.

Hopping into bed, she had only the emerald green lamp with the white lampshade and simple lace fringe with eyelets to turn off. With the covers perfectly straightened, Emma turned to the nightstand to switch off the lamp when she noticed her watch sitting there. That's strange, she thought. Did I put that there? I never do. Why would I do that tonight?

It was then she remembered she was without it at the bookstore and that was the reason—she had left it someplace odd. Her mother must have found it and put it in her bedroom. That was the only explanation she could think of. It made perfect sense since her mother would not be able to settle down successfully with it hanging around downstairs cluttering up the kitchen or living room.

Taking a better look at the watch, she realized it

wasn't working. The time was stopped on two minutes after ten. She laid the watch back on the nightstand and vowed to deal with it tomorrow. Now was no time to worry about the battery being dead and there was nothing that could be done at this time of night. It was time for sleep.

*   *   *   *   *

David sat at his old maple desk and stared at the computer screen. It was blank. His fingers were poised and ready to start tapping away like the start of a race. But it was not to be. No words were coming. No grand ideas. No characters. No settings. He continued his staring contest with the screen.

There were lots of words and situations roaming around in his head. The problem was they were sappy words meant to write passionate scenes in romantic stories, not the stuff that made up best selling thrillers. "Okay, this isn't funny," he told himself.

He stretched his long lean body and took several trips around the small room. He settled back down once again and went from blank to love and passion in a matter of seconds with no way to stop the onslaught. An oath slipped from his lips. What am I supposed to do—start writing romance novels? Ha!

With those flowery words invading his thoughts, he realized that an image of Emma came along with them. The significance was not lost on him. He was fully aware of his feelings for her. What he wasn't willing to accept was an interruption to his work. That world was his and his alone. It had nothing to do with fame or money or any of the other bits that came to a successful writer. For him it was about inventing a world of his own that was entirely of his making and under his control. It was the challenge of putting scenery, ambiance, actions and emotions into words that would create the exact look and feel of what he wanted to convey. The kick he got out of pulling the reader into a world *he* thought of was the biggest payoff of his writing.

He set it aside for now. His plan of attack was finding land to purchase and getting himself set up in a place. So far, the realtor hadn't exactly shown him anything he wanted to call his own. What the particular properties were lacking was hard to put into words, he just knew they weren't right. David was convinced that there would be no doubt in his mind when the perfect place presented itself.

He phoned the realtor, Mr. Higgins. The man with the slight paunch and a silver ring of thinning hair on his head answered, "Higgins. What can I sell for you or to you?"

"Cute. This is Schlosser. I would love for you to sell me something. Problem is, I haven't seen the place I can't live without."

"I'm sure there'll be more to look at soon, Mr. Schlosser. Or maybe one of the properties you've seen could become the one you need if the price was more attractive."

"Mr. Higgins. You're missing my point. I don't want or need a better price. What I need is more properties to view."

"Well, there just aren't—"

"There would be if you extended the radius of the search. I'm looking to settle into a home soon. So if you would be so kind as to get on that for me, I'd appreciate it."

"I'm confident the perfect property will surface in the near future. Good day."

"It had better. Bye."

With the assurance of Mr. Higgins, he felt certain that his plans were under control. There was no more he could do about it currently so he nabbed a beer from the fridge, located a wooden rocker on the porch that faced west and proceeded to get comfortable. His booted feet rested on the porch rail crossed at the ankles, his body casually slouched in the chair and his elbow on the armrest with the beer hoisted up wrapped in his strong hand.

He nursed the beer as he watched every star come to life, filling the sky with the sparkle of a kindergartner's art project. The simple pleasure of being able to actually see the moon and stars so clearly was one of the many reasons he moved back. He allowed his mind to wander to the future—a place he rarely visited. It was safer not to go there. The dreams were usually just that—a dream and nothing more. To bet on what the future might be like, or worse, what you want it to be like was like betting on a mule in a horse race—it always came up short. The best way to insulate oneself from the inevitable beating that reality gave you is to dispense with the dreaming in the first place. His fictional thinking was put into his books, not his life, and he was the better for it.

On this occasion though, he let his thoughts run where they may. The picture his futuristic thoughts offered him was wonderful and scary at the same time. At a long pine table sat what appeared to be the members of a family—David, Emma, an athletic boy with straw blond hair about eleven and a girl with hair the color of a mink and eyes that mirrored David's around age six or seven. The surroundings were familiar to him since he had dreamed of them before. The kitchen was warm and open, just as his feelings. David pulled the girl to his lap and Emma mussed the boy's hair affectionately. He allowed himself to fall headlong into the fantasy with little regard for the consequences. David was thoroughly enveloped by the overwhelming sense of seeing the future that was right for him that he didn't hear the truck approaching.

Sloshing his beer with the slam of the truck doors, he snapped to the present. "What are you doing here?"

"We came to drag you off for some real fun. You haven't had a proper homecoming yet." The short one was Charles, but everyone called him Choppy. He did the urging. Hank, the offensive lineman type, followed Choppy up the stairs nodding enthusiastically.

Choppy went straight for David's propped up feet and knocked them to the porch. "Come on let's get a move on! What are you, an old man sitting in the rocker on the front porch? It's time to act your young age." He leaned against the railing as he waited for David.

"I'm afraid of what you think acting our age might

include doing."

"You should remember. It's not *that* far from high school."

"I don't think I'm up to cruising Main Street tonight, guys." David slugged down the remainder of his beer.

Hank finally put a word into the conversation. "You got one of those for us?" That was about as much as Hank usually offered.

"No. I don't. I wasn't planning on company. And if I had been planning on some it wouldn't have been the likes of you two. I believe I prefer my company to be of the female variety." David offered a wry smile.

"Very funny. And no, I wasn't gonna take you cruising, you worthless lump." Choppy fixed his hands to the back of the rocker and dumped David off of his comfortable perch.

"Watch it, man. You're treading in dangerous waters, my friend." As fast as a flash of lightning, he had Choppy in a headlock and gave him several playful jabs to the side.

Choppy took it in stride and said from his rather precarious position, "Well, now that you're up let's go."

David let go as quickly as he grabbed him and Choppy nearly went face first into the porch floorboards. "Dude, you gotta watch your temper."

"Stupidity brings it out of me."

"That was harsh." Choppy took the free porch rocker.

"I only tease those I love."

"Yeah, well, stop having such affection for me, will ya? Get a move on. The night's a wastin'. I'd like to hunt up some sweet thing just waiting for the right man to come along."

"Why, you going to introduce her to me?" David let the screen door slam behind him as he entered the house to grab his keys.

Twenty minutes later inside Jesse's Watering Hole, they found a table in the middle of the dimly lit bar. The place was busy enough that it was a surprise to score an empty table. It was the kind of place with a handful of nightly regulars and then the weekly crowd, along with the occasional drop in.

Not likely to get Joanie's, the gal from school still waiting tables, attention on a night like this, David waded his way through tables, people gathered in groups and the rather deep wall of patrons at the bar. "Three beers on tap." He held up his hand as he hollered over the din.

"Comin' up!" Jesse bellowed. "Man, where have you been hiding yourself the past umpteen years?" He slapped David on the shoulder and shook his head, not really looking for an answer as he whirled around to fill the order.

Jesse was back before the encounter had played back in David's mind. Jesse took the money without another word and David snatched up the mugs and set off toward the table.

Along the way, he felt a hand on his forearm and an accompanying trill voice that cut through any amount of noise that Jesse's could provide. "Hey, stranger! And, I must add, celebrity!" The hand and voice belonged to none other than his girlfriend from high school, Becca Silvers.

"Hi, I need to set—"

Becca was too thrilled to see him to consider letting him finish his statement, let alone actually escape to the table. She wrapped her arms around his neck with all the enthusiasm of her former cheerleader days, sloshing the beers he held. "It is sooo good to see you! After graduation, I didn't see or hear from you again! If I didn't know better I might take it personally. You just visiting the folks?" She ran her hand along his arm.

"Well, no, I'm here to stay. Becca, it's good to bump into you, but I really have to set these beers down before I lose even more." He made a break for the table. "I'll catch up with you later," he called over his shoulder with no intention of actually doing so. He thought, whatever did I see in her? Must have been a high school thing.

He could see the table so safety was in sight. The relief of making it back with the beers fairly intact began to wash over him as a slap on the back jolted him right back out. "Man, haven't seen you in here in . . ." The guy trailed off, clearly having spent the evening at the joint.

"Yeah, it's been a long time." David was annoyed with the experience and extracted himself quickly. "Catch ya later." He had no idea it would be such an adventure to make the trip to the bar and back.

He plopped the drinks on the table with a look of disgust.

Choppy grabbed his beer and proceeded to add to David's mood. "What took so long, man? I got parched waiting for you." He took a long swig.

"Next time *you* get them and let's see how quickly you return." He continued sarcastically, "I'm having such a blast I can't wait to do it again." David was more used to fancy restaurants and parties that catered to a guest's every need. It wasn't that he was only champagne and designer clothes, he was boots and beer also. It was just that he wasn't used to fighting his way through a crowd of drunks and schoolmates to reach his seat and have his beer.

"Shut up and drink your beer. The fun is just beginning," Choppy urged his friend in his ever-tactful way.

"Oh great. You mean there's more? I can hardly wait for . . . what, the barmaids dance to begin?"

Hank chimed in, "That'd be cool."

"No, it wouldn't, Hank. And that's not helping anyway." Choppy turned his attention to David. "When the band comes back and the dancing starts, you can get nice and cozy with a beautiful female."

"I'm not interested." David slugged the rest of his beer down.

"Since when? You were always interested in high school."

"Things change. I'm focused on my writing and I don't have time for extras."

"This isn't just any old extra, this is a *woman* we're talking about here. You can't just go swearing off women. What kind of farm boy would you be? You're a disgrace to our kind!" Choppy made a sound of disgust, threw back the remainder of his beer and was off to the bar for another round.

David turned to Hank, "So, how's life treating you these days?"

"Good." Hank swallowed the last of his beer.

David knew that was all he was going to get so he proceeded to survey the scene, a habit of his, as it could come in handy in his writing. He saw a very young, maybe too young, brunette flirting with the young twenties cowboy type. A middle-aged woman who'd had too much to drink was ordering another with a smile that covered a sad face. A thirty-something average-looking man tried to interest a very bored, princess-like, blonde twenty-something.

None of those scenes interested him so he scanned the room for a more intriguing situation and landed on a pair of big brown eyes staring straight back at his. He took a careful look and did not recognize his flatterer. He considered asking Hank but he didn't want to appear interested, which he wasn't. His nature dictated his curiosity and sometimes drove him to do crazy things, but he concluded this would not be one of those occasions.

Choppy plunked down two beers per person. "There, that ought to keep us happy for awhile. Anything interesting while I was gone?" He settled in his chair.

"Nothing more than when you were here—same old, same old."

"Oh *contraire*! That lady over there," Hank

pointed discreetly, "has been staring at David for the past however long you've been gone."

"Now that's something to take note of. She doesn't look familiar to me. Not the same old everyday fare tonight." Choppy rubbed his hands together in delight.

"You're crude, man." David had matured quite a lot since school, but his friend Choppy was altogether a different story. He generally took the overall approach of why do it if you can get away with not, although he also had a generous heart and cared deeply for his family and friends. His demonstration of such might not be the average person's idea of it, but it was there all the same.

"Well, if you're not going to look out for yourself, who better than me?"

"That's a scary thought." David gave his attention to his two beers, then said, "After I'm done with these you can take me home."

Choppy laughed. "Not a chance, my friend. Not until I've seen you dance several dances with a very friendly female."

"No way. I can find another way home. Forget the whole thing."

"I brought you here to have some fun and you're going to." Choppy slammed down his mug for emphasis.

"Okay, one dance."

"Five."

"Two, but that's as far as I'll go."

"Four."

David's irritation began to well up. "I said two and no more." Challenge was in his eyes.

"Okay, okay. Two, but I pick the woman."

"That could be frightening. Oh well, I can handle myself. All right." Resigned, David nursed his beer.

Choppy didn't give him time to enjoy his drink and prodded him to get on with it. "She's the one." He pointed out the woman that was eying David. "And you have to get close and personal, none of this kind of dancing where you never make contact."

"I don't think you can change the deal now that I've already agreed. And why can't I choose the woman? *I'm* the one doing the dancing."

"We came to an agreement on this and if you renege now you might find it difficult to get home."

"You would, wouldn't you?"

"You know me well enough to know that sure as you're sittin' there I would." Choppy sat grinning like a cat that'd just caught his first mouse.

David stood proudly, as if being sent on a mission of great importance. "We'll do it your way, but when I'm done, we go. Deal?"

"Deal. But you're going to want to stay after you get a hold of her."

David ignored him and confidently went off to get it over with. It's not like he had trouble getting a woman to go out with him or dance, he just wasn't interested. Always the gentleman, he made polite conversation while dancing the required two dances. He thanked her and left her to her friends.

With the task done, he slapped Choppy on the back. "Done. Now let's go."

"You drive a hard bargain my friend." Reluctantly, he and Hank stood. "Fine, let's go. But are you *absolutely* sure?"

"I'm outta here, with or without you." David went out the door.

Choppy and Hank followed his lead. I tried, that's all you could ask of a fellow, Choppy thought. There was nothing else left to do.

Chapter 9

Emma opened her eyelids to the sound of a dripping faucet. As her consciousness gradually grew to full comprehension, she realized it was the gentle sound of light rain. It pleased her.

God's bounteous land was thirsty for nourishment. The rich earth waited to be tilled and prepared for seeding. This year's bounty had to be exceptional; it was essential to the farm's survival.

Emma was determined to do everything in her power to ensure the security of the farm. The problem was, not everything that impacted the farm was in her power. That detail frustrated her.

This situation was not foreign to Emma. Many times while growing up, the fate of the crop depended on the weather. She knew her mother did the only, and best, thing there was to do—pray. Emma's habit was to do so on a regular basis at set times but, when there was a pressing matter, she handed the mess completely over through prayer right then and there. She was fully aware that a lot of things in life were not up to her or in her hands at all, which provided her with ample fuel for frustration.

This basic fact gnawed at her A-type personality a majority of the time. Emma was at her best when she had a plan mapped out before her and she tackled each step as it arose. She was a doer, not a whiner, not a "poor me" person, she didn't covet and didn't shy away from hard work. The problem came when she couldn't turn her energy into action. That's when the feeling of helplessness reared its ugly head. She detested it.

In the case of the farm, there were plenty of tasks to keep Emma busy, it was what she couldn't do that picked at her brain and drove her to want to scream at times. Those nagging thoughts came from various sources. The bank, the weather, even her mother could be quite unpredictable on occasion.

Another major item she had no control over was David. She wished she solely held the reins, but the problem of David seemed less likely to be reined in than the weather. That made her very uneasy.

Emma found her mother humming in the kitchen as she fetched the milk, eggs and bacon from the refrigerator. "What's got you so happy?" She knew her mother was generally an easy-going person but this appeared to go beyond her daily contentment.

"Nothing in particular, just you home and the rain coming down outside. It makes me happy is all." Smoke spewed up from the frying pan as Nancy meticulously laid each piece of bacon.

"Well, that's as good a reason as any, I can't fault you for that." Emma put the coffee to brewing. "Hey, did you pick up my watch yesterday and put it in my room?"

"No. I don't recall doing so." She turned the bacon, sending less smoke up this time. "Did you lose it?"

"No, but that's just it, I found it on my nightstand last night."

"Well good, then it's not lost." She extracted the bacon from the grease and set it on a paper towel lined plate.

"No, it's not. I mean it's good that I have it, but I *never* put my watch there. *And* the time was stopped on it." Emma got the plates and mugs from the white cupboards and started setting the places at the kitchen table. She let the statement hang in the air, wondering what her mother might say about it. "I really didn't think too much of it until you said you didn't put it there." She poured them each a cup of the grocery store coffee. "It's just odd. And it makes me the slightest bit weirded out by it."

They both sat ready to eat and prayed together. "I think you're making way too much out of forgetting what you did with your watch. Now eat up."

As Emma ate, she decided she was doing just what her mother said she was—making a big deal out of forgetfulness.

The watch had to be fixed so she stuffed it in her

pocket on the way out the door. Rain was falling steadily, but not so hard that visibility was bad. She rather enjoyed being in the midst of it. Various types of weather are like the moods of a person, every one had to be experienced in order to know the whole person. Emma preferred well-rounded people and considered herself one.

She parked on the street in front of the jeweler, jumped from the farm truck and rounded the bed to get under the small overhang. In a rush of wind and rain, Emma went through the door.

"Hi, what can I do for you?" The voice came from behind the case displaying the shiny gold and silver, sparkling gems and polished rocks and minerals. A man that looked as neat and refined as his wares was ready for business, but made you think he was your long lost friend.

"I have this watch," she pulled it from her pocket, "that quit working yesterday and I was hoping it was just the battery. Could you . . ." She heard the faint tick of the watch, studied it and found it working perfectly well. "That's odd. It wasn't working last night when I went to bed. Now it is. *And* it's on the right time. How could that be?"

"Sometimes the battery is going and stops and starts. I can test it for you."

"Yes, thanks." Emma's thoughts were filled with amazement and confusion. How could the thing be on the right time? Weird. Oh,well, if it's working then I don't have to buy a battery. That's good for me.

The impeccably kept man came back from the

workroom and said, "It checks out fine. The battery is perfectly good and the watch seems to be keeping the correct time. If you have any more problems with it bring it back and I'll do a more extensive study of the watch's workings. But otherwise you should be all set."

"Do I owe you anything?"

"No. You have a good day."

Unbeknownst to Emma, she was holding her breath in hopes of the answer he would give. She didn't want to spend money on nothing. "Oh, thank you. You have a great day yourself." She left the jeweler and stared at the watch like it was an alien latched onto her wrist. Oh, well, she thought. Don't look for trouble where there is none.

She drove past the lumberyard to the outskirts of town and pulled into the feed store. Stepping from the old, reliable truck, she took note of the gravel lot sparse with trucks. It was a skosh early to expect many folks there for seed but she didn't care, her enthusiasm could not be contained. There was a plethora of chores she could control and do to the best of her ability, among which was being fully prepared and stocked and she would be if she had anything to say about it.

She strolled through the front door and would have known where she was even if she'd been blindfolded because it smelled like the feed store—it was dusty, musty and filled with Bill's booming voice. He had owned and ran the feed store as long as Emma could recall. He was always there; it wouldn't be a stretch of the imagination to conceive of him sleeping, showering, and eating there. There was no need for time for hobbies, the store *was* his hobby, and he lived it and loved it.

"Hiya! It's been awhile. Glad to see you back helpin' your mother out."

Bill was never too shy where his opinion was concerned. "Yeah, I'm taking a real run at ironing things out and getting 'em settled so Mom won't have to worry about it."

"Why? You plannin' on runnin' off again? Dat lady you call Mom's got a lot a reason to want you stayin' put. Dat farm over dere's been pretty rough on her since you gone off. Anyway, enough of me spoutin' off. What can I do ya fer?"

"I need seed so we can be ready to plant the first chance we get. The truck's around the side. Do you want me to pull it in back for loading?"

"Give me da keys. I'll take care of it fer ya. Best be careful about plantin' though. You'd be better off not jumpin' on the first openin'. Dat weather we can have late in the season can ruin a crop before it even gets a goin'. Dat wouldn't do ya no good." Bill took the keys from her and spun around halfway to the back door. "If you be wantin' to do anythin' else in town den off with ya. It'll take me awhile."

Emma thought the time it took to take two breaths. "Yeah, I think I will. I'll be back in, what, a half hour?"

"Good, now get outta here." Bill was sweet as the day was long, but he was never demonstrative about it.

Emma wandered the wet sidewalk of Main Street

as the chill seemed to penetrate her jacket *and* her skin. When it was damp and in the forties, it felt colder than when the mercury dipped below freezing. She wrapped her arms around her midsection and ducked into a nearby store, which ended up being the dress shop. This was not the place Emma had ever spent much time or money. The need almost never arose for her to have a fancy dress, although there was the time she was forced to go to a distant cousin's wedding and be the greeter to the guests, making sure they signed the guest book. She bought that hideous dress they made her wear from this very shop. It put a smile on her face to think of it, it was humorous and appalling at the same time.

She waded through the dresses on the nearest rack to the door, hoping no one would notice her and offer help. As dress after dress slid past her discerning eye, a woman appeared beside her. "Need some help locating the perfect dress?"

Emma looked up and straight into Becca's eyes. Sudden bursts of recognition formed on both faces but there were no sisterly hugs here. Not that there were any hard feelings between the two but they never ran in the same circles in high school, with Emma being a bookworm and Becca being the consummate cheerleader. Becca did everything with the utmost enthusiasm— clerking at the dress shop was no exception.

"Emma!" Her voice was as sweet as honey poured on thickly. "I heard you were back in town. Have you come in for a little something special? We just got some new dresses in that are to die for." Becca grabbed Emma by the hand and began dragging her to the other side of the store.

Emma resisted, gently attempting to free her hand but to no avail. "I don't think . . ."

Becca picked up a peach colored, tea length dress and held it up to Emma. "This would look just marvelous on you. You can try it on right through there."

Emma took the dress into the little changing room, figuring that if she did she might escape Becca for a few seconds—no such luck.

"So does that one seem to fit or should I get you another size?"

"I'm still getting into it. I'm good on my own. You can help someone else if you'd like." She needed to stifle a laugh upon seeing the dress in her reflection, almost as hideous as the one she remembered being forced to wear in the past.

"I'm all yours. I don't think there's another soul in the place. The weather really affects our business. So, are you going to come out and show me? I know it'll look just perfect. I want to see you show it off."

I'd rather just have it off, she thought. She suppressed another laugh. "Ah, I don't know about this one."

"Just come out and let me see. I wouldn't steer you wrong."

As Emma left the dressing room, she detected an audible gasp and thought, that's exactly how I felt when I dared to look in the mirror.

Becca surprised her and said, with all sincerity,

"You're stunning in that. I can't imagine it on anyone else." She put her hands over her mouth contemplating. "It was made for you. No one else should be allowed to wear this design."

Emma thought, I agree, but I think I'm going to include myself in that too. "I don't think it's me."

"Trust me. It is." Becca looked on in awe.

"I'm really not in the market for a dress like this right now."

Returning to the dressing room, she heard Becca protest, "When there's such perfection you don't need to be in the market. Well, think about it."

Emma put on her outerwear and contemplated how to ease out of the situation. She vowed that she would be polite but adamant on the issue of the dress and kindly, but quickly, exit the store.

Much to Emma's surprise, Becca didn't mention the dress. Emma was grateful for the reprieve and felt confident as she strode toward the front door. She noticed that the rain had given way to the occasional flash of sunlight as the clouds cruised past.

Becca put her arm across Emma's shoulders as old friends do, but Emma was never and probably would never be Becca's buddy. "It was really good to see you Emma. You should come out with us sometime to Jesse's. It's a whole heap of fun."

"No, I don't think so. Thanks for the invite, but that's not exactly my thing." Whether it was or not didn't really matter, it was more that she couldn't, in this lifetime, see herself and Becca hanging out together.

"I was there last night and had a great time. You'll never guess who I ran into there. He hasn't been around in ages. David! David Schlosser!"

"Really." Emma went into a semi-trance with a picture of David stuck in the forefront.

Becca wore a wide grin as she said. "Yeah, he's even dreamier than ever. He kind of ran off on me though. I didn't get to dance with him, but someone else did."

Emma came back to the present. "Oh, yeah? Who?"

"I don't know, but she was a looker. And they danced more than once." Suddenly Becca was bounding off to the back. "I don't want to keep you. See ya."

Emma stood frozen—physically and mentally. Nothing would work.

Finally, she shook her head and willed her feet to move. What did she care anyway? She had no claim on David and was in no frame of mind to stake one either. The problem was there was no way to control her instant, visceral reaction to his presence. And in this case, hearing about him was enough to produce the undesired response.

Anger began to creep into the mix. First, to the unwanted and uncontrolled reaction and secondly, to his thinking that he can swoop in and kiss her whenever he felt the urge and then turn his whims to another. She was, in no stretch of the imagination, going to put up with that. There was no interest on her part and she certainly didn't need the hassle of a man that chases whatever is before him.

With renewed determination, she put him out of her mind with the intention of barring the door to her emotions. Nothing would get through that was not desired—especially David.

She headed toward the seed store in hopes that Bill had completed the loading. All she wanted now was to get home and relax a spell with a hot cup of tea. The thought warmed her already.

Sure enough, the load was ready and waiting for her to haul it off home. After thanking Bill and signing the addition to her account she hummed her way back to the farm and up the lane leading to the barn. Getting prepared for the planting had her spirits running aloft.

Rounding the truck, she spied a bag that had split open sending seed across the truck bed and spilling out through the small space between the tailgate and the bottom and sides of the bed. The tear was on a bag underneath, straight down the side of it. So much for the euphoric feeling of being ahead of schedule with a firm command of the control panel, she thought. She scooped up the seed that remained in the truck, tossing it into an old seed sack. The loss was significant. There was less than half a sack.

Emma decided that it would be foolish to let this wheedle its way too far into her mood. Things like this came up all the time in the running of a farm, she just had to get back into the right frame of mind about it. It had been a long time since she dealt with the day-to-day workings of the farm. The correct method was to handle the problems that came along then move on to the next task. She would be wise to remember that, for it was certain the blight of mishaps and nuisances would rear its ugly head again.

*　*　*　*　*

David unloaded a box full of canned goods his mother was entering into the judging at the rodeo. The anticipation was palpable, flowing through the crowd of ladies bringing their wares to be scrutinized in hopes of a ribbon. All of them were clucking about, giving specific directions to their helpers, mainly their husbands and sons. They would have to wait until near the end of the next day, Saturday, for the results.

Carolyn and David watched the commotion, gaining a degree of contentment from it all. There was Jean with her blue ribbon apple pie in hopes of a repeat. Marilyn sauntered over to the needlepoint table to put the most excellent example of cross-stitch in the mix. A line of ladies filed in with jars of pickles, beets, cauliflower, peppers, pearl onions, okra, sauerkraut, pretty much anything one could imagine canning.

"Hi, Carolyn!" Nancy called over the chatter.

"Oh, hi, Nancy. I see you've quite a few items to enter. You must have been busy." She placed the card containing her information with her pickled beets.

"I love doing it. And it keeps me out of trouble." Nancy set her mixed-berry pie among the others on the long table covered in red and white checked tablecloths.

"That looks wonderful," Carolyn said upon seeing the golden-crusted pie. "Remind me never to enter that contest. Yours is sure to win."

Feeling rather proud Nancy replied, "It does tend to win, but you never know. I'd be happy to bake you one sometime. In fact, better yet, why don't I serve it when you all come to dinner? How about next week?"

"I'll have to check our schedule, but I'm pretty sure that'd be great."

While Carolyn and Nancy were busy inspecting the entrants in the wide variety of categories, David and Emma were attempting to hold a civil conversation.

David's annoyance meter was rising quickly. "*What* is your problem?"

"Me? I don't have any problem. *You're* the one afflicted by one." Emma spun toward the door to make a break for it.

David made a mild attempt to grab her wrist but to no avail. He didn't want to make a scene in front of the ladies lest they'd have large amounts of fuel to keep the gossip machinery running.

He stood still, took a cleansing breath, then followed Emma out the door and paused, scanning the immediate area in the crisp afternoon air. It was just a reminder that the last puffs of winter were squeezing themselves out to make way for the warmth of spring and summer. Not seeing her, David strode around the side of the building in time to see her dash a tear away from her cheek. Do I acknowledge it or ignore it? The answer is tricky either way, he thought.

Figuring he was probably the last person she wanted to discuss anything personal with he chose a different topic. "Hey, I didn't mean to irritate you, I just was trying to ascertain why you seem to have a target on my back right now. Can we have a chat without casting verbal stones?"

"We can try." Emma kept her eyes down. She didn't want to risk him seeing more than she could offer.

"So what's up with the attitude toward me?" The silence spanned more time than he was comfortable allowing, but he did so with patience.

In an accusatory tone she said, "I ran into Becca at the dress shop today."

"Great, but I have no idea what that has to do with me."

"She mentioned how she ran into you at Jesse's."

"And?"

Amazed at how dense he was being, she went on. "Becca was there the whole evening and saw you." She crossed her arms in front of her.

A light bulb went on. "Oh," he said in a knowing way. "Are you jealous?"

"I . . . most certainly am not. I just don't need you hanging around me when you'd be much better off with someone you find there. Besides, it seems like you already have. And I don't want to get in the way, that's all." She didn't dare look up because she could feel him leaning closer.

"Believe me, you wouldn't be able to come between me and what I want. And I know exactly what it is and you're just where you should be." He ran his hand softly across one cheek into her thick, lush hair and then did the same with the other. With his hands tangled in her hair, he slowly tilted her head back so Emma could read his face and know he was entirely honest about it all.

She couldn't for the life of her dam the flow of warmth, well-being, and overall belonging. She didn't want to. An incredibly strong force told her to let go but she couldn't, not completely. The only thing that ever happened when she did was sorrow, pain and misery. The here and now was just that. She would pay for this down the road. She knew it.

David seemed to burrow right to her soul with his unwavering gaze and generous countenance. Lowering his mouth to hers, the heat rose between them until the touch of their lips sparked the ignition. David was lost in her velvety, moist, pliant mouth.

She could feel his arms wrap around her and give what felt like protection along with deep, strong feelings never before felt. His tongue was active and his arms strong and sure. Emma could linger in this moment, forgetting her qualms and forgoing her fears. If only it was possible.

Reality came screeching back with the abrupt departure of David's confident and enticing mouth. He took a brusque step away, paused to make a thorough study of Emma, then walked back inside the building.

Emma, dazed by the experience and his sudden departure, held herself steady by leaning against the red brick wall. In the midst of calming her system, a small voice called out. "Emma? Emma? Are you coming to the rodeo this weekend?"

She looked down into the big brown eyes of

Abby, her cousin's child. "Why, yes. I wouldn't miss it for the world." She ran a hand over the silky skin of her pixie face and asked, "Are you?"

"You bet. I can't wait," Abby said with excited anticipation and ran off.

If only life could be as simple as it was for a child, Emma thought. But then most of us would probably go off looking for something to complicate it out of sheer boredom. Children already do as soon as they think themselves old enough to handle it, which usually ends up being premature for the majority. Emma realized that no good came from wishing things different. Change came in one's life through action.

She would put the whole David thing out of her head and get on with her life, starting with getting home and getting ready for work tonight. One day at a time, focus on the moment at hand. That was the only way to handle David.

Finding her mother was easy. The hard part was in removing her from the gossip group, at least that's how Emma thought of it. They really did have a good time together and supported one another. The fact was that Emma was somewhat jealous of the bond the women had. A community like that could get you through a lot of junk in life. She dreamed of someday being a part of a group such as that, but her life was in such disarray and limbo that she couldn't see it coming true any time soon. Her life was her mother's life these days. The life she envisioned couldn't be pursued until the pieces of her mother's life were put together well enough to stay.

Chapter 10

David wandered through the rides with Choppy
and Hank. Lights stretched into the clear sky as the Ferris
wheel crawled to a stop to exchange riders. He could
have been home staring at his computer screen if it hadn't
been for Choppy and Hank insisting he come. The music
box sound of the merry-go-round invaded his thoughts.

The three swaggered through the carnival area,
Choppy checking out every woman that passed by, Hank
engrossed in his corn dog and David swallowed up by
thoughts of Emma. Aren't we a motley group—
wandering through the fair grounds without children,
wives, or dates? David realized with sudden clarity that
he would rather be almost anywhere with Emma than at
the rodeo without her. Convincing her that they should be
there together might be altogether an insurmountable feat.
This lame evening needs to come to an end, *now*.

"I'm taking off guys. I've had enough of the

wandering aimlessly shtick." David began to walk toward the lot and waved over his shoulder. "See ya."

"Wait!" Choppy hollered. "You can't just take off."

"Watch me." David continued walking.

"What about the women we could meet here? Aren't you interested in having any fun?" Choppy went into a mumbling rant. "First the bar thing, now this. Doesn't he believe in fun? What happened to him in New York? Whatever it was it totally killed the fun side of him and smashed it to bits."

Hank stared at Choppy after throwing the stick from his corn dog away. "You okay?"

"Yeah, I'm okay. I just don't understand that guy. He's like dysfunctional now or something." Shaking his head, he moved on. "We don't need him to have fun. We've gotten along just fine without him for the past several years. Let's go."

David wrote off the whole incident with a forceful exhale of air. The whole rodeo experience seemed to be missing something without Emma. He'd been looking forward to it since his long absence from the experience, but it hadn't lived up to the hype his imagination had conjured. All he did know for sure was that he, unquestionably, was not into it.

A drive—that's what he needed. Back in the day, he used to do that when he was frustrated, concerned about an issue or just restless. The habit stopped in New York for obvious reasons, no time like the present to reinstate the custom and off he went with no destination in mind.

The rural Wisconsin road stretched out straight in front of him, disappearing into the black of the night. Darkness swallowed the edge of everything he saw— fields, houses, barns, fences, utility lines, trees, cars. Solitude was exactly what he sought. Solitude was exactly what he had. Now that it was his, he was still left with the feeling of emptiness.

He turned onto Highway N, continuing his quest for what eluded him.

David drove in silence. He drove in a state of basic contentment from his environment. He drove with a sense of urgency. He drove with a need for more. He drove because he could. He drove because he was driven.

Eventually, without awareness, he drove into the tiny parking lot at the bookstore. Before he even exited the car, he felt more settled than he had all evening.

When David walked through the door, Emma discreetly tossed his book that she had been reading under the counter. She opted for the surprised stare after stashing the evidence. "Hey, what brings you here?"

"I thought I'd check up on my books and see how they were selling." He sauntered to the shelf to put up a good front. "Doing pretty well, I guess."

"I figured you'd be at the rodeo tonight." She straightened a stack of books near the register.

"I was, but it didn't seem to be the same as I remembered it." He looked around, browsing half-heartedly. "Maybe it's because I'm an adult now. Maybe it's being with those two puerile beings. I don't know, maybe it's just my mood." He replaced the book that he'd been perusing back on the shelf and made his way to the counter.

"There might be a bit of each of those involved in the let down of the experience."

"Maybe." Placing his elbows on the counter and his chin in his hands, he effectively moved closer to Emma without taking a step.

Feeling a little tentative at being alone with him, she vowed to keep the conversation light. "So what *are* you in the mood for—marbles?" she said teasingly.

"Ha, ha! I don't know exactly, just not what I was doing."

"Well, since you're here you can help me get some boxes out of the back. It'll keep your mind from niggling at you." She led him back to the stock room.

"Okay, those two," she pointed to a couple of medium-sized boxes, "need to go in the mystery aisle. And that one goes up by the front door where there's a special display for it."

He carted the boxes with ease and returned for additional instructions to the stock room. Not finding her, he looked around one corner, then another. Nowhere to be found, he hesitantly called out, "Emma?" He used only a conversational voice so tried again. "Emma?"

"Yes." She stepped out of the bathroom and appeared to be even lovelier than the image in his mind. "I'm right here."

"Oh, I'm done with that. Is there anything else I can help you with before you help me out?"

Confused, she answered the initial question. "No,

I believe that's it. We don't get a lot in on any given day."
She pivoted to leave the stockroom. "I really appreciate
it. I can do it my—"

Catching her while they were still in relative
obscurity, David hooked his arm around her waist as she
was about to enter the sales floor and swung her into his
arms. "Not so fast, my lady. Now it's your turn to help
me."

"Whatever do you mean?" She was in a rare
playful mood. Circumstances had not warranted much of
the trait in the recent past, but she was tired of being
serious in every situation as of late.

Pulling her tightly against him, he elaborated for
her. "I mean this." He dove in without preamble. His lips
moved toward hers with force yet connected with
gentleness. The pillow softness of her lips enticed him
into deepening the kiss. One arm firmly held her as he
brought the other hand to her hair, brushing it from her
face. He let his hand get lost in the silky strands of her
abundant auburn hair.

All thought slipped silently into nothing as her
senses heightened and emotions took over. She was
rooted in the here and now. There were no lingering
notions of what might take place later and she wanted to
soak up the feel of this strong, intelligent man enthralled
with her.

Now both hands roamed the copious shafts of
feathery hair. Like a horse with blinders, all he could see
was her, all he could sense was her. She touched him to
the core by her giving, her responsiveness.

David broke the connection reluctantly, but for self-preservation. Holding her at arms-length, he studied her flushed face and took in her scent. Abruptly, yet silently, he left the storeroom and her.

She stood still, unable to move just yet. She was unsure of her ability to do so without undesired consequences. Second, she chose to allow herself the luxury of soaking in the lush feel of the moment.

Hearing the door jolted her out of the warm cozy place she inhabited in her mind and spurred her to action. Emerging from the back quickly, but not rushed, she scanned the store for David. No sign of him, and her stomach sank and her head spun. She hustled to the door to scan the parking lot for his car. Before she even opened the door she saw him leaning against his car in a casually, unknowingly smoldering way. Her heart skipped and within the next beat she scolded herself for behaving like such a schoolgirl. "Grow up, Emma," she muttered, "he's just a guy."

Thinking that he'd seen her, she thought she'd better join him. "Hey, what're you doing out here?" She leaned against the car next to him, out of arms reach.

"Just thought I'd get some cool, crisp, spring air." To clear my head, he thought. "I should probably let you to your work."

"Yeah, I'm supposed to have those boxes stocked." She looked at her watch keeping perfect time. If she hurried, she'd get it done by closing time. Spinning on her heels, the crunch of the gravel announced her intention to leave. "See ya."

"Wait!" He reached out as if to grab her, despite the distance. "Speaking of seeing you, are you going to the rodeo this weekend?"

"Yeah, I intend to."

"Well, let's go together. Save some fuel. We can be environmentally conscious citizens." Energized by the promise of spending more time with her he sprang from his leaning stance to one of attention. "I'll pick you up at seven. Bring your appetite, you don't want to miss out on all the wonderful rodeo food." A hint of sarcasm laced the comment. He reached for the door handle, pleased with himself and the upcoming outing.

"You might want to hang on before tearing off with the assumption you just made." She raised her brows in anticipation of his reaction.

He didn't move a muscle. "What assumption? You said you were going. I just made the arrangements as to how you were going to get there." Perfectly happy with himself he mentally lobbed the ball back to her side of the court.

"I may have said I was going, but I never said anything about going with you. And you may want to brush up on your asking-someone-out etiquette. It leaves a lot to be desired—like actually asking." The challenging look was there again.

"Sorry, guess I jumped the gun. Let me try that with a little more eloquence." He hung his head and held up one finger indicating his transformation. With the lifting of his head, the metamorphosis was complete. "Emma, would you do me the honor of allowing me to escort you to the rodeo tomorrow night?" His arms were clasped behind his back.

"Very funny. But that *is* more pleasant than being ordered around."

"So?" The irritation was creeping into his lighthearted play.

"So, sure, I'd love to. Besides, we want to be good citizens now, don't we?" She smirked and scampered off to resume her duties inside the bookstore.

He shook his head, baffled by the encounter. The woman was difficult to read—one minute she was friendly and playful and the next she wanted nothing to do with him. Not willing to let the weirdness ruin his mood, he smiled at the conflict within her and chose to focus on the date he had made.

The following morning Emma woke to a bright yellow shaft of sun streaming through the crack in her curtains. Lifted by the sun and the prospect of tonight, she gladly watched the dust motes dance in the invading light. They were light and airy, like her mood. The omen was a good one.

After chores, lunch, watching her mother fret over some last minute entries for judging and assuring Crystal that she would be there shortly, Emma encouraged her mother to focus on the current objective—getting out the door. Nancy could easily get sidetracked and devote a great deal of time to superfluous tasks. The ultimate goal was to take her mother to the rodeo to check on her entries, drop off the remaining items and get back in time to leisurely bath, dress and look utterly amazing for this evening. Emma was not convinced that she would achieve the desired result. She sighed.

"Okay, I'm coming." Nancy rushed around like she was being unduly hurried and harried in the process. "I just had to finish what I was doing."

"Mom, I don't think the sheets *had* to be folded before we left the house. They'll still be here when you get back." By Emma's power, the door closed with a thud.

Nancy trailed behind her with her arms loaded. "I always found my mother's favorite saying to be true—'No time like the present.' I hear the phrase in her voice."

Emma opened the trunk.

"You don't have to roll your eyes," Nancy said as she placed the last of her armful down.

"Mama, I didn't." A slight chuckle escaped her lips. "I'm not fourteen anymore. I only thought it rather interesting the way your mind works sometimes." Emma reached across the seat and hugged her mother.

"We're not in a hurry, are we?" Her mother was puzzled by the minute impatience she detected.

"Well, not exactly. I wanted to take my time getting ready for this evening." She paused, knowing how her mother would react to knowing the rest. "I'm going with David."

"Oh," Nancy said.

"Is that it? Are you feeling okay? Do we need to find a doctor? Where's the usual jumping straight ahead to marriage and grandchildren?" Even though her marriage didn't last, Nancy was still like most farm mothers in that she took marriage and kids as the next natural step when adulthood was achieved. With the dreamy expression she normally displayed at the mere mention of those occasions, one would think she had the best of marriages.

"Aren't you the funny one? I know you don't like it when I do that so I'm trying to respect that. Instead, all I seem to be getting is grief." Nancy deflected the inquiry with a deft maneuver. The thought that really ran rampant through her head was that, although she liked David, he would likely take Emma halfway across the country. Being a big time writer and having lived in New York, she was certain of her suspicions. She had just gotten her back; she was not about to lose her again. There had been enough losses in her life and Emma's.

They took the relatively short drive, at least for rural Wisconsin, lost in their own worlds. Nancy was contemplating her losses and Emma was regarding her recent past as mostly positive. Before either of them could consider a topic of conversation after wading through their worries, triumphs and joys, they arrived at the rodeo parking—an open field cordoned off with rope between barrels. Parking was not a problem this time of day.

As they headed for the building that contained the majority of the displays set for judging, Crystal met them with a look of anger. "Emma, Aunt Nancy, you need to come to the baked goods section. Your pie has been ruined." She began pulling Emma along faster. "Come on!"

"What are you talking about? And slow down. It's

not going to get up and walk off on its own."

"Sorry, I'm a little riled up." Crystal let go of Emma's hand and slowed her pace. "It appears to be deliberate."

Nancy brushed the thought aside and said, "Someone probably tripped or was off balance and accidentally stuck a finger in it." You didn't always know which trait would come to the forefront at a given moment. She was, for the most part, easy going. But there were times when Emma feared that worry would put her in the hospital. Emma was kept guessing.

Upon nearing the baked entries, Emma noted the appearance of her mother's pie. It didn't look accidental to her either. A shiver traveled slowly up her spine. Hoping her expression didn't give her away, she attempted as light a tone as she could muster. "Well, you have a lot of other items to win you ribbons, Mom."

"Yeah, you're right. There's always next year for the pie." She placed a hand over her mouth. "I hope the person is all right."

"I'm sure they're fine." Just not in the head, Emma thought.

"This doesn't look like an accident to me. It's too messed up. It's like someone stirred it with their finger." Crystal was concerned.

Emma turned her back to her mother to glare at Crystal. "I'm sure no one would have done this on purpose around here." She hoped she was convincing enough to keep her mother from catching on to what she thought was obvious.

"I'm sure that's true. I've just been watching too much television." Crystal glanced at Emma, hoping to find the expression that said she did a good job in covering.

Crystal captured her Aunt Nancy's hand to drag her away. "Show me what else you brought to wow the judges."

Emma seized the opportunity to dispose of the remains and clean the pan. "I can't believe someone would do that. It's just a fun competition, not high stakes poker," she mumbled under her breath.

By the time Crystal returned with Nancy the whole mess was gone, including the pan stashed in the car. "All your stuff registered and ready for winning?"

"I believe so. Let's go so I don't get accused of taking up too much of your time allotted for primping."

"Oh, what's all this about?" Crystal swiveled her head from Emma to Nancy and back to Emma in anticipation of an explanation.

Emma said, "We're just coming back tonight. That's all." As soon as she saw her mom, she knew it was unlikely that she would get away with leaving it at that.

"Noooo, that's definitely not all." Nancy's eyes had a twinkle to them. "Emma *is* coming back tonight, but not with me." She paused for effect.

Crystal couldn't stand it and was about to go out of her skin. "Tell me, tell me!" She quickly moved her attention to Nancy, concluding that she wouldn't get any satisfaction from Emma on the subject.

Nancy loved having her daughter back. Along

with the familiarity comes a healthy dose of teasing, which Emma usually took in stride. "Well, remember David?" Nancy was talking to Crystal like they were trading spy stories. "You know, the one who organized the rebuilding of our barn?" She touched Crystal's arm and leaned closer. "And it wasn't for my benefit."

"Okay, that's enough. I'm standing right here, you know."

They both looked at her, pausing only a second, then back to each other. "That's okay, dear, we'll be done in a minute." Knowing how it irked Emma was part of the fun, although not to the point of exasperation.

Determined not to let them get under her skin Emma said, "I'm going to the car. Come out when you're done." She had gone only a few feet, then realized she had better qualify it. "But soon."

They giggled like two schoolgirls with Emma out of earshot. "So they're going out tonight? That's great, I'm happy for her."

"Me too. She needs some fun in her life. There's plenty of serious to go around the farm and I like David, but I'm torn." Nancy read the confused expression of Crystal's face. "If they hit it off she might leave. I quickly came to love having her in the area again. I didn't understand how much I had missed her." Nancy's gaze fell to the floor.

Crystal touched her shoulder, looking her straight in the eye. "It's one date. It's not like they're getting married. Besides, I thought he lived here now?"

"Yes, but he used to live in New York. Do you

think he's going to hang in this part of the country for very long?"

"There must have been a significant reason he came back. Everything's going to be fantastic, you'll see."

Nancy was suddenly ready to drop the whole thing. She wanted to be thrilled for her daughter. And she was. But a small reserved spot remained skeptical. "Let's go before she sends out the search and rescue teams after us."

Grinning at their inside information they strolled out arm in arm to join Emma.

A few yards after rounding the corner, the two saw Emma in a confused state with the back door of the car open. She peered into the vehicle, then examined the door like it was a foreign object. Circling the car, she tried the other doors that appeared to be locked. She shook her head before she realized she was being watched.

"Hey, guys." She plastered on a smile. "Glad you decided to join me."

"What's going on?" her mother asked.

"Oh, nothing." Emma glanced briefly at Crystal. "I must have locked the other doors and left this one wide open. Weird, huh?"

The exchange between Crystal and Emma didn't go entirely unnoticed by Nancy, but she couldn't see anything to concern her so she acted oblivious to it.

Emma and Nancy got in and began to roll up the windows as Crystal bid them farewell.

Crystal couldn't resist one last jab. "I'll see you

tonight…unless you're stuck on the Ferris wheel making out with David."

"We're not in high school." Emma put the car in gear. "Bye."

Hours later she was ready to go to the rodeo with David. She felt like a teenager waiting for her date to pick her up. Thinking about it made her stomach churn, but in a good way. The idea that it may not all be worth it popped in and out of her thoughts. She had vacillated so much by the time David arrived that she was on the brink of finding a flower and alternating the phrases—'I'll go' and 'I won't go.' Convention made it a moot point now, for which she was somewhat grateful.

"David's here!" Her mother called from the kitchen.

She descended the stairs with as much grace as her body allowed. Suddenly incredibly self-conscious, she whirled, running back up the stairs to her room. The blouse was now inexplicably too provocative for the occasion. She corrected the mistake and threw on a sapphire blue V-neck with a cocoa brown, suede short jacket. Her appearance in the mirror told her that she was ready now—at least clothing wise.

If only she could calm her racing nerves. It'd been a long time since she'd been on a date with someone, especially someone that interested her. It wasn't like she had been in a cave with no social contact. She did go out with groups of people and attend the occasional party, but not date—not since what she'd rather forget occurred. Here goes nothing—and everything, she thought.

Chapter 11

In the car after the usual greetings, silence filled the air. It wasn't uncomfortable, like one would expect, but somehow felt right and natural. Staring out the window into the gulf of darkness, only to be interrupted by one of the many yard lights that dotted the farmland, her thoughts organized into coherent streams. "Have you been doing any writing since you've been home or are you taking a break from it?"

"It seems I'm taking a forced break." David flashed her a grin that had no right to be as appealing as it was.

"Oh, not coming smoothly from brain to computer?" Emma twisted in her seat to watch the shadows play across his face.

"You could say that. I seem to be slightly distracted since my return."

"Has this happened to you before? And what do

you do?"

"No, it's never come up before so I'm not entirely sure what to do. I do know that I've been successful in writing four books thus far, so it may just be time for a much-needed break. From what I can figure, it's best not to force the writing. Not only does it become tedious, but the end result would probably reflect the struggle. Not in a good way either." He kept his eyes on the two-lane highway that had virtually no shoulder at this point.

She wasn't quite sure where to go from there. On one hand, he didn't really seem too concerned, but she detected a slight hesitation in his nonchalance. It had to affect him in some way. His profession was *writing.* "I'm sure it'll come to you soon." She shifted back in her seat as they pulled into the lot.

"Let's hope you're right." He swung the small car into a space with ease.

She jumped from the car and didn't wait for him to even consider opening the door for her. "Oh, I'm right. You should learn that up front. It'll make life a lot easier for you." She gave him a playful expression, as he did make it over in time to *close* the door for her.

He grabbed her hand and led her toward the carnival area. "So what first? You hungry?" They neared the edge of the games. "You want me to win you a little teddy bear?"

"I can win my own animal. And, by the way, it would be that so-funny-looking-it's-cute frog. Not the bear."

"Why doesn't that surprise me. Let's walk around

and see what all they have."

They wound their way through games of skill, games of chance and games of impossibility. They strolled into the section with the rides and passed the merry-go-round, the tilt-o-whirl, the bumper cars and straight into Crystal and Jeff with Alan and Abby trailing behind.

"Watch where you're walking, will you, lady!" Crystal sneered playfully.

Emma gave her cousin a hug. "Are you stalking us?"

"How'd you know?" She not so subtly looked from Emma to David and back.

"Oh, Crystal, Jeff, this is David." She spoke directly to David. "You've met Alan and Abby. These are their parents, my cousin Crystal and her husband Jeff."

"We've met. The barn fixing, remember? Good to see you again, David."

Abby went to the other side of David, put her hand in his and looked up with big expectant eyes. David was compelled to respond to such an earnest face. He crouched down to her level. "You been to the park lately?"

"No, but you could take us."

"Well, I'm glad you had such a good time with Emma and me. We'll have to check with your mom."

Abby instantly began tugging on her mother's shirt. "Mom, Mom! Can we make a play date with David and Emma?" When her mom didn't reply immediately she tugged harder and raised her voice to be heard above the adult chatter. "Please Mom, please! Can we?"

"Abby," Crystal held the child's wrist firmly, "I don't think that David and Emma have time for a play date." Attempting to distract Abby she asked, "What do you want to ride next?"

David volunteered. "I'd—," he took in Emma next to him, "—*we'd* love to take them to the park again. Maybe you two could make a date, plan something you haven't been able to do in some time."

Emma joined in. "Yeah, just let me know when you want to and David and I will take the little monsters." She ruffled Alan and Abby's hair so they'd know she was teasing.

"If you guys are sure." Crystal glanced at Jeff and shrugged. "Thanks, we'll let you know. Hey David, did Emma tell you what happened this afternoon?"

"No, what?"

Before Crystal could open her mouth, Emma jumped in. "It was nothing. Some idiot decided to stick his fingers in my mom's pie. That's all."

Crystal told David the story along with the suspicion that it might have been more intentional than accidental.

"Hmm. That's odd."

"Yeah, well, I wouldn't dwell on it." Emma cast her attention on Crystal and abruptly changed the subject. "We'd better not keep the kids from more rides."

"They only get a few more and then it's off to home we go."

A chorus of "Aww!" rang through the festive

noise.

Crystal shrugged and said her goodbyes to David and Emma. "Have fun." With a whisper and a wink, she gathered her family and left.

"That was kind of like a small powerful storm blowing in quickly and out again with just as much intensity." David placed his hand in hers and led her to the concessions.

"So what kind of awful-for-you, rodeo food would you like to start with?" He surveyed the area. "My personal favorite is the funnel cakes."

"Sounds good to me." Emma loved them almost as much as caramel corn.

He pointed to a picnic table in the distance and said, "You save the seats and I'll get the contraband." He flashed a grin involving his entire face. It was such a lovely smile—Emma could stare at it indefinitely. Luckily, he had gone before she could make a fool of herself.

Waiting for him to arrive with the funnel cakes gave her a little too much time to become serious and leave easiness behind. What on earth was she doing thinking of him like that? No good would come of it. He was just a friend and should remain as such.

As David approached the table, he could see the change in her countenance. Leave her alone for a minute and she reverts to building that wall high and deep, he thought. Well, I'll have to keep breaking it down, I guess —until one of these days she comes to accept the fact that she doesn't need a wall between us.

"Man, that line was long. I think every teenager within a fifty mile radius is here tonight."

Emma picked at the funnel cake. "You're probably right."

"Something wrong with it?" He gestured to the funnel cake in front of her.

"Oh." She studied what she had done to it unaware. "No. Sorry, I'm lost in thought."

"About what—that weird scenario this afternoon?"

Not wanting to go there, she offered another explanation. "I was thinking about when I should get home tonight."

"We just got here. You're ready to leave already? Am I that boring?"

"No!" Stillness and quiet took over. "Sorry, everything's getting messed up. That's why we shouldn't even be here together."

"Let me get this straight. Because there's a long line and you're lost in your own little world, that you won't let me anywhere near, you think we should forget the whole thing?" He paused, incredulous, then sarcastic. "Yeah, I can see how that would make sense." He stuffed a giant bite into his mouth so he wouldn't say any more and tucked his hands in his lap so the temptation to strangle her wouldn't take over.

It did sound rather stupid when he said it out loud. "Okay, scratch everything up to this point. Stand up." She held out her hand to him. They stood facing each other. "Hey, imagine running into you here. You want to hang out together?"

He didn't want to make it too easy on her. "Depends."

"On what?"

"Are you going to be nice to me?"

"Of course." Emma hit him playfully on the arm.

"See, you're already at it." Rubbing his arm he continued, "I'm going to have a bruise."

"Yeah, right. You want me to show you how you can really end up with one?"

He cowered with his hands over his head. "No, I think I'll pass. Would you like some funnel cake?" He swept his hand across the table, waiting till Emma sat.

"Expecting someone? Maybe I should go." Glancing from under her lashes, she stifled a giggle.

He ignored her comment. "Where to after food? You want to go on rides and see if we can diet that way?"

"Gross."

"Or would something more calm suit your mood?"

"I think that's a much better idea. Let's check on the judging. Maybe they've gotten to some of my mom's stuff already."

He rose from the table, snatched the plates and headed for the trash can.

Upon returning he sat on the bench beside Emma, with one leg on either side facing her. Emma turned her head to see what he was doing and ended up with her face inches from his. He didn't move, he didn't speak. She was locked in place; his power over her was more than she

wanted to admit. He knew she expected him and even
wanted him to speak, but he stood his ground. Gazing
into her ocean-blue eyes, he could see the conflict to
which her ever-changing moods alluded. I would love to
confront whomever it was that made her so skittish, he
thought. Then he let that train leave the station before it
spoiled the evening.

Looking in David's eyes was like getting lost in a
forest of green. She saw want, she saw need, she saw
passion. Was there a hint of anger there too? Parts of him
were hard to read, and at this point, she needed to know
everything she possibly could about him.

His strong hands claimed her face and he tilted
her head to allow his lips to capture hers. The suddenness
of it thrilled her, the strength and heat emitted from his
gesture ignited her senses into responding with the only
option her body and mind would allow—openness and
returned passion. Her arms went around his waist over his
hard muscles to rest on his firm back. Feeling the need to
move, she brought one hand back, trailing up his rippled
stomach and rock-hard chest to settle on his shoulder.

Her hand was like a hot poker blazing a trail over
his body—not painful, but gloriously full of feeling.
Although her hand was motionless, he could still feel the
exact spots she touched and the effect it was creating. The
trail spread its warmth throughout his body until he felt as
though he might be consumed by flames. Kissing each
corner of her lips, he slowed the pace as he rained soft
kisses from chin up her jaw line to her ear, then started on
the opposite side and back down, only to light on her lips

once again. Little kisses traced her lips. The legato tempo did little to calm his racing heartbeat.

Rising as quickly as the whole thing started, he held out his hand to her. "Let's check out the judging."

Once inside the building the anger boiled just under the surface and threatened to overflow. Emma hoped she was adept at covering her hostility toward the individual capable of ruining her mother's pie entry. As they viewed the copious array of categories, she could feel it begin to bubble just beneath her skin and her pulse pound. The thought of how stupid and senseless it was fueled the ire. "I'm going to the ladies' room, be right back."

In the relative obscurity of the bathroom she took deep, cleansing breaths and closed her eyes, visualizing meadows of tall grasses, butter cream and lavender flowers swaying in the gentle breezes and a large shady oak tree. The sky was as blue as ever and the shade of the tree was inviting. Her system calmed under the influence of these mellowing techniques until she saw David in her vision, lounging under the tree. Although the image was relaxing in one way, it only served to agitate in another.

Opening her eyes, she studied her reflection with satisfaction. The obvious signs of irritation were gone and she could join him without fear of discovery. Her retreat was swift.

Stepping through the doorway was like walking through some kind of transforming device. The minute she was exposed to the room, there was an immediate and visceral reaction that could not to be deterred. She hoped he wouldn't notice.

As soon as she approached David, he put his hand on her shoulder with an expression of concern on his face. "Hey, what's wrong?"

"Well, that didn't work at all," she muttered.

"I beg your pardon?"

"Oh, I guess I was a little more upset by what happened this afternoon than I thought. It's nothing, it'll pass. It just seems so senseless. How come no one else's pies were disturbed? If it were kids messing around wouldn't they want to do as much damage as they could if it were for fun?"

"I don't know. Who knows how a teenage boy's brain works? Certainly not I." His eyes didn't leave her face. "You don't think someone did this on purpose, do you?"

"I'm trying to conjure up another explanation, but I'm at a loss for any others that make sense." Emma stared in puzzlement at the display of pies.

"I don't think any answers are going to jump out of the pies so let's try to forget it for now. Come over here, I've got something to show you." David led the way.

Emma couldn't help but smile at the big blue ribbon she saw hanging on her mother's cross-stitch work. It was a farm scene with horses in the field, the sun setting behind a beautiful maple tree dripping with fall color. "She'll be thrilled. I wonder if she's already seen it. She needs this." Her frustration about the earlier incident gave way to elation.

As though it was the most natural thing, David

leaned over, kissed her cheek, and put his hand on the small of her back, leading her out. "Let's see if we can make ourselves sick on the rides." He flashed a boyish grin her way.

"How could I refuse an offer like that? I can't contain my excitement over the possibilities."

"Well, we'd better make sure it lives up to your anticipation. How about we start with the tilt-o-whirl?"

"Trying to scramble my brain like a couple of eggs, eh?"

"That way I figure you'll be more inclined to kiss me on the haunted drive ride."

"You do, do you? Believe it or not, I can still think even with my brain feeling like it was put in a blender. So let's do it."

"Yes, ma'am." He followed her to their seats.

"That's what I like to hear," she said with a smirk.

"If you do, you'd better keep that one burned into you memory 'cause it's not likely to be heard again."

"Aren't you the smart aleck."

The ride crept to a start but, before either of them could glance in the other's direction, they were going so fast all they could do was hold on for dear life. As each seat followed the other around the circle, it undulated over humps and whirled individually. Sometimes quickly, sometimes slowly. Just like that, it was over. Getting out of his seat, he waited for Emma. She stepped out and stumbled, nearly falling on her face, save the fact that she landed right in David's arms.

"See, you couldn't even wait till we got on the

haunted ride!" He steadied her as they made their way off the platform.

"Right," she scoffed, trying to regain her dignity.

They took hardly more than a few steps before someone ran into Emma with enough force to knock out a grunt from between her lips.

Before she could say anything David had his hand on the man, only to turn him and make him aware of what he had done. "Hey, buddy. You ran—" He stopped mid-sentence when he was hit with the fact that he had grabbed Choppy. And Hank was just past him.

"Dude, what're you doing grabbing me like that? You're lucky I didn't haul off and slug you."

David could tell that he'd had his share of beer already. "*I'm* lucky, I believe *you* are the one who's fortunate in this case. Seriously, you need to watch where you're going."

"Sorry, man."

"I think that goes to Emma, not me."

Choppy nodded his head in a genteel manner. "Sorry, miss. I do beg your pardon." He glared at David. "We good?"

"Yeah. Here I am worried about you being inconsiderate and I haven't introduced you. Emma, this is Choppy and Hank. Choppy, Hank—Emma."

"Nice to meet you. Friends of David's, are you?"

"Why, has he told you that?" Choppy said with a wide, uneven grin.

David chimed in. "Yeah, occasionally we are." He slapped Choppy on the back.

"So you're the reason he didn't want to hang with us tonight." Choppy nodded a look of approval to David. "Guess we understand your reasons, man."

"Yeah, whatever. Why don't you guys slink off back to where you came from and leave us to enjoy our evening." He spun them both around and gave them a shove.

"We can take a hint. Don't do nothing I wouldn't." Choppy winked at David. "Bye, Emma." He nodded politely.

"Choppy, that doesn't count much out. I think we're good. Take off, eh." Without a word from Hank they were off.

"Interesting friends, David." She couldn't disguise a smirk.

"They really are fascinating, aren't they? They're good guys, though, a little rough around the edges, but loyal and there when you really need them." David and Emma joined the line for the Haunted Drive.

"Does Hank speak?" Emma couldn't contain her curiosity over the complete silence of his friend.

"He's a man of few words, but Choppy more than makes up for it. We were friends in high school and just reconnected the night we went to Jesse's. I've changed a lot since then."

"How so?"

"You don't really want to hear about all that. So you think you'll be able to plant soon?"

"Oh no. You're not ducking the topic that easily. Really, I want to know about you." She watched and waited.

That did it. He had to explain now. Refusing would be dumb. "Okay, you twisted my arm, but I warn you it's not pretty. I was a bit wild then. All I cared about was trying to dig up some fun in this place. I couldn't grasp why anyone would want to live here. I always brought home good grades, but that came easy to me. The discipline part I rebelled against. I thought I knew better than these Podunk town dwellers. And Choppy and Hank helped me find trouble. I told you that I couldn't wait to leave this place and, well, my dislike of it started early on. For what reason I cannot tell you, it was just a part of me.

"I don't know, maybe it had to do with wanting to know more about the world—places, people, cultures. Being a writer I especially wanted to know about people and the different ways they interacted with one another, the various types of relationships in which a person could be a part. It fascinated me, it made me hunger for more knowledge and understanding." David appeared pensive.

Emma brushed his arm with her hand.

"I became disillusioned with it all. Don't get me wrong, I would never take the experiences I had after leaving and erase them, but it was time for me to come home. That was the thing I slowly, but eventually, came to embrace—that this was *home.* And, of course, it wasn't this corner of the country alone that I came back for, it was family and community." David smiled at her unwavering attention. "I should probably finish with the diatribe lest you run away screaming."

"There is a chance of that, but only because we're about to enter the spooky Haunted Drive. Here goes nothing." Emma let out a mild yell for fun.

The evening was a great success and David wasn't in the mood to let it end. "I think I'm done with the carnival, how about you?"

"Yes, I think it's time to leave while we still have our hearing. Besides, I think we're getting too old for the crowd that's filling the grounds now."

"You want anything to go, like popcorn or soda?" He paused near the concessions.

"No, I don't think so, after the rides and all." They sauntered toward his car, the noise fading incrementally as they went. "Have you found a farm yet?"

"No, but the realtor has some land for me to look at that may turn out to be perfect. I'm definitely ready to settle in to my own house and make it mine."

The floor of Emma's stomach fell out with nothing but nerves left in its place. Tapping David as he focused on her, she could only point.

"What? What is it?" He followed her direction and saw the source of her reaction.

His car was in her sights sporting two flat tires and the side mirrors were hanging from a wire. It went from an impeccably kept car to a junker in a few hours.

His anger went from zero to warp speed in a split second. Speech eluded him, the plug was pulled on his tub full of thoughts. A high-pitched sound began to break through and he finally realized it was Emma's voice. Specific words he could not decipher, all that was audible was a blazing fast stream of words that sounded alternately livid and scared.

Reining in the anger, he faced Emma and pulled her in. He would put a tight lid on the outward signs of anger for her sake. "It's okay. I'll call someone and have you home in no time." He stroked her hair as he held her in his arms.

"No! I don't want to go home. I *want* to know what's going on. Who would do this? And *why*?" Attempting to hide her fear, without much success, she put her energy into frustration and sleuth-like tasks. "This has gone past the prank stage, we need to call the police. What's the deal, somebody got something against the rodeo?"

"Yeah, well, we seem to be caught right in the middle of it this time. You go call the police and I'm going to take a look."

"All right." She raced off knowing that it wasn't an emergency, but needing somewhere to place the abundance of energy she had trapped inside straining to bubble over.

By the time she got back to the car, she could already hear sirens. "That was quick."

"Yeah, there must be enough nearby because of the rodeo. I doubt anything will come of this, but it needs to be reported. I'll have someone take you home, it could be awhile." He stood with his arm draped across her shoulders. It felt incredibly natural for him to be connected to her—in every way.

"For a smart person you're pretty dense on this

one. I told you. I'm not leaving. I wouldn't be able to sleep anyhow." She spoke softly. "Besides, I want to be here to support you." Her gaze pierced through to his soul and touched him deeply.

He definitely saw more than a neighborly concern for him in her eyes before she averted them. "Thank you. I'd love to have you here with me." He cast a fleeting smile in her direction that did not mask the thoughts beneath.

David was inspecting the tires as the officers approached. "What happened here?" asked the tall, skinny one that looked more like a professional basketball player than a police officer. His name tag read 'T. Stewart' and the one with an average build, but very young features, read 'S. Bittle.'

"Good question. My first guess was a bunch of hoodlums 'having fun'. But the more I thought about it, it seemed a bit extreme for that. So I guess I'm back to the beginning." David considered what he was saying and didn't like the outcome. If it wasn't a gang of kids or even one kid looking for trouble that meant that it was someone with an agenda. That thought distressed him, more because of Emma than his own worries.

Emma fidgeted with her purse zipper in an attempt to keep her hands busy. Unfortunately, she had nothing other than what confronted them to entertain her mind. "So if it wasn't kids and no one has anything against David, then why would someone do this?" She caught an exchange between David and Officer Stewart that puzzled her. "What? Tell me what's going on!"

David took her aside. "There isn't anything to tell. They haven't done their investigation yet."

"But I saw you and Officer Stewart, like you knew something." Her eyes begged.

In a light tone he said, "No. I think you saw something that wasn't there. We weren't passing any kind of silent messages. I don't even know the guy. I was looking to him to take the lead, that's all." David rubbed her arms, spun on his heels and left her there to ponder— well, everything.

Officer Bittle approached David as he returned to the car. "Anyone have any reason to be ticked at you?" He asked in an almost accusing manner.

"No. I recently moved back here. I haven't had enough time to make enemies here yet."

"You never know, it doesn't take much for some people. Anyone from years back make any threats or had any run ins with?" He wrote notes in his hand-sized flip pad of paper.

Growing tired of the questioning, David let out a long sigh. "No. I told you there's no one." After a long silence he added, "Joey Baducci and I never got along in school, but we were just kids and I think he moved out of the area about five years ago. That is the only 'enemy' I can think of. I am a pretty likable guy."

"I'm sure you are, but someone seems to have it in for you. And maybe still does. You should be careful."

Officer Stewart stopped his partner. "Yeah, well we don't know that that's the case. We'll have to investigate and let you know." He glared at the junior officer next to him. "Is there someone you can call to get you home and to take care of the car?"

"Yeah, we're fine. So you're done for now?"

"Yep, we've got your information, we'll call you and let you know what we find." He handed David a business card and put his pen and paper away. "Call me if you or your lady friend remember anything that might be helpful—even if it sounds crazy or like it wouldn't pertain. You'd be surprised at what small details can lead to solving a case. I hope you get your car back to working order soon. Take care." Officers Stewart and Bittle headed toward the surrounding area to interview bystanders. Of course, the people who were there now were not likely to be the ones that were there when it occurred, except the workers.

Knowing his car would have to be left until morning, he concentrated on getting them home. "Let me give my parents a call. It's late enough that they would be home by now. I wouldn't bother them, but I'm sure the few other people I know are here."

They sat in silence while they awaited John's arrival, lost in their own thoughts. Different versions of the incident flitted through each mind. David remembered considering the evening a success at one point. That, of course, was before this. In consternation, he considered what Emma might conclude about the night now. He hoped she would recall the good parts— the laughing and joking, the snuggling and kissing. That was going in his permanent memory file. He hoped in hers as well.

Wild images ran across her mind's screen. Men like savages ravaged David's car, there was fear trickling down her spine as she contemplated if the pie deal and this were connected. If they were, the guy would have to know that she and David were going out, which meant that he was watching. Shivers ran rampant through her entire being at that thought and her mind went temporarily blank.

Enough with the drama, she silently berated her behavior. Her mind flicked the switch and threw her headlong into the embraces, touches and kisses that dotted the evening. Suddenly the warmth, like a hot bath, encased her. She was content. Maybe David would stay. He had talked of buying land. A man that's leaving doesn't buy land, she reasoned. Then again, it's easy enough to do an about face and sell it. She couldn't afford to let herself believe that he would stay—no one else did.

Chapter 12

For a spot on earth that was normally crime-free, she certainly had been touched by enough of it recently. Her night was fitful and her dreams were filled with scenes across the board, from romantic ones with David to terrible acts of crime she could not escape—neither in her dream nor by waking.

The day was alternately gloomy and cheery. The heavy threatening clouds whipped past the sun so that one minute it would be dark gray and the next bright, sunny yellow. It fit her dreams and her mood this morning. She couldn't light in one place with her mood being flighty and fidgety.

The experience had her questioning her sanity. It was totally out of character for her to go with the whims of her moods and she rarely gave into the urge. She was a woman of decision and action, but those were things that didn't submit well to the practice.

David was one that she hadn't cornered into the neat method yet. The little crime spree was also one of them. There was no decision to make, there was nothing to do. She was forced to sit and wait for answers instead of playing an active role. Feeling like a pawn in a game did not sit well with her, hence the mood hopping.

If there was no outlet for her activity-ridden disposition on the crime front, then she would have to disregard the subject altogether and pick one in which she could put thoughts into action. Although she was tired from the fretful sleep, she felt energy racing through her veins that would not quit. She resolved to put it to good use after church and Sunday dinner—they were an institution on Sundays in this part of the country. Watch out for odds and ends that never seem to get done, she thought.

Nearing the steps of the gleaming white building with a taller than proportionate steeple, Asa Landis appeared out of nowhere. David's cousin was usually in church with his family every Sunday and this one was no different. As the rest of them filed in, he asked if he could talk to Emma for a second. "Mom, you go ahead and save me a seat. I'll be right there." Her attention went back to Asa. "Yes?"

"Hey, I heard about what happened with David's car at the rodeo. That bites."

"I think I would have to agree with you. We don't really know what happened yet, we're waiting on the police to investigate." Asa's behavior came off like it was more than curiosity that had him asking.

"That's what I want to talk to you about. Jason, Stan and Pat were bragging about messing with some cars last night. They're such idiots." He shook his head in disgust. "They're a couple of years younger than me and I don't hang with them or anything, but I ran into them at the rodeo and they couldn't keep from shooting off their mouths. That's good for us though, huh?" He laughed nervously.

She was surprised by the information and processed it quickly. "Yes, I suppose. Did they say that they did this to David's car? Or that they targeted certain ones?"

"No, but how many people are running around doing that sort of thing in Brooks?"

"Yes, but did they admit to slashing tires and breaking side mirrors?" She found it hard to buy into kids doing the damage she'd seen.

"No, but once again the pieces seem to fit. And there aren't that many possible solutions to it." Perturbed with her apparent apprehension, he fidgeted with his hands and shifted his weight.

"You should tell the police."

"I don't want to talk to them. Then they'll start wondering if I was in on it! I've watched those TV shows and I know how it works. No way, that's why I told *you*." Asa stuffed his hands in his pockets and started kicking at the gravel.

"Don't get all worked up here. Those shows don't portray the real world, Asa. They exaggerate everything. You really need to tell them yourself. If I report this, they'll want to know why *you* didn't and then the police *will* be looking for you. You don't want that now, do you? I'll tell you what. I'll go with you and we'll do it together. It's the right thing to do. And I know you want to do what's expected of you."

She put a hand on his shoulder, reassuring him.

"Let's go to church." Simultaneously, they headed to the steep stairs. "I heard you're working for Doc Stevens. How's that going?"

Asa's body eased visibly. "Great. He's easy going and pays well. I'm kind of doing odd jobs—mostly whatever comes to his mind. He wants to put in a vegetable garden this spring so that's what I start on Monday."

It pleased her to know that he was employed after having had to let him go from their farm. She smiled, content with how God worked things out for the better for Asa. "Sounds like it's going fabulously. I'll pick you up at about two, okay?" The casual conversation did enough to ease his nerves.

"Sure." He was halfway up the aisle before Emma could locate her mother. In her scan of the church, she caught David's eye. He didn't change his expression as he let his eyes rove the entire length of her body and he kept them glued to her as she made her way up the center aisle, just before the minister. It made her nervous knowing that he was watching her every step of the way *and* that he was sitting behind her, which gave him the advantage. She didn't like it one bit.

Emma walked past him begrudgingly. She

preferred having the upper hand, especially where David was concerned. But you don't always get what you want, she mused. That's a slight understatement.

After church, David was waiting for her at her car, which now had the driver and front passenger windows rolled down. Emma lifted her gaze from the car and glared at him. "What'd you open the windows for?"

"I didn't touch your windows. Didn't you leave them down?"

She moved cautiously to the driver's side of the car, peered through the open window and let out a perplexed grunt.

"You sure you didn't put them down when you got here to let the nice spring air into the car?" He watched her reaction carefully.

Her hands were on her hips and her patience with the nonsensical was waning. "No. I think I would know if I opened my own car windows. It was too cool to have them down and I don't have a habit of leaving them open for thieves and vandals. If I leave them open at all it's never more than an inch. What are you doing by my car anyway?"

"You still don't trust me?" Incredulous, he sighed. "What do I have to do, give you a kidney?" He shook his head, wandering in the direction of his car.

Part of her wanted to let him go, but a larger part knew that would be wrong. "Wait!" He studied her as her thoughts gelled. "Sorry," she whispered. "I guess I'm a little suspicious after yesterday." She hung her head then picked it back up to look David straight in the eye. "I know I have no reason to suspect you. I apologize."

David took her delicate but sturdy hands in his, brushing his thumbs across the backs. The sweetness of it pulled on her heart. Taking a step closer, he captured her attention. "You've had a lot of stressful things happen lately. It must be tough." His right hand shot up to stop the inevitable comment. "I know you can handle it. But it's still tough, you can't deny that. Well, you could but it wouldn't be the truth." Flashing a quick smile so she knew he was playing, he quickly continued. "I mean with the attempted robbery gone awry and the recovery from that, the stress of the farm—running it and making sure it stays afloat, the car thing last night and then you come out and find this weirdness."

"And then there's you." She pursed her lips together in a smothered smile.

"And yet you can still make jokes. It's good to know that I don't have to worry about your mental health."

"Yeah, but it's a shame that I have to add worrying about yours to my laundry list of stresses." She hadn't told him of the odd impression she got from the seed bag being cut and the watch episode.

David raised his eyebrows above his green eyes showing brilliant in the sunlight. The weather had finally decided on sunny and warm—a gorgeous spring day. The leaves were out on the majority of the trees as they stubbornly held onto the yellow-green of early spring. Soon there would be more warm days than cool.

"You are so lucky that I'm a gentleman, otherwise

you could have a serious problem on your hands."

"We're in the church parking lot. What are you going to do to me here? Wouldn't that be sacrilegious or something?"

"Look around." He looked smug. "I didn't say it would be sinful, anyhow."

To her amazement, the lot was virtually empty. "Okay, so most everyone is gone. But my mom is still here and evidently the pastor too."

"There's always later." He smiled a wicked grin.

"Oh, I wanted to let you know, I was talking with Asa and he told me some interesting information." She relayed the story while David offered his full attention.

"That *is* interesting." I'd be surprised if it were kids, he thought. "I want to go with you." He leaned against her car.

"That'd be fine. I'm leaving at one-thirty."

"I'll be there."

Nancy came to the passenger side of the car. "You'll be where?"

"By your house to pick up Emma."

"If that's the case, why don't you come by right now and have Sunday dinner with us? No sense in going home and then getting right back in the car to come to our house."

"You are most certainly correct. I would love to join you for dinner, but only if Emma wants me there too." He leaned forward and looked into her eyes with his brows raised in question.

He smelled good. It was just soap and shaving gel,

191

but the combination on him was subtly intoxicating. Her mind was muddled. "Sure, whatever." She stepped into the vehicle to get away from the mind-altering attack on her olfactory nerves. "See you there." Her escape was thwarted when he leaned in the window and whispered in her ear.

On the drive home, Emma explained what they would be doing in the afternoon and Nancy was quiet halfway there. After ten minutes Nancy gave up on the idea of not saying anything, she never was very good at it. "David is so sweet. Don't you think so, dear? Wouldn't it be great if you and he got married? Oh, I think that'd be marvelous." Giddy, she twisted in her seat to share her joy with Emma.

"Aren't you at the finish line before the starting gun sounds? Besides, I wouldn't waste your enthusiasm on that idea, he's more than likely going to end up leaving."

Confusion took over Nancy's expression. "I thought he was searching for a place to buy here? A man that does that is not running off in the near future."

"Yeah, well, I wouldn't be too sure about that. He's lived in New York for several years so I hardly think that Brooks is going to hold onto him. Besides, he's just another man, so he'll pick up and move on—if not physically, then mentally and socially. I don't intend to put myself into that path only to be run over. No, thanks." She swung onto the gravel driveway, her disgust of the male species fully uncloaked.

"That's a rather pessimistic view. Look at all he's

done for you already. A guy like that doesn't leave you for road kill, Emma." Nancy hopped out of the car before Emma and made a beeline to David. "I'm so glad you agreed to come. You're welcome anytime, you hear, anytime." She walked him inside, leaving Emma to fend for herself since she was so fond of it.

Fine, Emma thought, if she stayed here any longer I might have been tempted to point out that although her husband was wonderful for many years that didn't keep him from leaving eventually. It's a wonder anyone stays married with the track record of the opposite sex.

Emma lingered in the vehicle trying to wrap her head around the chaos surrounding her life, now that she was back in her childhood home. So much had transpired in such a relatively short period, and this to a woman, to whom very little usually happened. She thought, how did I attract these unsolicited events? I never did . . .

"Wait a minute," she said aloud. "It's him." The venom was in her voice. "David's been around for every incident thus far. Why didn't I connect the two before? Well, no more. He may hold some kind of attraction for me, but I'll just have to curb that." It was only since she had known David that her life was spinning out of control.

Satisfied with her conclusion and her resolution, she exited the car and went to spend dinner with the irritant of her life.

Dinner passed without too much hassle to her. Emma paid him as little attention as possible and yet remained the polite hostess. He put on the charm, with her mother lapping up every last bit of it as she tossed a smile Emma's direction that announced silently, see how great he is? You could do a lot worse than him. Fabulous, now he has an advocate in my mother. It'll never cease to be the topic of conversation, she thought with a sigh.

"Anything wrong?" David said.

"No, why?"

"You sighed."

"What, a person can't sigh without there being something wrong? Well, then I guess I have a whole heap wrong cause I do an awful lot of sighing." She did little to hide the irritation she felt. The problem was that it was mostly at herself for falling prey to his charms. The longer she remained in his company the more impact it seemed to have. If she was going to succeed in putting emotional distance between them then she'd better make some physical distance first.

She rose, clearing plates along the way. Grabbing her mother's, her own and finally David's, she proceeded to the kitchen as she heard the complaint.

"Hey, I wasn't done with that yet."

"Are you serious? How long have you been eating anyway?" She came back with his plate, plopping it in front of him.

"Emma." Her mother used an authoritative voice that was rarely displayed in Emma's twenty-four years. "Get him a clean plate and mind your manners."

The reprimand from her mother was of no consequence to Emma, but the enjoyment that David got from it was humiliating. He sat there with a smirk on his face that he purposefully changed too slowly when Emma peeked at him. Emma snatched up the plate only to have David grab her wrist firmly, yet gently. Yeah, like this'll help, she mused. Her gaze found his to demand release.

"Thank you." David spoke in a soft, soothing tone with kind-hearted eyes.

The resolve she fortified when she left the car and throughout dinner melted in an instant. So much for plan A, she thought. "Sure."

She replaced his plate and moved on to washing the dishes. Noticing the time on the Felix the Cat clock that swished it's tail for every passing second, she kicked it into high gear to finish up in time to get Asa. "I'll finish the wiping down later, Mom. We've got to get going or we're gonna be late." She rushed around getting her stuff together and remembered her watch at the last minute. "I need to run upstairs and get my watch. I'll be right back," she said as she raced by him on her way. With her need for organization, she was lost without her watch.

In her room she held the small, carved, wood box that served as a supplemental jewelry case—not that she had so much that it wouldn't fit in one, it was that she had two small boxes that handled the job. The other one was made of stone interspersed with fossils and was more than a box, it was a connection to her dad, who had gotten it for her when she was five and suffering a broken heart after the loss of her pet rabbit JoJo. She had a sentimental attachment to it, but it also brought the pain along with it. How she viewed her father was an elusive thing. It was sweet like the memory of the stone box at times and then hopelessness, pain and abandonment at others. She couldn't define her feelings easily. They would always be in a state of confusion when it came to him.

Opening the lid to retrieve her watch, she was faced with the fact that it wasn't there—*again.* What is the deal with my watch lately? Why can't I keep track of it? I must be losing my mind. Okay, if it's not there, where would it be?

Before going downstairs and inquiring, and in effect announcing that she was becoming very forgetful, she scanned her room. Sure enough, there it was sitting on her nightstand with the battery sitting next to it. Picking it up, she saw the time stopped on a couple minutes past ten. A trickle of fear ran up from her stomach and down her spine. What are the odds that it would stop on the same time it did before? Besides, who took the battery out of it? Like the vibration of sound, a sense of dread spread throughout her system. Staring at the watch, she was frozen for what felt like an eternity but in reality was only a minute or two.

Jumping almost off the bed at the movement in her peripheral vision, she calmed only slightly at seeing it was David in the doorway. "Hey, jumpy, you ready to go?" he teased. Offering no immediate answer and seeing that her relief was not significant, he came to her and sat beside her on the bed. "What's up?" The backs of his fingers caressed her arm, finding their way into her hand.

It took her a spell to gather her senses as David patiently waited, recognizing her need for some space and time to gather her thoughts. Emma explained every detail of the watch story leaning her head against his arm at the end. She mumbled, "I don't want my mom to know anything just yet. I know her and she'll freak out. She's mellow ninety-nine percent of the time, but when she loses it she does a good job of it." Lifting her head, she looked to him for compliance.

"That's fine. But we need to get her to keep the doors and windows locked." He wrapped his arm around her so her head rested in the crook of his arm.

"How are we going to do that without telling her the reason?"

"We tell her *a* reason, not *the* reason." He gave Emma a squeeze, conveying that it would be okay.

"And what reason might that be?"

"I don't know just yet, but I'll have it by the time we get downstairs. You ready? If we don't leave soon we're going to be late, and we don't want Asa to get cold feet." He rose, holding out his hand to offer reassurance.

"Yeah, I'm ready. The sooner we give this information to the police the sooner they can get going on solving it." She let him pull her up, then gathered the watch and battery into a bag and headed for the door. "Let's go."

Downstairs, Emma stalled by appearing to search for something. She located her purse and swung it over her shoulder, keys ready in her hand, then leaned against the counter and looked to David with expectation. "We're leaving, Mom."

Her mom appeared in the kitchen doorway that

led to the washroom. "Okay, bye. Drive safe."

"I will," David answered. "And speaking of being safe, I would suggest that you keep your doors and windows locked. I know the folks around here are used to leaving with open windows and unlocked doors, but there have been a few incidents in the surrounding towns as of late and I think it would be for the best if we were all a little extra cautious. We don't want to make it easier for the criminal element. May as well make it as difficult as possible." He held his breath in anticipation of her acquiescence.

"Yes, I agree." Nancy thought for a brief moment. "What kind of incidents?"

David knew what she was getting at and proceeded to minimize her fears to whatever extent he could, without causing her to relax too much. "Just some robberies and property damage, but no violence. They took place when no one was home. So keep 'em locked up tight, okay?" He motioned to Emma to come.

"I will. Bye." Nancy wrung the towel in her hand that she had been about to throw in the washing machine.

They passed the pots filled with crocus. On the verge of bursting into full bloom, the rotund buds splashed color like a Pollock painting. "That seemed to work. I think it worked better coming from you. She would have asked me a zillion questions." Emma said.

"You just have to act incredibly confident and convincing, like you're an authority on the subject. I mean, I *am* pretty much an authority in most areas."

"Hah!" It sounded like she was choking as she

said it. "You really are delusional, aren't you? Really though, I appreciate it. I think she'll listen to what you said. Thanks." Standing at the passenger door of the old truck that David was driving, she pondered the situation. "Let's take my car. We've got to pick up Asa."

"No, I'm good. Hop in." The engine roared to life and Emma didn't have much of a choice so she sat in the seat.

On the way to Asa's they each pondered the circumstances. It was like some kind of alternate reality. Life here in the comforts of familiarity and simplicity had never and should never contain frustration, fear, insecurity, and helplessness. The two sides couldn't reconcile in a place like this—they shouldn't. The events appeared random until the two episodes with her watch. There *had* to be a connection—*but what*? This had to be solved—she couldn't take it with all the other stress that was in her life. Emma stared out the window in a subtle state of shock, watching the fields stretch endlessly into the horizon.

David could sense the tension and worry. He could see it in her posture and far away look. The upbeat tunes he put on were an attempt to distract her—well, both of them. As he finished with the knobs on the tuner he dropped his hand to hers, encompassing it in his firm grasp. Conversation continued its absence in the truck. The comfort of uniting over a common cause was solace enough for the time being.

Upon picking up Asa, the atmosphere became charged with excitement tinged with uneasiness. Hearing about the watch thing didn't help calm Asa's agitation. He was already nervous about involving his name in any of this, but his morals wouldn't let him back out of helping his fellow mankind. A good kid he was and a good kid he wanted to stay. "So there's no other way of doing this than me reporting this myself?" Asa asked.

"I'm afraid that's the best way. No one will find out that you relayed what you heard. It was so crowded at the rodeo anyone could have picked up on the conversation. The thing to do is give the police what information we have and let them do their job." At the same time David used this to convince Asa of being a good citizen, he told himself that he wasn't going to let it go at that. He couldn't sit idly by and wait for something else to happen, especially with Emma involved. It was time to engage his powers of deduction, which were sharpened from writing mysteries. It was imperative that he achieve success. Their mental health and security depended upon it.

Chapter 13

"Asa seemed to relax after Officer Stewart told him that his name would not be mentioned to anyone." David put his arm across Emma's shoulders to prevent her from sliding across to the passenger seat after Asa departed the truck.

"Yeah, I thought he was going to have a fit on the way there." She twisted in the seat to face David. "Do you think you or I am the target or it's just a coincidence that these things have happened to us?"

She fidgeted while awaiting his answer into which, surprisingly, she knew she was going to put great stock.

"I'm not the first to jump to conspiracy theories, but this is turning out to be a big enough coincidence. Your thing and my thing may not be related, but the two occurrences with your watch are most definitely connected." A quick glance in her direction told him that his opinion was disconcerting yet enlightening. "We'll get the creep who's doing this. I promise." He stroked the hair that draped down her cheek and hung in front of her shoulder. It had the ability to soothe him and her simultaneously.

He refused to let anything bad happen to the woman he seemed to be falling for with every breath he took. It wouldn't occur on his guard.

"I hope sooner than later. I've got enough on my plate with the farm and working at the bookstore and making sure my mom is taken care of. Life has never been easy." She allowed herself a rare pout. "It sometimes feels like things will never be settled enough to afford me the opportunity to move on to what I want to do. I mean, I love helping out. And it would do me good to be able to be there for her for once, instead of vice versa, but I want the experience of doing something entirely for myself. Saying that out loud sounds pretty selfish, huh?"

"It didn't to me. If you give yourself the permission to focus wholly on you to achieve a personal goal then, generally speaking, people around you will benefit from the endeavor."

The gravel he drove on was not her driveway, but the lot at the park. "Tell me what we're doing here before you explain that last insight of yours." Emma followed him out the driver's door.

"It's a park. It's a beautiful day. What's there to explain?" He took her hand, walking at a clip that implied he had some place he had to be. "As for the other, I think that if you suppress your yearnings forever you end up a bitter person. And if you indulge in pursuing them, no matter the outcome, you become a well-rounded and more fulfilled human being, more prepared to handle other people's garbage. That's it in a nutshell." His pace continued until they came upon a small burbling stream.

"I remember this spot. I haven't been here since . . ." Emma bent down to feel the water.

"Since?"

"Oh, sorry. It doesn't matter. It was a lifetime ago." Scooping up a handful of small rocks, she headed for the downed tree that had served as a bench to park goers for as long as she could remember. The rocks made a plunking sound each time one hit the water. Plunk, plunk, plunk, plunk. It soothed her to hear the sound as she drifted to memories that were good, instead of the initial one that plagued her mind upon arrival. That was best left in the past where it couldn't hurt her anymore.

"Tell me about your brother."

The sound was so soft she wondered if she imagined it. Or maybe insanity had finally taken over. Looking to David, she realized he was awaiting an answer.

"Do you mind?" He picked at the leaves on the ground.

"No. It does me good to remember him. I don't ever want to forget." Plunk, plunk. The stones were gone from her hand now. "He was an average student, though he might have been better, I just don't think that was of much importance to him at that age. The teachers usually loved his propensity to help in any way he could." She looked off wistfully into the distance. "I imagine him being a big brother to the little ones in heaven. You know, organizing a game of ball, leading the choir, passing out goodies, whatever he could do to make everyone feel welcome. That was him."

"Boy, were your parents lucky or what?"

"What are you talking about?" She glowered at him.

"Well, to have two such perfect children and all."

"Ha, ha. Believe me we weren't perfect by any stretch of the imagination. Mark had a lot of energy and that didn't always mean that he used it for good. I remember this time when he wanted to show my dad what a big boy he was, so he goes out to the cow pasture about ten minutes ahead of him." She grinned. "He was actually able to get most of the cows going in the direction of the barn. But there were a few stubborn ones. So he goes over to the one the farthest from the barn, because he figures if he gets behind them then they'll at least be moving in the right direction once they start. Well . . ."

Emma giggled at the memories. "As he approached the unwilling cow to move behind it she kept a wary eye on him. Once in place, he moved cautiously toward her without response. Closer yet, no movement. Finally, he thinks it a good idea to smack the cow on the backside to prompt her into motion. As soon as he does that, the cow whips her head around, letting out a snort, her big black eyes glaring at him. Mark sprinted to the closest fence without risking a glance behind him. My father showed up just in time to see him dive and roll under the barbed wire fence out of harms way, that wasn't even coming." Emma's head tilted back letting out a full bout of laughter.

It was a glorious sound. One he hadn't heard from her yet. He'd seen her chuckle or giggle, but not an all out laugh. There was something freeing about it, something refreshing and renewing. Joining her in laughter, he could feel her accepting him just a little bit more.

"You know, my dad laughed just as hard as I am at the stunt. He had a great laugh, my dad, it was a full, deep, belly laugh. I never heard a chuckle pass his lips after Mark died. He made himself lose his whole family instead of a son alone. Not that that wasn't bad enough, but he just made it that much worse. I don't understand it, and I probably never will." Hanging her head, she contemplated the dirt and rocks at her feet.

David rubbed her back as the depth of the memory washed over her.

Abruptly, Emma bounced off of the tree and yanked David up with her. She left the sorrow there as she dragged him down a sparsely used path. "I know a cool spot at the end of this trail. We may as well enjoy this weather while it's here."

Crunching dried leaves on the forest floor, snapping twigs, stepping over roots and branches, and hearing the brush rustle as anonymous creatures of the woods scurried about, they made their way to the spot Emma wished to share with David. There was a small clearing in the woods filled with tall, brown grasses left from last year and green grasses new this spring, swaying in the whisper of wind. It was simple, it was pure, it was God's creation.

"You know that I'm a writer, what is it *you* do when you're not saving farms?"

"I teach elementary and can teach middle school classes. Elementary age kids interest me the most, but if I taught middle school it would be science that I'm qualified to teach." She sauntered through the tall grasses.

"Science, wow. I always hated my science classes. Of course, that might have had something to do with the guy I had in ninth grade. I think he was the long lost, mad scientist. His hair was long and scraggly with none on top and he wore thick glasses inside of big black frames and dressed like he was straight out of the disco club. And if that wasn't enough right there, he constantly crunched his nose and sucked his teeth in between sentences that he spoke through his nose. Kids were always playing pranks on him. He was such a great target because he just about blew a gasket every time they did."

"Since you're a writer, did you like your English classes?"

"No. I hated those too. I really didn't want much to do with school at the time, although I did good enough to graduate and go on to college. The English classes, for the most part, didn't prepare me to be a writer of mystery novels. They taught me the basics, but the rest was pretty much through trial and error and God given talent. And I thank Him every day for it."

"You're just every teachers dream, aren't you?"

"Yeah, well, I did what I could."

Emma rolled her eyes at him. "We'd better get going, it'll be dark before we know it in the woods."

"Not yet. Let's watch the sun go down right here. It must be gorgeous."

Saying nary a word, she faced the west and waited. David stepped behind her and wrapped her up in his arms. The fit was ideal.

The yellow sky began to tinge pink, changing gradually to rose. Emma, almost imperceptibly, leaned back into David. She felt calm even though her heart sputtered and jumped. Purples and reds appeared as the sun sank below the tree line, with the final dash of color resembling an eggplant.

Compelled to act on the feeling that had welled up inside of him, David let go of the embrace, took one hand, and tugged so that she would face him. Once there, the electricity of the moment filled the air and spurred him on. The gaze was brief, the embrace of her face quick, the kiss commanding and the feeling intoxicating. He had never been confronted by the strength of emotion and the utter need that lie beneath it. It terrified him in one way, but also exhilarated him in another.

Emma let herself feel the vastness of her emotions. Parts of them had been in storage for such a long time they were all but forgotten and parts had never been awakened. She was frightened of awakening those segments of her life. It was infinitely safer to keep them closed off with the wall built high, than to risk acquiring battle scars of which there were a few already. But David made her trust when she was with him like this, he made her believe that there could be happy endings. Emma was absorbed into the moment.

David whispered in her ear, "We'd better get back, it's getting dark." Prior to starting the trek back to the truck, he couldn't resist the feel of her lips against his one more time. They were so warm and velvety.

She worried that if he continued her legs wouldn't make the trip back to the parking lot—sitting in the grass would be all that she could muster.

Just like that, they were off using their energy for transport.

The woods were dark, but not scary. They were magnificent in a different way than their walk into them. The sound of it was the same—crackling leaves, busting twigs, the whoosh of the brush that was disturbed as they passed. The look was like it was entirely a new place. Everything was in shadows. Objects were in light and dark and all the shades in between—color was absent.

Emerging from the woods, they were thrown back into the world of color. There the old aqua truck waited for their return alongside the shiny red sports car, which awaited the emergence of its people from the park. The contrast was significant.

* * * * *

The steaming hot water rolled over her shoulders and body, relaxing and refreshing her for the day ahead. Emma had already accomplished the morning farm chores, but her bookstore hours awaited. Sleep was an odd event the previous night, with the many dreams

produced by her subconscious. One was more trysts with
David offering simultaneously peace and excitement, and
another was of terrifying things around every corner she
passed. The warmth and aroma of the shower also
washed away the uneasiness of mind from the active
sleep she experienced and the cobwebs of doubt that
lurked in the recesses of her brain.

The shower and the process of readying herself
for the day ahead put her in the frame of mind necessary.
There was nothing that could be done about the odd
incidents that occurred as of late until more clues were
discovered or the person or people involved were found
out. As for the David issue, she had concluded that she
had no choice but to go along for the ride until it ended.
Then she would just have to pick up the pieces and move
on. However difficult that might be, she couldn't dwell on
that now. So with decisions made on two major fronts she
would go about her day working hard and striving for the
future.

"Mom, I'm going."

Her mom replied from the cellar. "Okay, when
will you be home?"

"I'll be home around six. I'll milk when I get
home, don't worry about them."

She swung the door and just before it latched, she
heard her mom yell, "Bye, be careful!" As she checked
and double-checked the lock on the door she thought,
you, too, Mom.

Pulling into the gravel lot with enough space for a
handful of cars, she bounced from the car, close to happy

to be working there. If she had to work someplace anyway, this was up on her list way above waitress, grocery store, hardware store, and miles above dress shop. She could browse the books they carried, have intelligent conversations about them with customers and read when the work was done. It was ideal in the sense that if she had to work outside of her profession, then this held the most attraction.

The bell on the door rang as Emma walked through. "Hey, Bobbi. Much business today?"

"Hi, no. I was waiting for you to get here." The ever serious, slight girl with short, jet-black hair and severely chopped bangs stated glumly.

Emma eyed the clock, then Bobbi, then searched the store for signs of a busy morning, looking for any indication of what might be the cause of Bobbi's mood. "I'm not late. You alright?"

"Yeah, I just couldn't wait to get out of here today. I'm spending the rest of the day with my boyfriend, Cory. Do you know him—big guy, rides a motorcycle?"

"No, but you can take off now. I'll punch your time card for you. I don't mind." She was much more comfortable alone than in the company of someone so opposite.

Bobbi smacked and cracked her gum as she fetched her things from the stockroom. "Thanks, Emma. I owe you one." Almost bouncing to the door, her mood was the polar opposite of what it had been.

Emma wistfully watched as Bobbi tore out of there enthusiastically anticipating her day. There were some days like that in Emma's life, but few stood out. Ever since the death of her brother, there were perpetual concerns that did not allow for the carefree attitude that Bobbi displayed so freely.

Better get to work, Emma. It usually gets busier later in the day, she thought. Maybe I'll have time to read some more of David's book. She smiled, setting off to check all the displays at the storefront.

Called Home

Chapter 14

David was at Mr. Higgins' office looking over the particulars on a couple of the properties that he had looked at in the morning. The office was quite basic in structure, although the furnishings were elaborate. Mr. Higgins had expensive tastes. He sat in a large, burgundy, beautifully-kept leather chair behind a giant mahogany desk atop of which stood a Tiffany lamp, a marble pen holder with wood, stone and gold pens, a leather portfolio and an old fashioned phone. The man filling the chair was impeccably dressed in a three-piece, tailored, charcoal-gray suit adorned with a blue silk tie and a diamond tie tack. The purpose for all of it was not only to impress clients, but also to feel like he was part of a big city firm while remaining in a small town.

For reasons of his own, David was drawn to one parcel of land more strongly than the others. It was a simple choice. If he bought now, found an architect and paid for speed he could be in by fall.

Excitement burst forth with the realization, but was soon tempered by a trail of regret. Unsure of the reason, he chose to ignore it and move forward with his plans to purchase his own land. "I think I'll take this one for the price we discussed."

"Are you sure?" Mr. Higgins knit his bushy brows together. "I can probably get the price reduced. The market is a bit soft right now."

"No, I have no intention in squeezing out every dime from some farmer who could use the money more than me." David pushed the papers back across the table to Mr. Higgins. "So, if you wouldn't mind, I'd like to finish this part of it as soon as you can make it happen." Standing, he shook Mr. Higgins' round hand. "I hope to hear from you in the next couple of days."

"Yes. Yes, of course. I'll get right on this." Mr. Higgins knew a good client when he saw one. He knew of David's wealth shortly after his arrival back in town. When David came to him he couldn't believe his luck.

When David knew what he wanted he went all-in without hesitation. "I thank you for your time and look forward to hearing from you." He strode to the door. "Bye."

Mr. Higgins scrambled from behind the desk to join David at the door. "Bye. You can be sure to hear from me soon."

Making his way down Main Street on foot, David was filled with a sense of accomplishment. He was more than satisfied with his decision, which aided him in getting things to move forward. The process was beginning to irritate him until the most recent property became available. His tolerance for the major events in life to get bogged down with the mundane details was on the extremely low side. He knew his parents didn't care how long he stayed with them, but he wanted a place he could call his own.

Slowing his pace to a stroll, he found himself drawn to Gail's diner. The aroma emitting from the establishment would make anyone's mouth water and he was no exception. Glancing at his watch, he concluded there was time and decided on an early lunch—a celebration of sorts.

He walked past the old timers talking loudly about the 'good ole days,' and Cindy and Jenny having a girls' lunch to catch up on the latest gossip, and made his way to his favorite booth in the corner. Mae, the ever-present waitress from his childhood, was there in a flash to take his order. Without preamble she took the pad and pencil from her apron and asked, "What can I get you?" Pencil poised, she impatiently awaited his answer. In the absence of an immediate one she tapped the pencil on the order pad—first the sharpened end, then switching it to the eraser.

"I'll have the lunch special and coffee."

"Okay, dear. Be right back with your coffee and rolls."

As David watched her retreat, he noticed Jim at the counter just settling in to have his lunch break from the lumberyard. He sat alone, scribbling notes on a

215

scratch piece of paper that looked like he had scrounged for it in the trash. It was torn and wrinkled. Weird, thought David.

Continuing his scan of the diner, he spied a couple that was obviously visiting the area. They were dressed in Bermuda shorts and knit shirts, had a map on the table, bags in the empty seats and the man wore a camera around his neck. Mid-fifties in age with a well-to-do look about them, they studied the diner like they'd never seen anything like it before.

In a booth across the way was a young couple holding hands in the middle of the table. They were locked onto each other and wouldn't have noticed if a bomb went off nearby. Then there was the lone farmer contemplating his coffee as he awaited his meal.

As his gaze scanned back, it passed Jim and flashed instantly back to him. Jim was, David thought, nervously alternating writing and taking peeks behind him. Then, noticing David, he glared without a flinch and went back to his writing.

"What odd behavior," David muttered. "I wonder what he could be up to." Before pondering it too long he added, "More than likely up to no good if you're that nervous."

Mae appeared suddenly like a hallucination out of nowhere, placing his food in front of him and disappearing like he'd imagined the whole thing. The efficient waitress knew her job well and performed it the same way. In seconds, she was back with a refill on coffee along with a perfunctory smile and to inquire about the status of his food.

"It's great, thanks." David dug into his food.

Without being aware of his mind's meanderings, he found himself face-to-face with the picture of sitting at a kitchen table that resembled the one that he had dreamed of having in his own kitchen. Emma was leaning against the door jamb with a content expression and a belly as big as a beach ball.

"Whoa. That came from out of the blue," he mumbled into his soup. "One thing at a time, buddy."

"Everything all right?" Mae looked at him like she was talking to an imbecile.

In his embarrassment, he answered curtly. "Fine."

"Okay, I'll leave you alone. You know where to find me if you need something." She spun to serve another table.

"I won't." He shoveled in another bite.

Just as he was about to finish his excellent meal, he strained to hear if what he thought he heard was real. Sure enough, the sound was getting closer and closer. His attention was glued to the street as the noise blared in his ears. The police car sped by in a blur. As it did, he was up and out the door staring after it. The siren soon went silent.

David reentered the restaurant and threw a ten on the table. Rushing back out, he could feel Jim glaring at his back. He didn't have time to consider Jim's disdain for him in his haste to find out what was going on in town. As he left the establishment, he had an uneasy feeling that he wished weren't there, for his feelings had a way of being right on in the past.

Wishing he would be wrong this time, he got in his truck and followed the path the police car had taken— at least as far as he could see. It wouldn't be hard to find them after that point since there wasn't much of the town in that direction and the siren had stopped shortly after. The objective side of his brain told him that, but at the same time his emotional side was needling him with dubiety over the whole thought process.

Before he could go too far down the dark path of doubt, he happened upon the police car in the bookstore parking lot. His stomach sank, his adrenaline pulled the stops and his brain went through all sorts of scary doors. He didn't like what it was telling him, but the flood had come, whether welcome or not.

The truck was barely stopped before he hastily exited the vehicle and almost tripped running into the bookstore where he found everyone calmly discussing something. The police officers were listening intently to Emma explain all she knew when he flew through the door, disrupting the scene.

"Can I help you sir?" one of the officers asked sternly.

"What's going on, Emma?" He was making his way toward her when the other cop impeded his progress.

David was not in the mood for games, he just wanted to get to Emma to find out if she was okay and what on earth the police were doing here. "Can I just talk to Emma?"

The officer didn't move but looked at Emma for

confirmation. With a nod of her head, he let David
through.

He was instantly at her side with concern in his
eyes. "You okay?" He could tell she'd been shaken by
whatever took place.

"Physically, yes."

"Explain. In detail please." David held her upper
arms in support as she spoke.

"Well, as I was just telling the officers I was
straightening up the stacks. I always start at the front and
move my way back."

"That's you—methodical."

"When I got to the mystery/thriller aisles I went
about my business until I got to the section with your
latest book in it. Nothing was noticeable from a distance,
but when I neared them, they looked funny somehow.
Not in an obvious way until I picked one up." She paused
and breathed deeply. David rubbed her arms. "Then it
became clear. Your name had been scratched out, like
with a sharp object, on the binding and the cover."

She shivered under David's grip.

"You need a break?"

"No, I'm okay. I proceeded to pick up the next
book with the same results. That's when I noticed every
binding had been ruined so I didn't touch anymore and
called the police straightaway." She let out a long sigh.
This is the second time that the police have had to come
to the bookstore. That had to stop.

"And the name has been crossed out on the others
as well. We'll take the books for evidence and see if there

are any clues left behind." The officer closed his notepad and stuffed it and his pen in his shirt pocket. "Thank you for your statement and cooperation. I'll be in touch." He shook David's and Emma's hands before joining his partner and hauling off the remaining books.

"Well, someone seems to have it out for me, huh?" He pulled her close and just held her for a minute, to calm her and himself. He was about to blurt it out but refrained and only thought, at least they're not after Emma.

"Maybe it was just a fan turned critic." She chuckled lightly.

"I see. You sure it wasn't you that did it?" David gave her a squeeze.

"Very funny. If it were me you'd know it."

"I have a feeling I would." He took a step back. "Why don't you lock up, I'll take you home."

Emma broke physical contact. "I'm not shirking my duties here at the bookstore. I have a few more hours to go and I intend to work them."

"Are you insane?"

"No, I'm just a reliable, hard-working person who is not going to be run off by some lunatic out to scare or hassle you without cause."

"Although that's very admirable, you need to be reasonable."

Color rose in her cheeks and her eyes narrowed. "Reasonable? You want me to be reasonable? I'll give you reasonable. You leave and let me get on with my work. No one asked you to come here and 'fix' things. I don't

need a hero. I just need someone to believe in me."
Fixing the counter displays after the police had shifted
them, she stopped and glared at David. "Why don't you
just take your 'help' elsewhere and leave me alone."

Not wanting to further irritate her, he left the store
vowing to stay nearby. To ease her stress and his mind,
he got in his truck and drove out of the lot, letting her
think that he had left. With the truck parked on a street in
close proximity to the store, he got comfortable for the
long haul. He would not leave her alone.

Emma busied herself putting the bookstore back
to rights. The books were straightened, the boxes stashed,
the accessories to books organized and then she began
dusting. She wouldn't leave until it was perfectly neat.

In the midst of her diligent cleanup, she felt a
twinge of guilt about the way she had treated David.
Picking up the phone she dialed his parents' number,
hearing it ring—one, two, three times. "Hello?"

"Hi. This is Emma, is David there?"

"No, he went into town. I don't know exactly
when to expect him."

"Oh, okay. I'll try to reach him later. Bye."

"Bye."

Great, now where am I going to find him? I really
want to let him know I appreciate him being such a good
friend. Her mind ran amuck with possibilities.

She finished out the day without many hassles.
The traffic was light and the customers agreeable.
Outside of the obvious flaw, she generally liked days like
today. The work got done efficiently and the customers

left the store as pleased as she could make them.

She was grateful once it was time to leave and Rob had made it in. She was proud of herself, but tired and ready to be home. Getting there was the first step, so she got in her car anxious for the freedom of the road. While pulling out of the parking lot, she saw David's truck parked across the street with him sitting inside. He was the faithful sentinel.

Her heart burst wide open for him at that very moment. His smile was weak because he probably thought he would be lit into again. Instead of keeping him in the dark about her change in attitude, she smiled and waved as she pulled up in front. They both left their vehicles and met between them.

"Have you been sitting there all day?"

"Yeah." He thought she might be mad. "I didn't want to leave you on your own after that. There seems to be too much happening around us lately."

"You are so sweet." Emma wrapped her arms around his neck and planted a big kiss on his cheek.

"You can put one of those right here." He pointed to his lips.

"I bet I can. Maybe I will." Her eyes searched his.

She did. It was a sweet kiss that hinted at the underlying heat.

He held her encased in his arms with her head on his chest. "You need to stop being so attractive to criminals."

"I can't help it though. My personality is so magnetic. What will I ever do?" She had to kid about it, if she focused on the possibilities too long she might give way to panic. Although it was his book and his name, it happened to be the place she worked.

"I know one thing that can be done." He held her back to see her face.

"What's that? Keep me in a cage?"

"No. But I'm not going to let you out of my sight when at all possible." Emma tensed instantly. He could feel it beneath his grip.

She raised her eyebrows. "That really isn't necessary. I'm a big girl and you can't hang out permanently with me. Don't you have things to do? Or are you on an extended vacation?"

"I am taking a bit of a break from the writing in order to get settled in here first. And I do have things to do, but maybe we could do some of them together. I don't think it would be so bad to be in each other's company for awhile. We're civilized adults, we ought to be able to handle it."

"Well, I know I am. Now you, the jury is still out on that one." The giggle burst out before she could contain it.

"Aren't you the funny one? Seriously though, I'm going to be your shadow whenever possible."

"I guess I can't really stop you. This is a public street with public sidewalks so you're free to roam wherever you like. One snag in the plan, you can't exactly go home with me. I don't think we could explain that one away to my mom."

"You're right. But I can drop in a lot and we'll just

make sure you're locked up tight before I take off." He could see the hesitation and doubt in her expression. "Humor me, okay?"

"Like I said, I don't have much of a choice. And I'm sure you'll charm my mom into letting you come by often, even if I don't make it easy for you." Fiddling with her keys, she found the ignition key and readied it in her hand for departure. "So, I guess I'm stuck seeing you whether I'm tortured by it or not."

"I can assure you it won't be torturous." He leaned in to kiss her.

"I'm not so convinced." Her mouth hovered over his lips for what seemed like an eternity. She then gave him a whisper of a kiss, spun and strolled to her car. The feeling was imprinted on her lips.

David watched her pull away before he snapped to, hopping into the truck and making the engine roar to life. Throwing it into gear, he stepped on the gas and was tailing her closely within a minute.

His mind made a thorough study of the possible criminal element as he went through the motions of driving. It made sense for him to assume that it was someone after him specifically. Emma was involved, but she was only collateral damage, as the criminal would see it. If it was someone targeting him, then it followed that it had to be someone who knew he was here, which wouldn't be an awful lot of people. And a person who hated him enough to do such things.

All those characteristics made sense, but who fit the profile? What would he have done, or not done, to make an individual hate him to that extent, causing this sort of action against him? He had no answers just yet. His mind was flooded with the images of all that had taken place thus far. There were plenty. The only thing was that no person came to mind. Not even one remote possibility. The whole thing was baffling, which in turn made it extremely frustrating.

David parked right behind her, feeling good about her being home safely.

Emma approached him. "I'm home now so you can take off and maybe I'll see you tomorrow."

"Oh you will see me tomorrow, but I am not leaving. We haven't been in the house yet to satisfy my curiosity. The house needs to pass inspection before I go anywhere." He confirmed his resolve by jumping out of the truck.

"Fine. Let's get it over with then. I feel like a little kid having mommy approve my every action." They neared the back door.

"You can either try to have fun with this," he winked at her, "or you can see every second of it as miserable. I vote for the first option."

Emma hit him playfully. "You would. I vote for the one that says it will be over with before we have time to become too annoyed by it all."

"So I'm annoying?" David pouted.

"You made that leap, not me."

They went through the door and into the kitchen. Nancy was at the sink peeling a couple of potatoes. "Hi, Mom."

"Hi, have a good day?"

"It was all right," she lied.

Nancy spun around at the sound of David's chuckle, highly pleased to see him. "Oh, hi. I didn't know Emma was bringing home company. I'll set another place for dinner."

Emma pounced on it like a cat getting into the milk. "No, David can't stay. He, ah, came by to borrow a book. I'm just going to get it for him and then he's out of here." She locked her gaze on his as she said it.

He figured he'd better play along if he didn't want Emma after his butt too. "Yes, that's right. I've got a lot to catch up on since the move, so I'll be off as soon as I get that book." Nodding conspiratorially to Emma, he offered her his boyish smile. "Maybe some other time, Ms. Benson, I'd love to join you again. Yesterday was great."

"Okay, but anytime you want you're welcome, David." Nancy tossed the potato pieces into the boiling water.

"Thank you, Ms. Benson. I promise you, I'll take you up on that soon." He shot Emma a satisfied grin.

She bared her teeth at him. For her mother's benefit she said, "Come on. I think it's upstairs."

"Following your lead, oh, omniscient one."

A glare came from under her lashes before she hustled to the stairs.

Once upstairs, David started to poke his head into every room and every closet. "What excuse can you make in order for me to check out the cellar before I leave?" He waited for the reply and added, "And I need that book that I came here to borrow."

"I'll check the cellar when we go back down from here." She gave him some unknown book from some unknown author that had been on the shelf in the extra room since the beginning of time.

"I wanted to borrow *this*?" He stared at the book, then at Emma.

"Yeah, my mom won't look that hard. She'll see you have a book and that's that. So finish your inspection of the house and get out."

"I love it when you talk to me that way." The poking around the upstairs was done so they went back down.

David entered the kitchen and Emma slipped down the cellar stairs. When she reappeared, she had a jar of peaches in her hand. "Can we have these tonight?"

Nancy was pleased that Emma wanted her canned peaches and didn't notice the odd behavior, which was Emma's plan in the first place. "Most definitely." She took the jar and popped it open right then. "David, would you like some before you have to go?"

He noticed the stern look from Emma and couldn't help it. "Yes, thank you, Ms. Benson. That's very kind of you." He smirked, not wanting to have a glimpse of Emma, lest he burst into laughter.

"Well, if you're going to sit around eating peaches then I'm going to make use of my time and milk the cows." She trounced out of the house and halfway to the barn.

Suddenly there was a hand on her shoulder and an

accompanying yelp escaped her lips—she was unable to plaster them shut in time. "What are you doing sneaking up on me like that? You're lucky I didn't mace you or something."

Looking smug, David retorted, "And where would it be that you're hiding that mace?" His eyes scanned her body down then back up.

"I believe that's my secret. What *are* you doing anyway?"

"I know what I'd like to do." He raised his brows.

"Hah! Now that really is funny. Seriously."

"Seriously, what do you think, I'm going to check the barn just like I did the house." He went through the barn door first.

Letting him go about his business, she headed for the opposite doors to let the cows in. By the time she had them all in their stalls, David came by and announced the premises secure.

"Thanks, bye." Attaching the milking machines kept her attention so she didn't bother looking up.

"Don't let the door hit me on the way out, huh? Just make sure you lock the door as soon as you get in the house."

"Yes, master." With all the machines attached, she went to the first one to remove it, empty it and move on to the next cow with a full udder.

"That's what I like to hear."

"Keep it in your memory bank 'cause you won't be hearing that again."

As she exited the stall, David grabbed her and

smashed his mouth to hers. Emma sunk into the luxuriousness of it and was left wanting more when he pulled away. "That's what I want stuck in *my* memory bank."

Without another word he did an about face and left with Emma staring after his receding figure. What a figure it is, Emma thought—fitted jeans on a tall lean man with a confident gait. She would have that vision stuck in her head for a while.

*   *   *   *   *

The next day was crystal clear, sunny and warm. Emma had to work the same hours as she had the day before at the bookstore. Upon leaving that morning, her nerves had been jumbled into knots at the thought of returning to the scene of two incidents—one solved and the other not. She ventured forth bravely and conquered her qualms without too much difficulty.

The afternoon in the bookstore was the polar opposite of what she'd expected. It was relaxing along with being productive. No weird happenstance occurred, not even the odd cranky customer materialized this afternoon. It was an all out excellent day working at the bookstore.

The bells on the door jangled, announcing another customer.

"Oh, hey. You been keeping busy today?" she greeted David nonchalantly.

"Busy with my bodyguard work." David handed Emma a coffee, then flexed his arm.

"Thanks. I told you that you didn't have to do that.

The police are keeping an eye on this place and I'm not working evening shifts anymore so it's all taken care of." She dislodged the lid and removed it, to let it cool from infernal to flaming.

"If you think that the three or four times a police car drives by here in an afternoon is going to deter a criminal with his mind set on coming here to make trouble, then you'd better think again." Sipping his coffee, he thought more about how to assure Emma that he needed to do this. "Think of it this way. You are not asking me to do this so you shouldn't feel guilty about the time I spend sitting in my truck *all alone*. No, seriously, I am doing this to make myself feel as comfortable as I can with you working here and this guy still on the loose. So humor me and don't worry. I'm good." He slugged down the remainder of his coffee.

"All right, but know that you really don't have to do it."

"Point taken." David gestured to her cup. "Better drink before it gets too cold to tolerate."

"I don't think there's much danger of that." She sipped carefully lest she burn her tongue. "Thank you, by the way. I seem to be saying that to you a lot lately."

"I'm sure you'll be able to find a way to thank me properly." That mischievous grin appeared.

"Right. Now let me get back to work." She tried to sound exasperated.

"Roger that. I'll see you in an hour to escort you home."

Chapter 15

The routine was similar to yesterday afternoon. David came home with her and checked the house under some kind of ruse, but this time Nancy insisted he stay for dinner. Nancy was too thrilled with his seemingly constant presence with Emma to question it. She wanted to see her daughter happy and, in her eyes, that meant married. Yes, her marriage ended prematurely, but that didn't mean that Emma's had to. She needed someone to share the ups and downs with her. She needed someone with whom to decipher solutions to life's problems. She needed someone to share her life—every aspect of it. Nancy concluded that she needed David.

"Well, you can make yourself useful and help me in the barn." Emma motioned to David to come with her.

"Emma. We don't ask guests to do chores."

Before Emma could make a snide comment about him not being a guest, David jumped in ahead. "I don't mind, Ms. Benson. I'm not very good at sitting around doing nothing."

Emma couldn't resist in light of the recent events. "That's not what I hear."

"We'll see. Let's go." He all but pushed her out the door.

Once outside, he confronted her. "You're feeling pretty saucy for someone who's going to be alone in the barn with me."

"If you know what's good for you you'll watch your step." Emma plowed ahead.

"Oh, I do know what's good for me and it has nothing to do with watching my step. It has more to do with stepping over the line, I believe."

"You try that and see where it gets you." Emma entered the barn and yelled, "No!" as she frantically took stock of the scene.

It was a mess. And it was a message. Harnesses, hay, feed, tools, blankets and the like were strewn across the entire barn floor. Workhorses were broken, water and feeding troughs were pulled out and turned over. Outside of the building being intact, it was in worse shape than after the tornado. It was the biggest mess she'd ever seen.

Scratched into the wall was the following, INTERFERE & BOTH WILL SUFFER. Underneath it read, 1002.

David took Emma into his arms to comfort her. The gesture was necessary only for a moment, then Emma had a surge of anger that required elbowroom. The animal-like scream came with an unexpected force that aided in purging her system. Her arms swung in wild gestures. One at a time, she picked up several items and chucked them as hard as she could. The tirade continued until she ran out of fuel. Spent, she slumped to the floor, dropping her head to her hands. She was too stunned and outraged to cry.

Instead of attempting to help her stand, David knelt down and gingerly wrapped his arm around her to test the waters. She welcomed the comfort at that point, soaking up every last drop. She lifted her head slowly and faced David. In a low dejected tone, she said, "My mom's going to have to know now. And it won't be pleasant."

He rubbed her back, conveying all the sympathy and support he had for her. "I know, but we'll get through this together. I'm not walking away from you no matter how much you push me to take off. I'll be here for whatever is needed of me. You're stuck with me whether you like it or not."

"Lucky me." She took a stab at kidding, but it only came out with a hint of the pathetic. "I'm not strong enough to push you out anyway. So you're safe for the time being." Emma rose, put her hands on her hips and stared at the disaster that lay before her. "The cows. How am I supposed to milk the cows this evening?" She looked to David with panic rising. That was something that couldn't wait until the next day. The cows *had* to be milked.

"*We*," he corrected. "*We* will get this cleared out just enough to do the job, but first the authorities have to be called." He patiently awaited a response but without one he asked, "Do you want me to call?"

"No, I was just thinking about how they've been doing such a fabulous job solving this whole mess." The sarcasm emphasized her disdain for the lack of movement by the police on any of the incidents that had previously taken place. She knew she had to, but she didn't see that much was going to come from calling, except a huge waste of time. "I would appreciate it if you would come in with me. My mom might not freak quite so intensely if you were there."

"Whatever you want, I'm here for you." He followed obediently: no wise cracks, no pushing her buttons, just quiet and total support which he realized could not have been staved off if he would have wanted. But of course, he didn't.

The routine was like *déjà vu*, only the details of the event were different. Emma was increasingly annoyed by each step because it felt like it was all for naught. Nothing would come of it *again*. By the end of the questioning she almost lost it when they said, "We'll look into it and let you know what we find." It was all she could do to refrain from an outburst that would do no good and only make her out to be a high-strung female who couldn't keep her emotions in check. That was the last thing she needed.

Playing the ever-polite hostess, she said, "Thank you. We can clean up in the barn now, right?"

"Yeah, we got what we need." They slugged down the last of the coffee that Nancy had given them and left them to deal with the aftermath.

Slightly down but never defeated, Emma breathed deeply and let a giant sigh fill the silence. "I guess we'd better get those cows milked before their udders explode." She chuckled at the ill humor. If she didn't laugh she might cry. That was the *last* thing she wanted.

"You order, I do." David offered his assistance in a way she would appreciate.

"I like the sound of that. You sure about that, huh?" Emma displayed a mischievous grin.

That's exactly what he was aiming for—a glimmer of light in her eyes.

In among the small catastrophe, the light left again. She looked tired and battle weary. He would allow her this and then proceed to bolster her reserves, but without a certain amount of time to mourn what took place, she wouldn't be ready for the rebuilding of her defenses. For now, they would do the necessary and when done they would figure it out from there.

The work was done in relative silence. Only questions involving the work or directions in answer were the rare disruptions to the silence. Their intent was to finish while they were still able to function.

Once the pile of stuff was set aside enough to invite the cows in, David helped her get started on the milking. After the initial surge, he put his energies into cleaning while she moved on with the evening chore, although it was now well past eight o'clock.

She was so focused on the cows that she paid little attention to what and how much David was doing. With the milking done for the day, Emma wiped her hands on her jeans as she surveyed the barn. It was almost back to normal. Looking at it now made the scenario seem like a dream—until she saw the writing again. Upon viewing it, a shiver ran the length of her spine causing her to shake.

David was aware of the response, but could see the determination set on her face. Best not to bring it up, he thought. "Ready to eat? I'm starving."

"Yeah, but aren't you always starving? How do you stay so skinny?" Emma scanned his body all the way down and back up. "You don't have an ounce extra."

"I do all right. Let's go attack that meal your mother has waiting for us."

"That's a plan I can get on board with."

With dinner complete and the chitchat winding down, Nancy excused herself to head off to bed. "You're welcome to stay the night, David. There's plenty of room around here."

"Thank you, Ms. Benson. I think I might take you up on that." He didn't see Emma's expression until Nancy had closed her bedroom door.

"What's that look for?" Even though he knew, he wanted her to articulate exactly what was the problem.

"Like you don't know. You can go home now." She put her hands on her hips.

"If you think I'm leaving you two here alone after all the garbage that's happened, then you really have gone around the bend."

"We're big girls, we don't need a babysitter. We're all locked up tight and it's not like he did anything in the house." She softened a bit, knowing that he'd been a huge support and only wanted to help. "I don't want you to have to hang here when you'd probably rather be somewhere else—like anywhere, but here."

David stepped closer, making sure he had eye contact before he replied. "There is no place I want to be than right here. I wouldn't be able to enjoy a thing knowing that I walked away from you in this situation." His hand brushed gently across the silken path of her hair, coming to rest on her shoulder. The other hand joined it on the other shoulder. "You are my only priority at present. If anything happened to you that I could have prevented I would never forgive myself." He gathered her up, wrapping her in his comfort and care that was beginning to feel very much like love. He was absolutely smitten.

"I beg your pardon?" she said against his chest.

"Oh, nothing. Just the ramblings of a tired lunatic." He stroked her hair and was so utterly filled with joy that he knew it couldn't be anything but love. Now, if only Emma could come to the same conclusion. "Okay, so where do I bunk?" His impish grin appeared again.

She knew what he was alluding to and said, "Since the barn is where the trouble was maybe you should make sure it's secure tonight." A smile was struggling to break free of her constraints.

"You're such the kidder." He eased closer to the stairs as a hint.

"What makes you think that I'm kidding? You should know me well enough by now to know that I'm perfectly capable of being serious about a statement like that."

"Just in case you are serious, my argument is that I'm here to keep you safe, not the cows or barn. So, if you would so kindly show me to my room, I'd be grateful." At the bottom of the stairs, he swept his arm from her to the steps to suggest her compliance.

"Fine, if you insist on staying in the house." She brushed past him.

"I definitely insist."

With him settled in the room farthest from hers, she readied herself for bed. Her mind wandered all over the place—a serpentine path if ever there was one. She skated from topic to topic, overshooting the target and then back past it to another. Her thoughts ranged from the violation of property crime, to the care and concern of David, to her life in upheaval, to spending her life with people that love her. Love, how did that word enter the meanderings of my brain, she wondered, ridiculous.

She shuffled her slippered feet back to her room. "I must be delirious," she mumbled as she entered her room. It now felt very empty and lonely. She couldn't fathom why. It was the same room it had always been but now she yearned for more.

She laid in her bed all comfy and cozy in the thick homemade quilt, with all light except moonlight extinguished and yet she could not sleep. After the wearing day with its various ups and downs, her body remained uninfluenced by the temptations of sleep. Making a pact with herself, she vowed to give it another hour after which she would do something other than frustrate herself by lying there unsuccessful in sleep.

Yep, it presented itself as a lost cause. Emma sat on the edge of her bed wondering, now what? She couldn't stay in her room in her bed. She was restless and craved movement. Exiting her room, she glanced to David's door without inducement. It was closed and his light was off. Much to her shock, she was disappointed at him not being up and available for conversation.

She flicked the switch for the stair light, which wouldn't disturb anyone. Once downstairs, she passed through the dining and living rooms with ease. She shuffled to the kitchen and headed for the refrigerator—not that she was hungry, just thirsty. Upon opening the refrigerator door, the light from within illuminated the area enough to catch a figure in Emma's peripheral vision. She jumped and let her mouth gape open without a sound.

"It's me," David whispered.

"What are you doing creeping around down here?"

"I think probably the same thing you are. I couldn't sleep and got up to roam when I thought that maybe I might find something in here to coax sleep to come more quickly." He grinned, holding up a glass of wine.

"That might work." She stared at it like it was a prize to be won.

"Would you like some?" He held up the bottle.

"I believe I will." She snagged a wineglass from the cabinet instead of a juice glass, which David was using. "We do own wineglasses, you know. This is a *civilized* farm."

"This is harder to knock over. How much?" he asked as he started pouring.

"However much will fit. I think this is the kind of day that deserves a full glass of wine, or maybe two. Let's sit in the living room. It's more comfortable and we won't disturb my mother as easily in there."

She made herself cozy in the big chair by the fireplace and even though it wasn't lit it warmed her anyway. David sunk into the couch and stretched out his legs. "So why are you up at this hour? Shouldn't you be tired after the day you've had?"

"You're up, shouldn't you?"

"Me? All I did was sat in a truck all day drinking too much coffee. The only thing I should need to do is go to the bathroom."

Emma quietly laughed. "Yeah, about that. I really do appreciate your vigilance. I know I discouraged you from being there, but it did the job in making me feel safer." She stared into the fireplace. "Before tonight I at least felt safe at home, but now . . ."

"Well, that so boosts my ego."

"No, that's not what I meant. If you weren't here . . ." She held her breath to see if she had made amends.

"It's too late. I already know how you feel about my abilities." He feigned hurt.

"You can add being a big baby to the list."

"Now you've done it. You're not my friend

anymore." David let out a satisfied sound that told of his self-proclaimed superior value.

After several minutes of companionable silence, Emma was ready to find out more about the man who seemed to be capturing her heart. "So what brought you back to dairy country anyway?"

"I just wanted to be here. Remember I told you that I got tired of the rat race. I grew up enough to accept that this is where I belong. I love it here. I know people who would choke on that, but I really do. Despite my resistance to this place growing up, I think it's a superb area to raise a family, et cetera, et cetera."

"That's all. You just picked up and moved on a whim, without everything set in place?"

"Not exactly on a whim. I'd been thinking about it for awhile."

Emma sipped at her wine and considered the casualness of his answer. Could it be that simple? "You explained that your writing could be done anywhere, but what about your friends and colleagues?"

"Colleagues are simple. There's phone, e-mail and the occasional trip that do the job on that front. And as far as friends go, I have good friends here. The ones I had in New York were fun and interesting, but there wasn't any deep connection that I feel lost without. And of course, the easiest part of the equation is that my family is here. You can never replace them." He tipped back the juice glass and drained the last of the wine.

Emma held out her glass to him. "While you're pouring, would you?"

"Hang on to it. I'll bring the bottle out here—much easier that way." He disappeared and then reappeared with the bottle. "So I was thinking, you know why I came back, but why did you?"

"I thought I told you that I was here to help my mother."

"Yes, but she'd been running the place for the past several years without your help, why now?"

She squirmed a bit in her seat, slightly uncomfortable with the direction of the conversation. "Look, I just thought I needed to be here *with* her and *for* her. Finances were part of it, but instead of just sending the occasional check, I thought we could both benefit from having the other around."

Scrutinizing her, he felt that there was almost certainly more to do with it than what she offered in explanation. Being the perceptive writer that he was, he left it where it lay. Another time, he thought.

She watched him, although not obviously. The relaxation she recognized in him she wished she could feel with him. His arm was laid across the back of the couch and she envisioned herself leaning back against him with that arm around her. They would enjoy a crackling fire, dry red wine and the comfort of familiarity. But that was the problem, they really didn't know each other all that well. And despite what he said, she was sure he would leave. He pulled up stakes and came here just like that. What's to keep him from doing the same thing about leaving?

Easing out of the chair, she got up and offered to

take his empty glass. "I think the wine did its job, so it's off to bed with me."

"Goodnight."

"I'll see you in the morning." She ascended the stairs ready for sleep to come quickly. All she wanted was for her brain to turn off.

The next morning was slightly weird with David in the house, using the bathroom, running around in his pajamas, eating breakfast with her and her mother. Emma didn't altogether dislike it, she just wasn't at all used to having a male living in the same quarters as her. He helped with everything. It surprised her that his abilities included many of the things that the men of the area considered women's work—washing dishes, making the bed, frying bacon, folding sheets, even dusting. The list grew as the day grew long. Emma was quite impressed, although she was going to keep that thought all to herself.

"Don't your parents expect you to live at their house while you're without your own residence?"

"I already explained the situation to them. They know that I'm not going anywhere for the time being. So you'd better get used to it."

"I'm good. Problem is, I might get too used to it and then you might be stuck doing dishes and making beds."

The phone rang and she smiled as she passed him on her way to pick it up.

"Hello? Um, sure," she spoke into the phone.

"Yeah, I'll be there. Bye." She hung up, unsure of how she felt about the call.

"So, where you going to be?"

"The girl scheduled for tonight can't make it in, she's sick. So I just agreed to work her shift, which I'm conflicted about. I could use the money, but I was looking forward to having the evening off." She shrugged it off. "Such is life, I guess."

"Yeah, but look at it this way. You get to spend the evening with me." He raised his brows. "Isn't that great?"

"Right, great." Emma couldn't have sounded less thrilled, but it was all in jest. "We'd better grab some dinner and get going."

"You're in charge." David waved her through to the kitchen ahead of him.

"You'd do well to remember that for the rest of the evening." She poked his arm and held her head high as she breezed past him to get dinner together.

It was quick and easy. The pork chops pan-fried in minutes and the potatoes from the other night took little to heat up. Once dinner had been consumed, Nancy kicked the two of them out the door, vowing not to allow them any part of cleaning up. "See you two later." Nancy never missed the opportunity to put the two together—in talk or in actual situation—she was ecstatic knowing that Emma was, at the very least, friends with someone like David. And she hoped with all that she had, that more would come of the friendship. It would be good for them both.

Work at the bookstore was going well, especially with David there. The work didn't seem like such, with good company and good conversation. Time ticked on by without dragging its feet and without much fanfare. Emma thought, I could get used to this. Better not start thinking that way. You know what happens then. As soon as you begin to expect someone to be there, that's when that person walks out of your life—for good. They become a fixture and then, poof, they're gone.

All the shipments were stocked, including the new one of David's books. It was put to rights now with the empty space refilled and his book once again available for sale. She had flashbacks to that night as she and David shelved them. Every few that went through her hands flashed in her mind with his name scratched off. A surge of energy pulsed through her system every time it happened and she slipped into a pensive state as a result.

David noticed and attempted to pull her out of the sudden mood by making fun of himself. "Can you believe that picture they made me put in my books? They tried to make me look like a movie star or model. It's pretty hilarious." He opened the book to show her the inside back cover.

"I think it's an awfully handsome picture."

She didn't razz him, now he knew for sure that something was up. "Leave the word handsome out and you got it right on." Her lips were all that much more enticing when she sported a pout.

"Maybe it'll attract some women to read it that normally wouldn't. That can't hurt the sales any." Going about her business, she failed to see the desire in his expression.

"Yeah, that's the only way to get people to read

it." Maybe if he engaged her mind elsewhere he would see the light come back to her eyes.

"That's not what I meant. You're just being the insecure artistic type. And you should know that's not true anyway. The things are huge sellers."

"The 'things', that pretty much describes them. They do have a way of taking on a life of their own. Enough about me, let's get this finished so we can take our break—hopefully without any customers interrupting it."

"Why? You planning on doing something that can't take interruption?"

"You bet I do. And it involves you." He caught her around the waist as she tried to scoot past him. "See what I mean."

"I'm beginning to, but I think I need a little more in the way of details."

"I like how you think." He ran a strand of her silky auburn hair through his first two fingers and thumb. It soothed him, and he hoped her as well.

"Oh, that's why." She looked into his eyes—green, full of life, all she wanted she saw. It mostly excited her, but offered a hint of uncertainty underneath. She didn't like uncertainty, although that was the only way some things came. The more time she spent with him, the more they did as a team, the more she couldn't imagine going back to being without him. But that's likely what would happen. Emma couldn't fathom him staying here in rural Wisconsin when he had the world at his fingertips. Losing the thought, all that was left were his eyes—

brilliant green with desire, his face—strong, confident and oh, so kissable. Which is exactly what she did before she over-analyzed it.

David felt her soft, warm lips light on his cheek, working their way to his temple to his nose, across to the opposite temple and down to his chin. The sensation of her taking charge, he could most definitely live with. Each spot her lips touched was warmed by a minute shock of electricity and he thought, I could endure this for some time. He had to contain the urge to jump in and take over lest he lose this feeling. His soul had never been reached to this extent before. He liked it, very much. It scared him, very much. The liking won at present. And presumably always would, he hoped.

Emma made her way to his mouth that waited in anticipation. The feel of his lips—firm, but gentle—made her just want more. She enticed his tongue into action. Slow and lazy with spurts of energy, they explored the art of kissing. His hands stroked her back, arms, shoulders, and neck and ran into her hair with such care it made her bones melt. She returned the favor caressing his back, arms, shoulders and neck following the contour of every muscle. And there were plenty, especially for a writer.

The bell on the front door rang with a ding and a voice followed on its heels. "Sorry to bother you, but we have some information the two of you will be interested in." It was Officer Stewart and Officer Bittle.

Scrambling free of David, the embarrassment showed only slightly on her cheeks. "Yes, we want any information there is. Would you like some water or soda first?"

"Oh, no, thank you."

"Well, what have you got?" David waited impatiently with his thumbs hooked in his back pockets.

"I'm going to warn you up front, it's not good news." Officer Stewart had a very serious, business-like air about him.

Emma looked on nervously while David sighed and offered his commentary. "So what else is new lately? That's all we seem to be getting."

"You'll want to know this though. Kenny Fallon."

"Who?" David had never heard the name.

Officer Stewart continued, "He's the guy that attacked Miss Benson."

"What about him? He's in prison in state custody." David's body went rigid at the mention of the word "attack."

"He was." The officer paused for the inevitable reaction.

Emma didn't make a sound, the color drained out of her before David's eyes. "Emma, why don't you sit down."

"Not unless you all come over with me. I want to hear everything you have to say." She was talking to Officer Stewart now.

"You lead." Officer Bittle gestured for her to lead the way.

Once they huddled around the chair, Officer Stewart said, "He escaped from the courthouse and he's been out for at least a week. The state didn't seem to think that we needed to be in the loop since he was in their custody. Why we shouldn't be informed, I could not even begin to explain." He bent down to look Emma in the eye. "I apologize to you, miss. There's no excuse worthy of this muck up. Sir," he offered his hand to David, "Sorry."

"So what do you suggest we do?"

Officer Bittle fielded that one. "I recommend you keep your eyes open and your doors locked. And let us know of anything suspicious. We're doing everything we can to find him."

"You folks have a good evening." Officer Stewart waved a hand over his shoulder on the way out.

David called after them. "It's a little late for that now."

He looked to Emma and saw her appearing fragile, like she never had before to him. Kneeling down, he took her hand in his. "I'll be with you." He covered it with his other hand. "Don't worry. They'll find this guy now that they know he's here." Her small hand remained in his for several moments.

She sighed heavily and sprang to her feet. "He is *not* going to scare me out of my daily activities." Pushing past David, she added, "*not*," for emphasis.

Chapter 16

The following days went as routinely as one could expect with a criminal on the loose. Outside of them being each other's shadows, they did the tasks that were required of them and even some that weren't. The experience was more pleasant than originally expected.

They picked up feed in the truck, they ate at Gail's for lunch, they went grocery shopping together, and they went to Mr. Higgins' office so the realtor could have David sign some papers. The hunt for a birthday present for Nancy was, you could say, fun.

It all seemed normal, even under the umbrella of stress and fear the situation created. The whole thing should have felt odd to Emma, but instead it came across as so comfortable that she knew it would be painful when it was over.

She undoubtedly wanted Fallon found, though for obvious reasons. She couldn't go on with the uncertainty of him popping up out of nowhere at anytime. Her outlook was confident on that front. If he was hanging around hassling them then he should be easier to catch. She was fearful of one thing though—when the case was over, might *they* not be over, too?

Not willing to peer into the future, she chose to be content with the present. It followed her today as they ducked into another shop in search of the perfect birthday present. Nancy liked pretty things—knick-knacks to set around, fancy towels, handmade mugs, doilies, place mats, and wall hangings. But nothing struck Emma as being the one that had Nancy written all over it. If it didn't show up soon they'd find themselves having to go to another town. Emma wasn't up to going through that much effort. Her reserves were currently pretty low and it wouldn't take much to completely deplete them.

"What about this?" David held up a large set of metal wind chimes that sounded like they were from a monastery.

"That's it!" Emma all but yelled it. "She loves those." Suddenly, her countenance darkened. "You'd better put them back. I know how expensive those things are and I can't justify buying them with so many other places for the money to go." She allowed herself to feel defeated on the gift front. It was perfect but for the ever-pesky detail of money, which never took a break.

"I was planning on pitching in. Seeing as I've been staying in her house, I wasn't going to ignore the fact that it was her birthday. So you put in what you planned on spending and I'll make up the difference.

Matter of fact, you don't have to put anything in. I mean, what do I have money for anyway."

"Oh, no, Mr. Moneybags, I'm not going to let you buy *my* gift for *my* mom. I do have some pride."

People glanced at the conversation going on in the homey gift shop. Not that they were being loud, it was just that people could tell the tone of it was at least semi-serious. David and Emma were in their own world though and blithely went about their business.

"Fine. Just give me a few bucks and then it'll be from both of us and then you can say you contributed and all that. Besides, I should be paying you room and board for staying at your house, so please let me do this." He was hitting her weak spot. "You'd be doing me a favor." That did it. She couldn't pass up a favor for a friend.

"Fine, if spending a lot of money means that much to you I wouldn't want to stand in your way."

He grinned, grabbed the chimes and paid for them before she could think about changing her mind.

On the way home, Emma thanked him for his kindness.

"No, really, I'm telling you the truth. You did me a favor by allowing me to do this. Your mother is such a sweet lady. She has taken me staying there indefinitely in stride. She's great and I wanted her to have a really great present that she wholeheartedly deserves. So there."

"Well, I guess that closes that subject. I'll take care of making dinner then."

"Nope, sorry. I've got that one covered too."

"What do I get left with?"

David thought purposefully while he drove. "Buy her a huge card. And if you want, some flowers." He was smugly satisfied with his answer.

"You're pleased with yourself, aren't you? Well, I must admit, you put a lot of thought into this. My mom will love every last detail of it. She loves surprises and gifts." Emma had a faraway look about her. Too bad her life had offered few people who cared enough to make the effort.

"What's going through that complicated brain of yours?"

"I was thinking about what I said last. Although she loves those kinds of things she hasn't had anyone around to provide her with those special days."

"She has you."

"I know, but I was referring to a partner to share life's good times and bad times." She became quiet and road noise filled the cab. "She had it until my father decided that he didn't want to work through those tough times with anyone. The bottle became his friend. And it left my mother with a farm and a small child along with her grief. It's a good thing she had her faith. It got her through the most difficult of times. And the church community offered help and support every step of the way."

"That's the kind of thing that I was referring to when you asked me why I would want to move back here and leave the excitement of New York behind. It's a sense of community and family that's not the same there. You can find a form of it, but it didn't cut it for me. I guess you have to be a particular type of person to make it work. I'm glad I had the experience. I think it helped form the human being I am now, but I think it would have started to have an adverse effect if I had stayed much longer."

"Then I do believe you're where you should be."

David pulled the truck into the driveway. "Oh, I believe I am." He studied her, knowing that he meant much more than she suspected by that statement.

* * * * *

Nancy was ecstatic with every detail of the birthday celebration and let them know again on the way to the bus station. David and Emma couldn't have done any better if they'd invited the residents of Brooks. The fact that it provided such joy for her mom made her, in turn, filled with satisfaction at the occasion. David and Emma had dropped Nancy off at the station so that she might visit her rarely seen sister in Iowa.

On the way home, Emma became anxious at the realization that she was going to be alone in the house with David staying there. It wasn't that she didn't trust David. The problem stemmed more from her own inadequacies and possible lack of control of her desires than any misstep on his part.

At the house they carried on as normal, with an edge.

At dinner, there was a slight air of tension that neither one of them acknowledged. With dinner eaten and the kitchen cleaned up, they had time to relax. Emma didn't know how much she was actually going relax, though.

Emma and David watched television for a while. She sat across the room from him, hoping that it was a safe distance. At the end of the eight-thirty show she decided that she had hung out long enough and made her excuses to go on up to bed.

"I'll see you in the morning. Goodnight."

"Goodnight." David didn't mind being alone. His system needed a reprieve from her charms. And as far as he was concerned, there were many—she was smart, witty, funny, strong, sensitive and the list could go on.

The night proved to be a long one, full of sensual dreams leading to waking in a fitful condition only to lie awake with similar notions playing on his mind. With the scenario rewinding and playing several times over, he relented to the fact that sleep would not come peacefully this night and got up to hopefully wear himself out enough to fall into a restful state. Although his outlook on the real possibilities of it happening was not positive, he thought it the only choice.

Downstairs he poured the whiskey, which he had made sure was in the house, into a glass straight and brought it to his lips, slugging it down in one svelte move. He repeated the first part again with the intention of nursing it while reading. It didn't achieve the results he wished for, it only proved to sharpen the focus on Emma. Where would he be once they caught Fallon? Nowhere, he thought. He'd be out of this house and, he feared, if Emma had anything to say about it, pushed further away inch by inch. He couldn't let that take place.

Emma slept surprisingly well. She woke in the morning well rested and ready to face whatever today threw at her. She descended the stairs in her fuzzy slippers and chartreuse pajamas, letting out a cut-off yell at seeing a figure reclining on the couch, but not enough to see it was David in the split second before the noise escaped her lips. With her hand on her chest she felt her heart beat strong and quick and watched as David jumped up ready to fight.

"What? Who is it?" David was alert with the remnants of sleep lurking in the background.

"It's just me. Sorry. I didn't expect anyone to be down here and you just surprised me, so a silly reaction was the result. You okay?" She neared him, with an apology written all over her face.

"Nothing that some coffee won't fix." He stretched, exposing his stomach and displaying every taut muscle.

Emma couldn't look away. She hoped that he was too caught up in waking each muscle and nerve to notice her gawking. Snapping back to reality, she willed her body into motion. "Coffee it is."

He heard water running, dishes clanking, and coffee brewing. Just the sound of it nudged him closer to wakefulness. It was going to be a long stay without her mother in the other room. Best put my mind to the business of the day, he thought.

Entering the kitchen, a surge of domesticity with the one he loved whacked him upside the head with tremendous force. What was he going to do? He knew

257

Emma enough to know that if he pushed, the only direction it would get him is opposite of where he wanted. "I'm going out for a run." The door was near so it was possible to escape.

"Like that?" Emma said, looking at his attire.

"Oh yeah, I guess pajamas aren't the thing to take a run in." Hustling through the kitchen, he took the stairs by two.

He was back before she could pour a cup of coffee.

Standing for inspection with his hands in the air and palms up, he said, "Better, huh?"

The picture before her of the slim, muscular body clad in running shorts and a T-shirt had joy welling up that she couldn't explain. Not a physical reaction, but an emotional one that touched her soul. "I think that'll do the trick. Now get going so we can have breakfast. I'm starving."

As soon as the door slammed behind him, Emma sighed in relief for the reprieve from David's presence. He was getting too close and if it weren't for her own inability to make a clear-cut decision about him, she wouldn't be so tortured. He was good, he was kind, he was strong, he was everything she wanted if she was pressed on the issue, but there was the inevitable, ready to rear its ugly reality at any given moment. She would be smart to never forget that for the sake of self-preservation. The sticky part was that she suspected that she was already lost and the pain would come no matter how much she tried to avoid it.

Cups, plates, silverware, and napkins were all out and set on the table. Pans, bacon, eggs, and bread were on the counter ready for making. With everything prepared, she contemplated what to do with her time, sat at the table and began to have a very pertinent and honest talk with God about what has been going on in her life. The more she rambled, the more the weight she felt lifted from her shoulders, and the more she felt bolstered for the day.

David came through the door all flushed from the exercise and calmly said, "We need to call the police again. He was busy last night."

"Okay, what is it this time?" She felt irritation and fear, but along with it was a healthy dose of anger. "I'm getting more sick of him being able to disrupt our lives than I am with any of the actual property damage being done." The anger visibly increased and burst through without restraint. "I'm sick of him running my life. *I'm* the one that gets to run it, not some two-bit criminal getting his jollies from making my life miserable." She stomped around the kitchen.

"You ready to take that energy outside and see what he did?" David led the way to the hidden side of his truck.

Emma stared at the truck. David stared at her.

"What on earth does that mean?" She pointed to the passenger door where the number 1002 was scratched in the paint.

"I have no idea. I was wondering if you did, but evidently not. He put that in the barn, also. I didn't see it

259

until I was coming back 'cause it's on the side facing the street. We'd better call our friends at the police station."

The shiver ran through her as the fingers of fear spread like creeping bugs. "I just made a connection. My watch, it was him." She turned and screamed, "He was in my house—my bedroom!"

Trying to understand and yet calm her, he asked in a soothing tone, "What are you talking about?"

"My watch stopped a couple of times, but I had the battery checked and it was fine."

"Watches do that sometimes, but what does that have to do with this?"

Her agitation continued. She wanted his immediate understanding. "I know that and that's why I didn't think anything of it at the time. I only had a slight hesitation when I found out that the battery was still good, but I shrugged it off as one of those unexplainable things of life—until now, when I put the two together. Both times my watch stopped on 10:02, which I also thought a bit too coincidental. Anyhow, that's the same number that's here and that was in the barn. I don't know what he's trying to say, but I'm beginning not to like the time 10:02. And it makes me nervous that I don't know whether he means morning or night or if it is even supposed to be a time."

He staved the rambling by actually putting his hand gently across her mouth. "Take a breath." Thoughts were flashing through her mind, visible on her face along with the urge to lash out. "We'll figure it out. It sounds a little too coincidental. This guys been busy." He paced behind her, racking his brain for answers.

"Yeah, and I'd like to relieve him of his overloaded schedule." She kicked the truck in frustration.

"Hey, it's not the truck's fault. You need to be gentle with it, it's an old man." The light tone and the caressing of the hood of the truck did nothing for Emma as she held on to the rage within.

"If we come across this guy before the police do, you'd better keep me away from him if you don't want to be visiting me in prison."

"You're kind of scaring me right now."

Emma faced David in time for him to see the rage on her face fade. "Sorry, I get a tinge over the top sometimes, but if there's a good reason then this is it." She grabbed his hand without thinking and dragged him to the house. "Let's call and get some clothes on before they show up." She looked down at her wardrobe and then to his with distinct disapproval. "They might get the wrong idea here."

"I don't think they care what the idea is at all as long as we're not naked." He winked.

"Well, *I* do. So get on it."

* * * * *

The soup was simple. It was superb in its understated character. She spooned up another bite of the chicken-based soup with thin noodles, potato pieces, garlic and cilantro. Debbie, the clerk at the Stop, Drop-in and Shop, sat across from her and was fast becoming a good friend. Emma or David went in there, usually more than once, every day when she was working at the bookstore.

"I finally got Jim to take me out last night." Debbie tossed her shoulder length, blonde hair out of her face with a shake of her head. "I had a great time. He, on the other hand, seems to be stuck on someone yet." Debbie raised her light eyebrows over her darkly painted lashes in suggestion.

"It's not my fault," Emma defended. "I have never encouraged him."

"I know, I'm just hassling you. I just wish he could let it go so he could move on." She took a bite of her burger. "With me, of course." She laughed a laugh that announced her love of life. Debbie was the kind of friend that suited Emma well. They complimented one another. Emma with her close to over-serious side and Debbie with the fun always near the surface, they somehow met on the middle ground, which pulled out the part of them that needed to appear more often.

"Maybe he'll snap out of it soon." Emma sucked the last of the noodles off of her spoon. "Man, this soup is fabulous."

"Hey, maybe Jim could get a push in the right direction with some help from us." Debbie's excitement at the thought of Jim getting a nudge in her direction was contagious. Emma and she discussed the particulars and, satisfied with the plan, hefted the large glasses to wash down their meals.

Debbie leaned over and whispered like it was a confidence that had to be kept. "Your gorgeous hunk of a man is coming over."

"He is *not* my—"

"Hey, can I join you?" David flashed the boyish smile that she had trouble resisting.

"Of course." Debbie answered before anyone could jump in and offer a different one. She gave Emma a look of satisfaction.

David slid in beside Emma. "You ladies leave me any food?"

"No." Debbie pulled her plate closer to her. "You'll have to fend for yourself." She shoved the last bite into her mouth and stood, throwing a ten on the table. "I'll see you later." She flounced off.

David turned in the booth to face Emma. "She's a whirlwind, isn't she?"

"Yeah, she's a trip. So what have you been up to?" She nibbled on her homemade bread with a generous spread of Wisconsin butter.

"Funny you should ask. I was just about to tell you that you need to be ready to celebrate tonight."

Taking a substantial hunk out of the slice of bread, she chewed and watched, waiting for him to elaborate.

"The deal on my piece of land is final. I'm a landowner." He announced it with pride in his voice and joy all around. It overflowed and came out in a hug. He squeezed Emma in front of the whole diner.

Flustered, she went with it hoping that not too many people noticed. When he let her go she saw Jim glaring at them from the doorway, where he froze in his tracks on his way in for lunch. Although he proceeded to smile at her, something bothered her about the encounter.

She hated hurting his feelings, but there was no way around it. And she *did* want to discourage his attention to her. Well, she thought, that pretty much takes care of any plan Debbie and I had to take me out of the running. Maybe she should reinforce it.

With that thought in mind, she took David's face in her hands, turned him to her and planted a solid kiss on his inviting lips. Outside of the raw surprise in David's expression, she saw out of the corner of her eye the controlled yet furious state that Jim was sporting.

"Sorry for my shock, but that was a bit out of character for you. Especially after how you just reacted to the hug seconds before that." He raised his hand to wave down the waitress.

"The hug caught me off guard, that's all. And then I decided to go with it. Maybe Debbie's rubbing off on me."

"That's fine with me anytime you feel so inclined." He turned to the new waitress and gave his order. "And that's to go. Thanks."

"Well, I guess it's back to work I go." She suggested he scoot out with her look. "Don't worry, I'm not going back without my babysitter."

"Good, you wouldn't want to get in trouble with me."

"You think?" She threw a playful grin over her shoulder for him to ponder.

On her way to the bathroom, Jim caught her wrist. "Hey, long time no chat. Why don't you sit down for a spell?" He patted the empty seat beside him with his free hand and pulling slightly with the one on her wrist.

"I don't really have time right now, Jim. I have to get back to work."

He didn't let go of her wrist. "You have time for him." Jim tossed his head in the direction of David.

"That's none of your business, Jim. You have no claim on me." Emma mustered up a stern expression and plastered it on her face. "Now unhand me before I involve others." Her tone was filled with quiet strength as she challenged him with her eyes.

At this point David caught the gist of the confrontation, but remained put for the time being in an attempt to avoid a scene that people would take centuries to forget. He knew Emma could handle most anything— she was a strong individual.

Jim let her go. "There's no need for that. We're having a friendly chat here." The friendly tone of his voice was unable to cover the contempt just beneath.

Her senses were left confused and without a clear conclusion. All she wanted was to get out. "Don't make a fuss," she muttered.

"Sorry?"

"I just said, 'bye', that's all." Emma made a feeble effort at a smile and spun to leave. As she did, she heard a low voice.

"See you around."

The whole thing was entirely too weird for her. Her system was buzzing with a whole gamut of emotions, unsure of which to land on and embrace.

Returning to the table, she saw that David had his

food so, in an effort to vacate the premises swiftly, she snagged his food bag and took off out the front door. She could feel Jim's eyes on her.

"What's the rush? Didn't you want Jim to give us anymore glares?" The attempt at humor was a futile endeavor.

"It's not funny. With everything going on it creeped me out."

"I can take care of him for you. I know—we'll put a hit out on him."

"Very funny, wise guy."

"Give the guy a break, he's got it bad for you and he sees you with a stud like me. What's a guy to do, but get in a bad way about it?" David stood with his arms wide to afford a good look.

"Stud. You've got a high opinion of yourself. More like also-ran."

"You're going to pay for that one. Remember, your mom's not at the house for a few days." His raised brows warning of the possibilities.

They reached the bookstore. "So what's going on with Debbie these days?"

"She went out with Jim, but has yet to break him out of his funk over me. We were conjuring up some stupid thing to give him a shove in the right direction, but I think I already managed that one."

"Enough about everyone else. Where should we celebrate tonight?"

Emma thought so long that he thought she hadn't heard him. "I don't really feel like going out tonight. Is that okay?"

"Alright, maybe tomorrow." His mind continued mulling it over.

The customer in the lot waited in his car for her return from lunch. Everyone in the area knew the bookstore was closed from one to two and no one ever minded.

"I hope I didn't keep you waiting long," she called to Mr. Segura.

"No. You need to eat. I've got time." Mr. Segura was a sweet man in his seventies who frequented the store.

"I don't have anything new, Mr. Segura."

"That's okay. I'll just browse." That was his favorite hobby outside of reading.

Emma straightened each book one by one.

Called Home

Chapter 17

After the evening chores of the farm, David and Emma were in the kitchen ready to prepare a meal. David glanced at the clock and calculated in his head that he would have time to accomplish what he needed to in order for success. "My turn to do dinner tonight."

"What do you mean, we usually do it together?"

This wouldn't be easy to do. It would be a trick to move her on out. "Well, not tonight. Why don't you relax upstairs for a bit and I'll let you know when it's ready." He prayed it would be the right button to push.

"Can you cook? I mean without help?" Having lived on his own she assumed he had some abilities, but was unsure as to how many.

"I'm good, don't worry about me."

"I'm not concerned about you. I want to make sure I'm going to get something edible." She said as seriously as possible, before she burst into laughter.

"I assure you, it will be more than edible."

"You sound like a pompous *maître d'*." She could barely talk for all the laughing she was doing. It felt good to laugh.

"If you've had your fun you can take off so I can be a master in peace."

Flitting out of the room, she took her breezy mood with her as she mounted the stairs to shower. She may as well, she figured. With him making dinner, there was more than enough time to shower.

Stepping into the tub, she let out a last laugh as she pondered how lovely it was for someone to make her dinner—not just someone, but *David*.

When she came down the stairs in her cut off sweat pants and old T-shirt, she winced at what she was wearing when she saw the presentation. There before her in the dining room, not the kitchen, was the table elaborately set with an oil lamp illuminating the place settings of china, silver and crystal. A single white rose adorned the table in a crystal vase with simple flowing lines like waves. The wine was open and waiting to be poured as it sat in the silver bucket surrounded by ice.

"What is all this? I thought you were down here bumbling around the kitchen making something like spaghetti."

"You like?"

"Yes, but I'm wearing rags. I need to go up and—"

"You do not have to dress up for this. That's the whole idea in bringing the celebration here. We can eat in any condition we wish and no one will be around to care.

So, before the food gets cold let's get to it." He pulled out a chair for her.

Emma found no reason to resist. She sat. "Thank you."

Pouring the wine, he bent down to kiss her cheek. He set down the wine, put his hands on her shoulders and blessed the food before he took his seat. "Dig in. I'm told it's really good."

"It looks fantastic. You most definitely surprised me, which isn't easy to do. I have a habit of discovering the truth even if I don't want or try to. Usually clues work in my head and go to the correct end. I love surprises, but have rarely received any. My mom and I are a lot alike." She giggled. "Thank you." The forkful of juicy pork smothered in a mushroom wine sauce perched on her fork finally went to her mouth.

Once it did, she looked at him with wonder. "What did they do to this? It's the most wonderful thing I've ever eaten. It's like chewing butter it's so tender." She never denied her enjoyment of food in front of a date. Not that this was a date, just two people enjoying dinner together. But she figured if they didn't like a female that ate, then that was their problem, not hers.

"I'm glad you like it. I hope it was all right to go ahead with a celebration here, but I couldn't help it. I never owned any property. My apartment in New York was rented and I left straight from my parent's home, so this is new and wonderful territory for me and I wanted to share it."

"My taste buds are ecstatic at the fact that you

271

chose to share this with me. They wouldn't want it any other way. The meat, the salad, the wine are all heaven for my mouth."

Noticing her wineglass was sparse on wine, he rose, brought the bottle over and poured her another glass. When he was close, the air thickened, making it hard to breathe. She had to order her breaths until the space grew between them. Just pretend you're having a burger over a picnic table, she ordered in her thoughts. It has to do with the man, though, not the food. "So, when do you get your car back?"

"It is back—at my folks. I thought I'd stick with the truck since I'm staying on a working farm. I really do like the farm life. Don't tell my parents that, they may just keel over on the spot. Ironically, it's the one thing I said I wouldn't be caught dead doing. It was the worst thing I could imagine. As if you know what you're saying when you're a teenager." David looked at her cleared plate.

"We have a truck here. You could get your car back."

"I suppose, but it's a good thing I didn't have it when the idiot decided to do some art work in the side of the truck. I would have had to send it back to the shop. Are you ready for dessert?" He gathered both plates and took them into the kitchen.

"I think I need to digest some of this food filling up the space before I can fit in dessert. How about we retire to the living room and work on the wine?"

"Sounds like a plan. I'll be there in a minute."

"Okay."

"Fill your glass before you leave the table," he called from the kitchen.

"Good idea." Filling hers, she turned to his and filled it. She brought both to the living room and set his on the little round table at one end of the couch. As she sat on the other end waiting for him, she thought it sad that this room didn't get used more often. It was inviting and warm, especially in the lamplight.

Emma's face lit by the glow of the oil lamp flame appeared as a vision to him. He was in awe of the power she held to pull him in and hold him in a vice grip, without any effort on her part. The thing was, he wanted to be there. There was nowhere else he wanted to be if she wasn't with him. He had to come up with a way to make her see that with her is where he wanted to be and he wasn't going anywhere. She had a right to be wary of people in her life, with the exception of her mother, because they all left one way or another. But not him, he would stay put.

He sat near his wine. Emma watched his stunning form as he relaxed against the back of the couch, his arm on the armrest. There were times it struck her as magnificent. This was one. Speak, Emma, she ordered. "Now that you have the land, what are your plans for it? Where is it? How big is it? Tell me everything."

"I'd like to find an architect as soon as possible. I'm anxious to get a house going so I can actually live on it. My plans for it aren't completely set yet. The house comes first, then some horses and past that it's up in the air. You know the land rather well actually. I bought the

273

track of land you were selling. You got your asking price and I got an excellent piece of property. It's a win for both of us." Her quiet unnerved him more than screaming would have. "You don't have anything to say about that?"

"That's not the problem." The effort to keep her voice even took a great deal. "It's that I have way too much to say about it. And it's not coming to mind in a very *polite* way." She fumed silently.

"Why would you have a problem with this? The land was up for sale, it's not like I stole it from you." David scooted to the edge of the couch trying, without success, to solve the puzzle of her reaction. It was utterly unprovoked. "I can't keep up with you. We'll be in the middle of having a decent time together and out of the blue a mood comes over you that I never see coming— like this whole thing." Standing, he felt lost. Needing to do something, he went to the kitchen to gather all the restaurant dishes and put them in the box provided.

"You can't say that and walk off." She followed him loudly. "I have my reasons. And just because I don't go blathering them from the rooftops doesn't mean they're not there and that they aren't very real and make perfect sense." She paced the kitchen, coming off as a mountain lion trapped in a cage.

After a void of any kind of communication, she sat and returned back to their conversation: "I'm sorry if you don't like it, but you don't have to be here." It hurt her to say that. She had become incredibly used to having him there and rather liked it. "You can leave anytime you want." It was costing her already. That's what she had feared.

"I'm not going anywhere except my room." His tone was stiffly polite. "The dessert's in the fridge if you want." He walked to the doorway and turned with a heavy sigh. "See you in the morning." Dejected he climbed the stairs like he was traversing Mt. Everest.

Emma stayed downstairs, pacing at first then reclining in the overstuffed chair. She drank the rest of the wine. Every thought possible on the subject of what happened went through her mind. To begin with, they came all at once then settled into a line as she proceeded to dissect each of them individually.

What was she doing pushing him away? She liked him. The only conclusion she could ascertain was that she was one of those flighty females that didn't know what they wanted. She cringed at the thought. That was *not* something to be proud of. Her problem was that although she knew what she wanted, it would inevitably be taken from her. She didn't know if she could handle that again. The whole property mess was probably for the best. It offered a plausible excuse for putting space between them, and that's exactly what she would do. She had to, for her sanity and survival.

Once in the bedroom, David stared in the mirror wondering what a glutton for punishment looked like. Why couldn't he just let it go? That was obviously what Emma wanted, well, at least, that's what she was saying. He was never the kind of guy that didn't know when to cut his losses and move on. Why was he hanging on so tightly now? When that guy is caught, I'll pick up where my life was before I ran into Emma Benson and get on with the things that I came back to do, he thought, forming the plan in his mind. He was very much in need of a plan in the midst of something so confusing. Attempting to turn off his brain, he went to bed.

After having had a fitful night of sleep, David woke while the sun had yet to greet the day. Sick of the effort he had to put forth to gain the poor sleep he had gotten, he got out of bed to dress for farm chores. He'd had enough of thinking and inactivity, now he had to *do* something to take his mind off of Emma.

In the barn, he set about organizing shelves, installing more hooks, and cleaning anything that he could. When the time came, he would milk the cows and get them to pasture before Emma wandered down. It satisfied him—the work, the accomplishment, the doing something right.

Maybe this would all be worth it in the long run. He would have the satisfaction of knowing that he helped someone in a time of need and he considered that he could use some of his experiences in a book. Anytime he came across a situation he could mold into his writing, it was an excellent occurrence. That's what he would take from this. And just maybe, the process would be cathartic and he would find himself on the other side, way better off than he was on this side of it.

David was done and hadn't seen any sign of Emma. That's odd, it's definitely past the time she usually came to the barn. He wondered how the atmosphere would be at breakfast—light and airy like nothing happened or thick like sludge like it all happened even worse than it had? Only one way to find out, he thought.

Vowing that he would not be the cause of it occurring like the latter, he breezed through the door with a smile on his face and a kind word on his tongue. "Good morning. Cows are happily out to pasture all milked." Emma was gathering her purse and keys and there was no breakfast in the works. "Where are you going?"

"I'm going into town early to get a few things done and to have breakfast with Debbie." She strolled to the door. Her demeanor was as congenial as you would expect of a hostess with a guest. "You can have whatever you can find for food around here. I don't know how much there is since I need to go shopping." Turning to go, she paused when she heard David grunt a sigh.

"Ahhh, did you just expect me to milk this morning?"

"No, but when I went out there and saw you, you were almost finished so I came back in and got ready. No sense in me getting all dirty when you had it nearly completed." Emma made perfect logic without any bite or harshness in her words. With that, she was out the door and in her car.

Stunned, he wondered what universe he had just walked into. Finding neither atmosphere he was expecting, he was baffled. It wasn't as if nothing happened and it wasn't as if the worst happened. She was acting polite but detached, and he didn't know what to do with that. Knowing that there wasn't much else to do he would follow her lead and be courteous, talk when spoken to and steer clear of touchy subjects.

Over breakfast, just coffee for her, she told Debbie everything that had taken place the previous night —the dinner, the conversation, how she felt about it and him, and then the awful way the evening ended. "I feel completely lost. I don't know where to go from here. I'd like to just walk away, but then I can't and I couldn't cause he's here and I'm here for the foreseeable future." Emma dropped her head to her hands. "Uhhhg!"

"Yeah, it is kind of a mess," Debbie said.

"Thanks. I was insightful enough to come up with that much myself," she said.

"I know you're smart enough to figure that out, but you don't seem to be intelligent enough to know that you're crazy for the guy—," Emma attempted to interrupt but Debbie put a hand up to dam the flow of objections. "—*and* you're scared to death it might not last. So instead of sticking around to see if it works, you want to fast forward past the middle part, which is the fun part by the way, and impose your self-made ending. That way you can say *see,* every single time it doesn't end happily ever after for you. You're scoring up points to prove your hypothesis is correct."

Now Emma held her hand up. "Okay, okay, I get it. I caused it. But I do *refuse* to accept that I had anything to do with what happened a couple of years ago."

"Oh, I agree. The only thing *that* has to do with this is that's part of the reason you go for the self-fulfilling prophecy technique." Debbie offered a half smile with a hint of poor girl thrown in the mix.

Emma hated that from most people, but somehow Debbie did it with a let's-kick-your-butt-into-gear along with it, that Emma loved and evidently needed now and then. "Yeah, you're right. But back to what to do about it now." She studied her coffee. "Now that I screwed it up."

"No one said it's screwed up. You were on the path to doing so, but you can be diverted back to the right path. So let's figure out how to do that."

They huddled together like they were solving world peace. They argued a bit, but mostly came to the same conclusions. They settled on what could be done and how to do it.

More importantly, Debbie offered advice on how to make sure she didn't chicken out. It had a lot to do with having Emma imagine herself as an old lady, with no one at Thanksgiving dinner with her, and sitting in a small room all alone with no pictures of kids or grandkids. No remembrances strewn about from special occasions and family get togethers. Debbie knew that family was very important to her, even though the only close family she had was her mother. It was an effective device to have Emma use. She knew that, although Emma didn't want to be hurt, it would also hurt her to end up alone, with no one to share life.

Time went by quickly when you were trying to solve problems and this was no exception. If she didn't get a move on Emma was going to be late for work— something she considered a flaw, which she had trouble accepting. She could get there in a couple of minutes, she thought, and since that's all she had, she'd better. It's only around the corner, for goodness sake.

Her little car blew into the parking lot, shocking Mrs. Pembroke, who stood staring from the other side of the lot. Emma bolted out of her car to check on the woman on her way past. "You okay, Mrs. Pembroke?"

"Yes, no thanks to you, young lady." She brushed off the front of her from the dust that Emma had kicked up in the lot.

"Sorry, I didn't mean to scare you, I'm just almost late."

Mrs. Pembroke hollered to her before she slipped through the door, "You shouldn't come close to killing a patron because you're late to work, you crazy girl!" Mrs. Pembroke shook her fist at Emma as she disappeared inside the bookstore.

Emma smiled at the incident, knowing Mrs. Pembroke for being prone to exaggeration and complaining. For some unknown reason, Emma liked the woman, probably because she usually entertained her when she encountered her. Suddenly the realization came to her that she may be that way because she was the epitome of the type of woman Emma was attempting to avoid becoming—lonely, childless, obviously bitter at the way life turned out.

The encounter proved to fortify Emma's resolve to do everything in her power not to become that woman. She wanted more from life than just to exist. That was no life.

David ate and showered, taking his time for each. There was no hurry since Emma was having breakfast with Debbie and she worked with George for the first couple of hours. He would mosey on in when he was done. And that was the way it was going to be, he told himself. He strove for a casual take on safekeeping Emma. He was in no way going to leave in the middle of this ordeal, but if she wanted distance then she would have it and still maintain protection from him.

It didn't work for long. He wasn't one who could keep a death grip on a bad mood. The decisions made during his bad mood would still hold true but being cantankerous and caustic was not something he could sustain. So, although adamant about his conclusions, he would carry them out with confidence and perseverance, not by being grumpy and ill-tempered.

Determining that he didn't want to waste the time he now had on his hands, he sat down with paper and pen. The words began to pour out of him, with his hand moving as speedily as humanly possible and yet unable to keep up. It felt so good to be writing again, to know he could.

He got so wrapped up in his writing that time passed by in chunks. The honk of a horn on the highway that passed the house brought him out of his writing-induced fog to the reality of where he was and what time the clock chimed.

"Oh, crud!" he said aloud. "I'm supposed to be there by now."

He hustled out the door with keys in hand, the door slamming behind him.

George had left the bookstore in Emma's capable

hands more than a half-hour ago. She straightened the little that needed it, stocked the box that George left out for her and picked up David's book to pick up where she had left off. Recent events had provided her with little time to explore the fictional world according to David Schlosser. It certainly was an interesting world—not one in which she would want to be a part, but she did love the excitement of it as long as it was confined to a fictional book.

When a customer entered, she put the book down under the counter. She watched the middle-aged man in the security mirror posted in the corner across the store. It seemed he was looking for a particular book in the biography section.

Part of the fun in this job was people-watching. Everyone had a different way of experiencing a bookstore. Some came in, went straight for, and picked up the one book they had come to get. Some picked up just about every book in a section and only looked at the cover—front and back. Others selectively plucked books from the shelf and perused several pages of each.

Some bought, some didn't. This one headed for the door without a purchase. Emma always thought it quite odd to go into a bookstore and not come out with something.

"Oh, well, to each his own," she pondered out loud.

Slow days were welcome once in awhile. For the most part she didn't like them. With people to talk with or watch, merchandise to stock, even the straightening and cleaning to do, all caused the time at work to melt away quickly and fluidly.

His book was the reason she looked forward to the lulls in traffic since she was caught up in the part of the story where tensions were heightening toward the climactic peak, at least in the reader's mind, hoping the resolution was mercifully near. It was the section in which it was necessary for someone else to remove it from the reader's hands as he clung to every twist and turn in the plot, trying to ascertain its meaning. Immersed in this fictional world according to David, she wanted to have the freedom to continue her quest for the story's solution to the puzzle.

Back at the counter, she snatched the book from the shelf below the register, coming close to dropping it in her rush. She caught it and knocked out a piece of paper the size of an index card that floated to the floor as she tossed the book on the counter. As far as she knew, she was the only one of the employees reading David's book there at the bookstore. Crouching down, she picked up the notepad-size scrap of paper, flipping it over to see if it was someone's to-do list or grocery list. As she did, the familiar twinge of fear ran through her when she saw the number 1002 written as large as the paper would allow. Slipping from her fingers, it floated gracefully back to rest on the floor.

She had to get out of there. It felt like the store was suddenly filled with unbreathable air that was attempting to suffocate her with every breath she drew into her lungs. Running to the lot, she automatically scanned the street with no sight of David or his truck. He was always there. Why not this time, when she actually needed him?

A splash of panic washed over her when she thought that he might not care what happened to her after the difficult time she gave him the previous night.

Now what? Think rationally, she ordered. It's only a piece of paper and it can't hurt you unless you get a paper cut. She chuckled at her odd humor at a time like this.

As she was contemplating her options, David drove into the parking lot. She was standing in the middle of it, looking like she'd seen a ghost.

The truck had barely stopped moving when David was already out of the door, leaving it to hang open, and to her side in a couple of strides. "What's wrong?"

"I'm making too big a deal out of it. It surprised me is all." She continued to stare at the gravel of the lot.

"What? I need to know." His mind offered possibilities his didn't like.

"I'll show you." Spinning on her heels, she marched to where the offending paper lay and solemnly watched as she saw David's fingers reach for it, pick it up, and flip it.

Throwing it down, a quiet stream of curses flowed out of his lips until he cut it off as quickly as it started and looked Emma in the eye. "You did not overreact. It's the same fool terrorizing you." His fist came down hard on the counter.

"Us," she corrected. "He's going after us. But

what is the deal with this number? I'm just not getting the clue. Or maybe it's some kind of criminal business card saying that he's been here."

"You could be right. I'm sorry I wasn't here earlier. The time slipped through my fingers, as it does at times when I get totally caught up in writing. You're never going to be out of my sight again." He pulled her to him and wrapped her in his protective arms. "Never. Nothing's going to happen to you as long as I'm around."

It felt so good to be in his arms and it made her believe every word he said. She knew at that moment that she didn't want to ever be in anyone else's. Emma hoped it wasn't too late, hoped that his response was out of love for her and not some sense of duty. Emma needed and wanted David. She prayed that David needed and wanted her.

Called Home

Chapter 18

David came into the bookstore to finish out the rest of her shift with her after the police questioning concluded. The idea that they were on their own with this, at the old routine with the authorities, hit him square in the face. They would solve just as much as they had with the other investigations—nothing. This couldn't go on. He wanted a return to some semblance of a normal life in the near future. The life he wanted was with Emma, but the way to that was full of relationship peril. He wasn't sure that they would both make it through the course.

Not being one to usually give in to self-pity, she felt ashamed for inviting it into the picture. The constant barrage of incident after incident was reaching its breaking point with her. She'd rather have some kind of change, whether that was a cooling down or a ramping up from the status quo. The unraveling of her very sanity was etching its effect into her psyche. At least with David on hand, she could borrow from his courage and strength.

The day was long and psychologically tiring. Emma wanted no part in having to make dinner or clean up. "How about we go to Cranton and take in a movie after dinner? I'm up for a break from, well, everything."

It didn't take David more than a tick of the clock to answer. "It couldn't hurt to take our minds off everything, as you said so eloquently. In fact, let me call Asa and see if he has time to milk your cows so we don't have to trek back to the house until we feel like it." He was already dialing the phone before she had a chance to verbalize the same sentiment.

David was smiling while on the phone with Asa, so Emma assumed that was good news. She was stoked at the prospect of spending a frivolous evening with David —no worries, no responsibilities. Their only focus would be each other. The sole purpose was having a grand time. And she intended to do her part to achieve those things.

"Let's go. No worries, I've been told. He said he'd be happy to help us out." David led her to her car and opened the driver's door for her. "Let's make it a night we won't forget."

"Sounds like an excellent idea. Let's see what we can do."

Dinner was spent in a steak house with a casual atmosphere, superb food, quiet booths and prompt service. The food was as good as any he'd eaten and the ambiance catered to the casual romantic. He couldn't have chosen a better place to bring Emma. This was what he would have ordered if he had his whims desire.

Conversation was easy. It was as if they'd been friends for their whole life. All Emma knew was that she never wanted to lose this. But she battled with her inner demons about the urge to hang on to him. They said to her that she might do all the hanging she wanted, but if he let go there was no stopping the separation and hurt. With all her might, she suppressed the strong draw to listen to every word those demons told her. She repeatedly lectured her brain that they were lying to her and that they only wanted her to be left alone with them as companions, for the rest of her life.

Emma vowed to give every ounce of determination to the cause of denying her demons and allowing her dreams to step forward and shine. Deciding that one of those steps in that process was to divulge her secret demons, thereby stripping them of their power, she resolved to start now.

"Hey, you know how I acted a bit funky when we went to that park with the river running through it?" Emma folded her hands in her lap.

"Yeah." He wondered where this could be going.

"Well, there's a good reason for it."

"You don't have to tell me anything you don't want to. I didn't mean to bring bad memories back to you."

"I don't want that place to conjure up memories I'd rather not remember. I always loved that spot before." She paused for thought as she sipped the merlot. "I want to love it again," she said wistfully, "without the threads of sadness woven into it. Ripping them out and burning them might do the trick, but I'll start with lightening the load, sharing the burden."

"You tell me what you want. Just know that I'm hear to listen anytime you need or want an ear." He picked up his wineglass, held it in the air and said, "To secrets and their demise."

Emma raised her glass to his, softly clanking them. "To their demise." After drinking a healthy swallow, she set it down, eyes glued to the glass and not on him. She was afraid that she might not even begin if he was boring into her with those exquisite green eyes.

To gently nudge her in the right direction with a bit of humor he said, "The floor is yours."

"May as well just jump in. It's usually less painful than the long-drawn-out method. So, I was in my sophomore year of college and met this guy, Matt, in my statistics class. We were partners for work done together and in the same group for a big project. He finally got the courage up to ask me out, which turned out to be easy for him, since I'd had a crush on him and said yes immediately. Conversation was easy, he was smart, he knew where he was going in life, he never raised his voice, I never saw him down. He was an incredibly even-tempered individual. I liked him. Our priorities were in the same place with similar goals. We never had a fight. Matt was everything the experts tell you to look for in a potential mate. We were happy." Emma dropped her eyes to her hands that had been twisting her napkin in her lap for some time.

David attempted to increase her comfort level. "You have me on the edge of my seat so far. I've got to hear how the story ends."

She sighed deeply in preparation. "He had met my mother several times in the almost two years we were going out. On the last trip we made to my mom's, Matt had been giving me all kinds of signals that I interpreted as suggesting a life together. I admit, I thought it was a bit early in my life for that just yet, but I knew that these things didn't always pick the ideal time either. I was blissfully happy. I knew that people didn't just walk into one's life all the time who could fit that partner bill, so I told myself to consider it carefully." The waiter picked up the dinner plates and offered an array of desserts.

"We would just like a couple of Irish coffees, please." David ordered some after-dinner drinks that sufficed as dessert anyway, in order to have more talk time.

"Sounds good. I haven't had one in awhile." After the waiter left, she knew it was her cue to finish the story. "Anyway, the day before we were to go back to school he asked me if we could go to the park, that he had something to tell me. My pulse charged full steam ahead answering, 'Sure.' When we got there, he opened the door for me and he held my hand as we walked to the riverside. Stopped and facing each other, he took both of my hands, looked me straight in the eye and began to tell me how wonderful I am. At this point, I can tell that there's something funny in his manner and his tone of voice. I ignore it. I came to the conclusion that I'm

291

imagining the peculiarities. You should never push your instincts out of a situation. Anyway, in the same breath he told me of my being exceptional, he tells me that he's met someone else and that this is the end of us. I don't think I moved a muscle, including breathing. There were so many emotions bursting to come out at the same time it froze me. I didn't know which one to deal with first." The waiter brought the coffees.

"Thank you." David raised his coffee. "To dispensing with assholes."

"I'll raise my glass to that. Problem was that I didn't think he was one at the time. I was so hurt. I wanted to slug him. I wanted to hold on to him so he couldn't leave me. I didn't know what I wanted." She sipped her coffee.

"He obviously didn't know what a rare creature he had. I know one when I see one. And I don't let it get away so easily." A soothing smile lit his face.

"I found out later that he'd been going out with her for six months. He was seeing her during the time he was seeing me, supposedly exclusively. Evidently, he didn't know what the word meant. To add insult to injury, he married her a year later. Not that I wanted him anymore, but it just appeared that he couldn't run to her fast enough and away from me far enough."

David took her silence as a sign of her being finished with the story. He knew her father left her and her mother. That had to play into the hurt that was felt from Matt leaving. He reached his hand across the table, holding it palm up in invitation of her hand. "I'm sorry someone treated you that way. You deserve so much better than that. We're not all scum, Emma." That was all he said on the subject. His temper was barely kept in check. His would have preferred to lash out and he wished it could be at Matt, the little twerp.

"I know that, but it's hard not to want to use the best armor I can to avoid that kind of thing. Letting my guard down in a relationship is like going to battle, without a weapon. I feel naked and exposed. I'm learning, though."

With their coffees done, they went to the movies with a greater understanding of one another. The movie was good, but the company was better.

Pulling into the driveway the headlights lit the house briefly. There was nary a light since they hadn't been there all day. Asa left the outdoor light on down by the barn, but it didn't help much near the house.

David felt like she opened up the possibility of them being together. And that was enough for now.

"Stop!" David inched away from her toward an object on the ground. He held up his hand. "Stay there."

She was pulled to his side by some innate impulse. They stared. They looked up. They stared once again. "Now what?"

"I think it's a rabbit." He took her by the hand. "It looks like someone broke his neck. You know what we have to do. I feel like I know the police personally."

"I know what you mean." They headed toward the house.

David stopped abruptly. There was something else

on the ground. "Looks like an opossum." Continuing on, he was forced to stop at the base of the stairs.

"Not another one." The strain was beginning to come through in her voice.

"Yeah, it's a dog. And there's something on it. We have to get the police out here."

With the police called, all there was to do was wait. Emma had never been very good at the task. Coffee, she thought. She would busy herself with making coffee.

As she sat waiting for it to brew, she kept seeing pictures of rabbits, opossums and dogs playing in different settings—all perfectly alive. Then the picture would go black and the lights would come up just enough to get a glimpse of those same animals, lifeless on the ground. A river of ice ran through her, causing her to shiver from the images and the thought it all brought. Now it's gone from property damage to taking lives. Where is this going to stop?

Just as that thought came to her, the police arrived, jarring her out of her trance. Getting up and heading for the door, she was stopped in her tracks by David putting his hands to her shoulders.

He spoke to her in a low voice, appearing somewhat remote. "I don't think it's a good idea for you to go out there."

Emma challenged his gaze with her own. Knowing he was thinking of her, she attempted to reassure him. "I know it's not pretty, but this is my property and I want to know what's been done. I have to see what we're dealing with." She took his hand. "Will you go out with me?"

David couldn't help but be somewhat proud of her, wanting to be a part of everything that took place on her land. No matter what it cost her, she was going to be involved. He could appreciate and respect that. Emma Benson was a stubborn and strong woman. He liked that about her—he liked her. "I'll be right there beside you."

What Emma saw when she went out *wasn't* pretty. She saw the dog first because it was the closest to the house. It was also the one with the note attached. There was a cut on the dog's neck and a pool of blood surrounded its head. The opossum and rabbit looked like they were asleep on the lawn. They must have had broken necks.

David's voice came through her haze. She could hear him explaining that they hadn't been there all day to the officers and the part about Asa doing the milking. The noise began to fade like it was on the other end of a tunnel, as her attention was pulled back to the dog. The blood—it was so red with the lights on. It must not have been there too long because it was darkening from the exposure to the air.

Moving away from the dog, she slowly walked to the other two victims. She took small, slow steps like she was in a viewing line at a funeral home. They looked so peaceful, like they would jump up and scamper off at any moment. She knew they wouldn't. Although they looked at peace, they also had an odd appearance. Realizing what it was, she backed away a step, then two. The heads of the two were at angles not consistent with a live, healthy animal. Straining, she tried to will them to breathe and felt the air go out of her lungs. It wouldn't happen.

When David finished giving them the information he had, which was very little, he came to Emma to encourage her to come in the house. "Let's go in, there's nothing left for us to do out here."

"I don't want to leave them." He walked her a few steps. "They died for nothing." They went a couple more steps.

She went rigid when her feet were near the dog. "Poor thing. Talk about being at the wrong place at the wrong time. What's the note say?"

"It's just a bunch of gibberish. Come on." David put a bit of pressure on her back in an attempt to move her on. It didn't work. She stayed put.

"I want to know everything. I can tell you know what the note said, so tell me. I have a right to know." Standing firm, she waited.

"Okay, it's short and not so sweet. It said, 'Get in the way and you're next.' That's it."

"What are we getting in the way of? He's the one after us." Satisfied in knowing, she went up to the door and into the kitchen. "Coffee." She spun around and flew out the door.

"Would any of you like some coffee? It's fresh, I brewed it while you were on your way." She waited for their answers, hoping it would be a "yes."

"Yes, thank you. I think we'll all take a cup," Officer Stewart answered. They knew that it was best for some victims to stay busy.

"I'll be right back."

It did help to think of something else, even if it was for a short span of time. She already dreaded the night, when the likelihood of nightmares was significant. Maybe I can talk David's ear off and stay up, she thought. I have to sleep sometime. Just play it cool, Emma, just play it cool. You've got a caring, strong man beside you. Good thing Mom isn't here.

She shifted the tray in her hand as she struggled slightly with the door. One of the officers noticed and got it for her. "You should have hollered for one of us to get it. We're more than happy to help when it comes to coffee." He grinned and with his light tone hoped that it would ease her just a tad.

"I'll leave this here for you. There's more if anyone would like." Her gaze skimming the men as she turned about-face to go in, she couldn't help but see the dog again. She couldn't keep her eyes from going to it, like a magnet pulling her gaze. Staring at it she first wanted to burst into tears, then that thought abruptly morphed into a strong hope that the dog got a chance to take a bite or more out of the perpetrator of his demise. Every ounce of her wished it to be true.

"I'm sure you guys have already thought about this, but if the dog got a piece of him he may have had to go to a hospital."

"Yeah, we did give that a thought and we're going to put calls out to the hospitals in the surrounding area. You're a smart one, maybe you should sign up for the job.

We could always use an intelligent person like yourself in this line of work." He smiled.

"Thanks, but I'm running everything I can through the processor," she pointed to her brain, "so this can be over with ASAP." She hung her head, contemplating her toes. "I need it to be."

"We'll get back to it and let you know when we leave." They all turned back to the job at hand.

It was so weird to see them on her lawn huddled around a crime scene. On her lawn, she thought again. The whole thing struck her like she was plopped in the middle of a television police drama and, although she was a part of it, it was also like having an out-of-body experience. She was in it, but she felt like she was also watching from a place away from it all, all alone. It was a very surreal feeling.

After all the commotion, the difference was stark and disconcerting with only her and David in the house. It gave her a sense of the ordeal being over, even though the culprit had yet to be caught. She didn't mind visiting with the police, but she wished she would never have to see them in an official capacity again.

"We're locked up tight. Do you want to have at the bathroom first? I'm a little too restless to push sleep and tempt insomnia." David watched her carefully to make sure she was handling it okay.

"I don't know what I should do now. It's not every day that happens."

"Good thing, too. Do you want to talk about it or go on our merry way as if nothing's wrong?" He would do whatever she wanted.

"I think I'd prefer to stick my head in the sand. At least for tonight I would. Tomorrow is soon enough to deal with the rest."

Racking his brain to come up with exactly what that should direct him to do, he fished for guidance. "So, wine?"

"No, I think I will go up and soak in the tub, but . . ." In her embarrassment she hesitated to ask.

"But what? You can ask me anything." With all his body and soul, he wanted her to leave the mess behind and be okay. If he could take the weight from her, he would.

"Could you hang out upstairs? I just want to know that you're close by. I wouldn't ask, but I know myself and left to my own devices my mind will wander, finding its way back to the incident." Emma thought it sounded kind of lame and she never wanted to be anything but a self-sufficient, capable-of-handling-anything kind of woman. She had always thought of herself as such. And here she was asking this guy she would rather impress to come upstairs and baby-sit her. Life did throw a person a lot of curve balls.

"Sure." David spoke in a kindly tone, not patronizing, but rather like he was her best friend and would do whatever she wanted. "I'll read in my room and you can soak all night if you'd like."

"Thanks. You're pretty incredible." Her smile was genuine, although it flashed out quickly with the weight of it all.

"Make sure you remember that the next time you're mad at me." His face lit with a quirky curve of his lips.

It was so sweet, and so was he. She could have stayed right there watching him.

"Bath's a waiting." He gestured to the stairs.

She hesitated. "Thank you." Emma went to him and his arms opened wide in welcome.

David held onto her conveying support and more than that—love. Taking a step back so he could see her delicate features over the strong disposition she possessed, he ran the back of his fingers down the side of her face. He cupped her chin and at the same time his eyes increased in intensity. "I'm not going anywhere." Remaining in a locked gaze with her, he was adamant in his effort for Emma to really believe it.

Numerous feelings rushed through her—gratitude, yes, relief at his being here, yes, companionship, yes. But more than all that, she couldn't deny there was love. It was a love she wanted, needed, yearned for, and had no idea she would ever have. She would not let it go and she was driven to make sure that no one took it from her.

Emma reached up on her toes to kiss his inviting lips. She hoped the whole of what was going through her head would be conveyed through the kiss.

Once his lips reacted, Emma began a gradual sinking into the softness of love. It took on the feel of descending into a cloud of warm cotton balls remaining suspended in the air. She felt a visceral reaction to an emotional state of being. It was glorious. It was hers. It was theirs.

He felt her skin warm and a peaceful drifting of the tension flow out of her body. With her calm, his followed. He wondered if she knew how swiftly and thoroughly she pulled him in and how deeply his emotions ran. Her dive into the sensual wonders that only a kiss and bodily contact with David could bring brought on his own dive, induced by Emma. She offered something he had never experienced before and never thought he would—a giving that was utterly selfless.

David was never one to pull out all the stops and go for flowers and candlelight. And although Emma didn't need it, since she was a very pragmatic person, she deserved it. He wanted to give it to her. So he insisted on drawing her bath for her.

While Emma was in her room, at first, getting nightclothes and a towel, she heard David run downstairs and back up. She then picked out clothes for the morning, straightened her jewelry boxes, organized her shoes, and couldn't fathom why she heard him on the stairs again. Before she had much of a chance to ponder the goings on too long, the knock at the door sounded.

"Hey, all set? Don't let the bath get cold."

Emma opened the door wide, retrieved her towel and pajamas from the bed and slung them over her arm. When she reached the doorway, David took the bundle off her arm. Throwing it over his own, he swept his arm to signal her to lead.

She could see the flickering yellowish light sneaking out into the hallway. Looking to David, she touched his arm and gave him a gentle smile, not wide, that brightened her entire face. At the bathroom door, she saw the candles she knew she would see and along with them a bath full of steaming water. The ledge of the tub supported a book and a glass of wine waiting for her to indulge in both, while she soaked her cares away. That same glow found her face once more as she entered the room without a word. She didn't need to say a one, for her message was well received from her expression.

His heart was full. Going to his room, he came to the conclusion that he was too wired to read yet, but he needed to stay close. He would lose his mind thinking of her in that tub if he just sat. Rummaging through his bag, he found what he was searching for—notebook and pen. He would write. With his mind focused on the story at hand, all other thoughts tended to either melt away or get folded into the writing of the story. Writing would do just fine.

Entrenched in a world of his own making, he didn't notice when Emma came to the door clad in her multi-colored, polka dot, fleece shorts and tank top sleepwear. She was nearly to him before he looked up and saw her there in front of him, with neatly combed wet hair and a freshness about her that came from more than a mere bath. "Hey. You look ready for a good night's sleep."

"Let's hope I can get one." She moved closer, and like a jumping spider on a fly, she pressed her lips to his. Her enthusiasm conveyed through her state altering approach.

Every movement of mouth, every flick of tongue had tiny arrows connecting with various spots throughout his system. The effect was widespread and catastrophic to his objective thinking. He didn't care. He had no choice but to allow his emotional side to take over and rule.

Emma detected the loss of control taking place and although she would love to join him, she knew she had to stop. Facing her reflection in the mirror in good conscience was a must. No matter how much she yearned to let go, she had to hold on. Respect for herself came before anything else. Pulling away was like separating two very strong magnets—hard, but she had the strength to do it. Disengaged, she took several steps back, smiled quickly and fully and whirled out of the room as stealth-like as she had entered.

Called Home

Chapter 19

The sunshine streamed through the space around the rose-flowered curtains. Awakening from one of his few bouts of rest, he wiped the sleep and the weariness out of his eyes. He was happy to be done with the night—happy to greet the day with intentions of making it a good one.

He crept downstairs in his shorts, for that's all he wore in bed. There she was pouring coffee and more beautiful than his mind recalled last night. Sneaking up behind her, he encompassed her in his arms and squeezed. "Morning." He kissed her hair, pulled it out of the way to find a sweet spot on her neck.

"Up late, must have slept well." She went about the business of breakfast.

"Not exactly, but good enough. You didn't already get the milking done, did you?" He asked a bit sheepishly, hoping that she hadn't.

"No. I can't say that I got up much before you."
The eggs sizzled in the pan with the bacon. This morning
she tossed it all together, causing a smell to inflict hunger
where there was none previously.

"I guess we're the lazy two this morning. Glad
your mother's not here to see it." Opening cupboard doors
he lifted out the plates and proceeded to set the table.

"I'm glad my mother's not here for a great many
reasons." She was referring to the plethora of crimes
perpetrated against them.

She didn't elaborate, which left him wondering
about the exact meaning of the statement.

They ate silently and efficiently. Being late on a
farm wasn't a smart idea, especially when there were
milking cows involved.

He finished with his meal before Emma was half
done with hers and hopped up to put his dishes on the
counter. He fled the room with the announcement, "Be
right back with clothes on."

He was, too. Before the dishes were completed,
David was in the kitchen clearing his throat. "Should we
have the last cup of coffee now or as a reward when we
come in from chores?"

"We'd better get out there." She wiped her hands
and tossed the dishcloth aside.

"Fine, as something to look forward to then." He
went to the door with Emma following.

Once they were both out, she locked the door. Her
mother and she never did that normally, but then again
this was not a normal time. She hated having to change so

many things for one guy that decided to create trouble. But she would do whatever it took to be safe. That was the first priority.

David and Emma walked through the beautiful spring weather. The blue of the sky, dotted with large puffy white clouds that were nowhere near threatening, met the green of the earth, dotted with splashes of color from blooms. It was stunning in a simple way. Birds called out to their neighbors and mates or potential mates. The air was charged with new life.

David said, "Do you have to work at the bookstore today?"

"Yes. It usually is yes unless it's a fluke." They took a few strides. "I'd rather have the work and feel like I'm getting somewhere with all of this." Her hand swept across in front of her, encompassing the land.

"If you need any help."

"You'll be there, won't you?" She was baffled by his offer, since he'd been glued to her lately.

"Yes. I mean with money." Not knowing whether he should have broached the subject, he knew he would soon find out with her answer.

Instead of getting mad, like he thought she might, she casually answered him. "No, thanks, we're good."

He knew she would be stubborn about this. That was part of the reason he bought the land he did and at asking price. The need to help was strong.

They were almost to the barn when Emma suggested he go up to the hayloft to drop some down. Since Asa was there last night, there probably was hardly any left to replenish the stalls.

"I'll get started on the milking while you do that."

"On it." He strode off toward the hill that led to the loft.

She liked this sharing the chores deal. Never did she mind doing them, but it certainly was a lot less like a chore when you had a partner to split the load.

As she strolled the length of the barn to let the cows in, her peripheral vision caught a foreign sight. She turned to look.

"AAAHHHH!" Emma let out a scream that could've been heard in town.

Hearing it, David ran faster than he even knew he could.

Now beside her, he saw what she saw—Jim, in one of the empty stalls, with obvious broken bones and what appeared to be a broken neck. Nothing else was out of place, nothing else was messed up. Only Jim was messed up and out of place . . . and dead.

Fear blazed the fastest and burned out quickly. Self-pity crept in quietly along the way and hovered for awhile. Anger built slowly, but now won out in the end for Emma. She was boiling mad. No one is going to do this to her, to her friends, to her family and get away with it. "This has *got* to stop. The other stuff was one thing, but now he's taken a human life. I am not going to cower in a corner and wait for this guy to make his move. If the police can't do it, then I'll have to find a way. How hard can it be to locate one guy that's out of place? He's got to stick out like a weed in a pristine garden around here."

David hopped on the anger train and pitched his fit in a more reserved manner. "We most definitely should do more about this than call the police. After we do that, I'll find a private investigator to do some digging. They're able to dig in places that the police aren't legally able. That may be what it's going to take to get this guy, before someone else gets hurt or worse." He turned her to leave the barn.

Emma couldn't leave, she just kept staring at Jim. No one deserves something like this. He may have manhandled her the last time she saw him, but she would never wish this on a single soul. May his soul rest in peace, Emma thought. She said a silent prayer on the spot for his family and friends.

Eyes fixed on Jim, David noticed a corner of paper sticking out of his pocket. He considered getting it, but knew the best course of action was to not touch anything. Clues could potentially be collected from anything. Curiosity was bubbling up through the dark edge of anger, but he knew better. Leave it, his conscience told him.

"We really should call. Let's get it done." Firmly steering her toward the door, they exited the barn.

Outside of some initial questions, she let David deal with the police and busied her hands with the coffee thing again. This was getting way old, she thought. How long is this going to go on? She poured half-and-half in a creamer and sugar in a bowl, placing them on the sturdy wood tray. The coffee went into two large thermoses that her mother kept handy for haying parties and the like.

Filling another tray with mugs, spoons and napkins, she carted the one tray out and returned for the other.

Now that the coffee task was done, her mind took over. The feeling of being trapped in a nightmare that she couldn't wake from played through her thoughts. In the nightmare the only way to escape was the one thing she didn't want to take place.

Her brain leaped from the nightmare only to land on the living one. She thought of Jim. Did he know it was coming? She thought he did from the damage that was done. What caused this sort of reaction from someone? And why was he here in her barn? Every thought was in question form. With no answers on the heels of them, it was an exercise in frustration.

Virtually every officer had a mug in his hand and was very adept at doing the job with coffee attached to them. They were finishing up their preliminary investigation, so the body could be removed. The initial conclusion from the detectives and the medical examiner was that he was murdered. It was no accident.

The word spoken out loud sent chills up her spine, out over her shoulders and spread down through her body. The more they threw words around like murderer, suspect, motive, weapon—or the lack thereof, career criminal and a host of other phrases, Emma felt her head begin to spin. Leaning against the post helped level her sense of balance, although it did nothing for her queasy stomach. This, she had the inclination to believe, was going to be with her for some time to come.

Emma watched as they lifted Jim's lifeless body to

a gurney, covered him and hauled him away like a piece of rubbish. It's sad, it's so premature, it's senseless, and it's beyond belief. Her thoughts naturally went from Jim to the perpetrator of such a vicious act. Who would do that? What kind of person would do that? Possible answers to the latter were the ones that unnerved her. The kind, she imagined, who was out there free to do it again. And, for some reason, he had it out for them. That sick and twisted individual was coming after them. Her knees gave way slowly as she slid down the post to sit on the barn floor.

David was there before she even made it all the way to the floor. "You okay?" He scrutinized her, looking for any detail that might alert him to her requiring more care than he could offer.

"I just had to sit for a minute." Dullness coated her eyes.

"That's a funny way to go about it." A hint of humor lit his face, in hopes that it would do the same for Emma.

"You came over to make jokes, did you?" With her focus solely on him, color was coming back to her cheeks.

"Well, I have to take my opportunity when I have it." He offered his hand. "Let's get you to the house and I'll start the milking."

"The poor cows. They've had their share of late milking. They're going to think that we can't take care of them properly."

"I think we're safe. Cows are generally stuck in

311

the moment and I don't think they hold grudges." The boyish smile flashed on his face.

"I'm not so sure about that. I've been around cows my whole life and I swear I've seen evidence of it. And, by the way, I'm not leaving you alone with the job. I can do it." She stood on wobbly legs, but they held. Pride spurred her on to take the next step and the next until she was ready to roll.

Sitting in the house alone with nothing to do but think was the last thing on her agenda. Action—that's one of the things that would help her cope. Her usual routines would contribute and the apprehension of the sick person responsible would clinch the deal. She knew already that she would never be the same person she was before the whole mess invaded her life, even after it was over. The bastard took something from her that would never be fully restored. Emma couldn't help but feel hatred for him and what he'd done. She knew it was wrong, but also that it would take time for her to separate the person from the act.

David and she had nearly completed the chores, before Emma remembered the paper in Jim's pocket. "Hey, I wanted to ask about the paper they found on him."

David looked apprehensive about answering the question even before she had spit it all out.

"Was it some stupid list or receipt or was it something we were supposed to find?" Emma didn't take her eyes off him so she could gauge his response.

"The latter." He stopped there, not really wanting

to tell her.

"You should know by now that I'm not going to settle for that as the answer. I know there's a lot more to it and I want to know what it is." Her eyebrows were raised in anticipation of a response.

"Fine, you're right. I do know you well enough to know that, but a man can hope." He plastered a feeble smile on his face. "It said, 'Get in my way you're next!' Pretty much the same sentiment he left before." Pondering his feet as well as the note, he considered possible conclusions. "I really don't know what he's trying to tell us. I don't think we're in anyone's way. It won't do much good to dwell on it, I'd rather focus on catching the lunatic."

The 'you're next' stuck in Emma's brain. Imagining it didn't offer relief of her condition. Her mind went nuts with the information. She visualized David like Jim ended up and then her mother, then herself and then everyone she knew well, on down to acquaintances. "Stop it." She said it loudly.

"Stop what?"

"Sorry, not you. Me. I'm not doing myself any good. My mind is running amuck."

"We're done here relieving the poor cow's close-to-leaking udders. Let's go call that investigator."

"That'll do me good. I do well with a plan and action."

"I will lock that little bit of information up tight in my memory banks. It has high potential for coming in very handy in the future." David smiled all the way back to the house.

* * * * *

Later in the day the phone shrilled through the silence. "Hi. Yeah, this is David Schlosser." Listening intently, he shifted his weight as he glanced in Emma's direction every few seconds.

"Yes, we knew some of it, but not very much. Keep digging."

"We will, thanks. Bye." He hung up the phone and let out a sigh.

Holding out a hand to her, he said, "Let's sit. That was the PI with what he's been able to find out, after a full day of digging."

"Tell me. I can't hold my breath any longer." Emma leaned forward on the table with keen attention paid to David's words.

"Well, there's the stuff we already knew, which isn't much. Like that Fallon is wanted in other states for aggravated robbery and that he escaped from court. But the additional info is awfully interesting. Fallon's been married and divorced twice. Neither ex had anything good to say about him and offered curses for him while Briggs, the PI, talked to each of them. He also found records of more than one report for abuse on the books. The authorities have positively connected him to a couple of robberies, but they also think he might be involved in one or two assault and rape cases that remain open. The guy's a real creep. Briggs suggested I not let you out of my sight, which I assured him was already the case." He held her hands across the table.

Emma wasn't even sure what should come out of her mouth. "So the 'stay out of the way' must be for you. He must be trying to get to me." The realization came without an emotion attached. Confusion ruled.

"I guess it is. Don't worry, though, he's going to have to try a lot harder than that to get me to leave you alone." David wore his determination well.

Sitting up straight, jaw clenched and muscles on the ready, he looked like a warrior to Emma—her warrior.

"That's what I'm afraid of. You come back to town and get mixed up in some chaos that sounds like it belongs in one of your books, all because you met *me*."

"Don't go there. I'm the better for knowing you. So you can drop the you'd-be-better-off-if-you-hadn't-met-me routine, right now. I'm a big boy, I can take care of myself."

"I don't know how I feel after figuring out that he wants you out of the way so he can get to me. That sounds so eerie when you say it out loud." She mulled it over. "I'm terrified of him getting to me, but I don't want anything to happen to you. But I don't want you to go away. I want you right here with me. But that puts you in harm's way, which makes me out to be awfully selfish."

"You can put that idea in the trash bin immediately. It doesn't fly with me. Oh, I almost forgot to tell you the most interesting tidbit. The note with the dog and the note on Jim were likely written by different people."

"What?" The confusion wouldn't come into any

315

semblance of order in her head. "Maybe he had someone else write it for him." Looking to the ceiling, she searched for answers. "That doesn't make sense. A man like that would likely be a loner—therefore, no partner."

"Maybe, maybe not, but the handwriting was different on each note. It wasn't even close, the slant was angled differently, loops were bigger on one than the other and also the pressure of the pen was at odds on them. They were definite about them coming from incompatible sources. Back to the part about you being responsible for my well being. I make my own choices and if I didn't want to be here, I *wouldn't* be here. But I do and I will stay. That's the end of that one."

"Getting a bit bossy as your comfort grows around me, aren't you?"

"Believe me, you make me anything but comfortable." He had his hands about her waist, lifting her from her chair. Eye to eye, he emphasized his point. "We're going to get through this *together*. You got that?"

"Yes, sir."

"Forever the smart aleck. Even when I'm about to do this." He gathered her in his arms and smothered her mouth with his.

It was a moment that seemed like forever, when his mouth explored and enticed hers. But then it was as short as a breath when he stopped. Emma relished the time in his arms. It brought so much to her, it was close to overwhelming.

David held her tightly. He didn't want to let her go —in any sense of the phrase.

The following day arrived in the usual way. With the lack of any further incidents, Emma should have been grateful. She was, in a way, but with nothing, the tension grew and grew. Maybe Briggs could find out more and they would be armed with information that would help protect them. Knowing it was wishful thinking didn't matter; what mattered was that she had a speck of hope on which to hang her hat.

Across eggs, bacon and biscuits Emma contemplated bringing up the issue. It's not like it wasn't there if she didn't, but they'd been expert at pretending recently. "Why don't you give Briggs a call today, see if he has any further info."

"Yeah, I can do that. You work this afternoon, right?" He buttered his biscuit while he chewed his bacon.

"Yes, I get off at seven."

"I'd better call now then." Finishing the last couple of bites that remained, he washed it down with the rest of his coffee before he rose to get the phone.

"Hi, it's David Schlosser. Anything new to report?" He listened intently. "Uh-huh . . . uh-huh . . . Okay. Thanks. Bye." David hung up the phone.

"Well, not much. He couldn't find any sign of credit card use since he was in jail. That's probably because they have his wallet at the prison. At least after his arrest, they have a current picture of him and that has been circulated all over creation. Someone thought they saw him heading out of town toward Cranton, the night we went there for dinner." He awaited some kind of

317

reaction.

"Kind of makes your skin crawl, thinking he could have been following us. I feel like I'm in a fish tank, waiting for someone to catch me."

"I know. At least they have signs up everywhere. Everyone is on the lookout. I kind of feel sorry for visitors now, until he's caught. Any person unknown is going to get seriously scrutinized."

"Yep. That's the way this place is."

"Good for us right now, though."

Emma drifted into silence as she contemplated why they were the lucky ones to be the target of such crimes.

As he watched the wheels turn, he realized that the circumstances more than suggested patience was required, but he also wanted her to be able to share her thoughts, troubles, and joys with him. In this moment, he was more than certain that it wasn't the latter. Okay, enough patience. "What's going through that pretty little head of yours?"

"Hm?" she uttered as she slowly swiveled her head around to him.

"I lost you there for a minute. You okay?" David tilted his head slightly to gather everything she was communicating above, beneath and around the words he hoped she would say.

Emma let out a cleansing sigh. "I was just allowing myself to indulge in a little self pity for a few minutes."

"Well, I think at this point you're entitled to

indulge in just about anything that might help."

She looked away sheepishly. "That's just it. My thoughts are not helpful in the least." Her hands caught the drop of her head. "I'm feeling sorry for myself and questioning things that don't have an answer."

"Such as?"

Lifting her head, Emma confessed. "Such as— why me? Why us?" She shook her head at the uselessness of such a line of questioning, but couldn't help her overriding urge to voice it.

"Good question. I'm afraid we may not know for a long time." He paused, not wanting to finish the thought. "We may never know." That one was hard to take for someone who thrived on being well informed.

"That's part of what bothers me. I may have a real hard time getting past this without knowing why. My brain tends to want to know everything."

"I had no idea."

Emma saw the stifled grin. "Oh, very funny. But I know that about myself and hope it doesn't get in my way."

"In all seriousness, I also know that when you put your mind to something it gets done. So even with this personality trait of yours I'm sure you'll be able to get past anything. You've already conquered a lot in your life."

"You're right about that. Let's get ready for work." She left him in the washroom cleaning off his boots.

Emma mounted the stairs, pleased with the information they were able to attain and where she and

David were at with each other.

Chapter 20

Delighted with the fact that she had extra time to get ready, she actually blew dry her hair, styling a slight curl on each side. The result was better than she'd anticipated. Now on to the clothes part, clothes for work anyway, since she was decked out in an old T-shirt and baggy sweat pants.

Visualizing her wardrobe, which was not vast by any means, on her way to rummage through it, she mentally picked out her outfit. Just inside her bedroom door, a sharp pain rose without warning in her head. Automatically putting her hand to her head, she felt the wet and became instantly aware of being hit by something really hard. The instant surge of fear smothered the pain.

"Sorry for the rude welcome, but I always have the upper hand that way." Fallon grinned scarily at her.

On the floor, she scooted on her butt in reverse in

a feeble attempt to flee. She had to do something, anything. He came at her again with what he used the first time he hit her—a book. Rolling just in time to avoid the blow, she saw it was David's book in hard cover.

"Oh, you noticed the weapon. I thought you'd appreciate the irony." He laughed maniacally as her eyes went wide at his obvious crazed character.

"David." Emma whispered. "Where's David?"

"It would have been too easy to take him out and then have at you, so instead I knocked him out cold. I figure he'd never let himself live it down if he were downstairs taking a little nap, while I did whatever I felt like with you. Ready?" He stepped forward.

She rolled from his side as he lunged for her, taking out his legs. Toppling over, he missed her narrowly, but shot his hand out to snag her shirt while she scrambled to get away. As he held on tightly to the wad of material in his hand, he inched toward her, changing hands on her shirt in order to grasp a bundle of her hair with his right hand.

Getting to his feet, he pulled her up with him by her hair and, as he had at the bookstore, led her like a horse with her hair as the reins.

She had no idea what he intended to do and where he was going, but Emma decided she wasn't going without a fight. Concentrating on the visual in her head, she followed his direction slowly enough to give her time to study it. As confident as she was going to be and running out of time, she kicked her left foot up and back hard, connecting with him. She didn't think she got a direct hit on the groin, but she got enough to cause him to let her go.

Whirling around quickly, she aimed and raised her foot again to ensure a direct hit. Instead of achieving it, he turned in time for her to kick his leg. She spun to run and instead was tackled like a running back. Falling hard, she heard her head hit the floor. It was very weird—she heard it like it occurred elsewhere and she felt it very much like it happened to her.

The wooziness of her head being hit twice was beginning to muddle her thoughts and efforts. Her body betrayed her by suggesting she give up, but her mind kept flashing images of David and her mother through her mixed-up brain. She knew then that she didn't want to give up the life that flashed before her, she wanted it. She wanted it badly enough to not give up, even when she was facing astronomical odds.

"Try that again and I'll take my time with you." He raised his hand to slap her face.

Realizing that this was her chance, she reacted without thinking it through—the only way to survive some situations. Emma was able to get her knee up fast enough and hard enough to knock the wind out of him and toss him backwards.

Ignoring the pain screaming in her head and the dizziness threatening to thwart her escape, she hopped up, hoping she would have time to get through the door—it was a start. The doorway gave the illusion of receding further into the distance throughout her effort.

Struggling for air, he saw her get up. He made

some sort of effort to move, with the only result being a grunt.

She slammed the door behind her as she stumbled to the stairs.

David's eyes opened, but his vision didn't focus. His mind was as fuzzy as his eyesight. Hearing a tripping noise on the stairs brought the unpleasant memory back, shocking his vision to functional, yet still blurred. He had to fight the nausea and dizziness to get to the stairs, where he saw the most beautiful sight—Emma.

"What did he do to you?" With clenched teeth, he spoke quickly.

"No time for that. He won't be down long. Phone." Emma used furniture for support and got to the phone. Her vision was blurry, but between the limited eyesight and knowing where the numbers were from the layout, she got it dialed. Watching David from the kitchen doorway, she saw him seriously think about going up the stairs and blurted out, "No! I can tell what you're thinking and—"

"What's your emergency?" The operator's voice sounded like she used a megaphone and had Emma's head pounding loudly with the reverberation of the echo.

"This is Emma Benson and Fallon is in the house, he's—" She heard him on the stairs and dropped the phone. "David."

They spun and ran through the kitchen. David grabbed keys on the way out. Once out the door, which they swung shut with them, the truck—safety—was in sight.

Barely in the truck, they saw Fallon flying out the door and stumbling toward them. David forced the engine to life, put it into gear and gunned it forward. The truck hit Fallon, tossing him several feet like a doll.

Stunned by the events and the flood of pain rushing back into their bodies, they slumped in their seats, not so unaware that they didn't each keep their eyes on Fallon.

After what seemed like ages, but wasn't, the most welcome sound was heard. The blare of the sirens grew louder by the second until they raced up the drive. Only then, did David and Emma catch their breath and allow the weariness to take over. Their hands clutched each other's and linked them more than physically for longer than the moment.

* * * * *

"Debbie wants to go into Cranton to hit some of the nightlife that's nonexistent here—her words, not mine. I don't know if I'm really up for that." Emma took a bite of the juicy, giant burger that they served at the quaint diner.

"Think about it. It'll be exciting." David grinned as she took another giant bite of the burger. "You know, that burger's not going anywhere. You don't have to eat it all at once."

"Very funny. I'm starving." Emma continued to chomp down again.

"When aren't you?" Chuckling, he took a bite of his own fully loaded burger that he was thoroughly enjoying.

"This from the man who can suck down a steak in five minutes."

"Yeah, but men are supposed to be pigs."

"Out of the mouth of the beast himself." Pleased with the repartee, she curved her lips gently, full of contentment.

"Now that we've hashed that out and you left me on the chopping block, let's get back to the question at hand—the nightlife."

"I believe I've had my share of 'exciting' lately. Let's tell her another time. I would love to double with her and her new obsession. Just not this weekend."

"You're right. I'm just in such a hurry to get things back to normal. Sorry, I'm rushing it." His motives were worthy.

"You should be." Emma teased him. "No, it's just that I feel more like kicking back and relaxing this weekend. I want to enjoy some of this spring weather before it gets too hot to enjoy it."

"Let me take care of the plans and you just show up. Tell Debbie another time and to have fun with Ted."

"I like a man who takes charge *sometimes*." She tried to give him a serious look and failed when she burst into a full facial grin, which led to an all-out laugh.

"I'll show you how I can take charge." David leaned across the table and planted a serious kiss on her, erasing any trace of laughter.

Emma felt even more pleasure than the laughter, although vastly different. Still, she tried to convince her brain that this man was with her, because of her. There was no more need to protect, but he was still here. The nagging thought of how long he might stay usually crept in, before too long. Just enjoy, Emma, she thought.

David walked her back to the bookstore. Kissing her on both cheeks, he couldn't stop there because he found her mouth so inviting. The velvet wonder of her sweet-tasting mouth sucked him in, without any awareness outside of it, until he felt a firm pressure on his chest.

The pushing didn't do it, not like she was trying that hard. David was immovable. Finally able to pull back, Emma glared at him playfully. "Gotta go."

"See you later." He stood right where he was, making her do the leaving.

"Okay, bye." Emma entered the store revived and rejuvenated from lunch, yes, but mostly from David.

At five o'clock on the dot, David strolled into the bookstore. "Hey."

"Hey, yourself. What are you doing here? I thought you were busy writing." Puzzled, she hoped nothing was wrong, she'd had enough of that in the recent past.

"Officer Stewart asked us to stop by. I thought this would be a good time—you're off work and in town. So, shall we?"

"Sure. I wonder what he wants." Emma grabbed her purse in a hurry, for she needed to find out soon what was up. She'd had enough suspense lately.

"I don't know, but I sure hope it's not anything about Fallon's sorry ass getting out on a technicality."

Almost simultaneously they jumped in the car, swinging the doors shut. David was back to driving his car again.

Emma was grateful that he had the truck that night. "I doubt it. Don't borrow trouble where there is none." Her outlook had gradually changed to the optimistic. "Weird, usually you're telling me that." She rather liked the new Emma. It wasn't that she would have called herself pessimistic in the past, just practical—to a point very nearly reaching over that line.

"I don't mind roll reversal." He kept his eyes forward.

She could see the smirk on his face as he made the turns to the police department.

Once inside the tiny building that served as a short-stay jail (overnights mainly) and base for the officers, they announced their arrival to the clerk at the front desk. Officer Stewart appeared in seconds. "Hi. How are the two of you?" Not allowing an answer, he went on. "You look great. Amazing what not having a crazy person on your tail can do for you." His laugh didn't match his persona, it was high-pitched squeaks coming out of a big guy.

Cop humor, she thought. The laugh was contagious, causing her to follow suit. "You're right about that. It does wonders for me, I know that much."

Stewart went around the functional metal desk to his seat. With his hand out palm up, he gestured to the chairs on the opposite side of the desk from him. "Have a seat."

David piped up a bit uptight. "So, what's this

about?"

Recognizing stress when he saw it, Officer Stewart said, "Nothing to worry about, just wanted to give you all the information we know on the case. The notes we knew were written by different hands, but we didn't know how it connected or if he had someone else write it to throw us off. The fact is that the two notes *did* come from different sources and not because Fallon had someone else do it for him. The first one was actually written by Jim." He saw the instant shock.

"Jim? What? Why?" Emma couldn't get much out that made a lot of sense.

"I'll tell you." Officer Stewart fiddled with a pen. "That whole event was on him. He killed the animals and set them out. He wrote the note and left it for you."

"But that doesn't answer the why." David was befuddled as to why Jim hopped on the criminal wagon. "Did Fallon recruit him or something? And how do you know it was Jim?"

"Fallon had nothing to do with what Jim did. We found a journal that detailed Jim's plans. He was more than miffed that you were always with Emma. He saw it as your fault that she didn't go out with him. *You* were the one in his way. It was his attempt to scare you out of the way."

Emma was stunned, but wanted to understand, *needed* to understand. "But that note was along the same lines as the other messages."

"Yeah, that's what we thought also. Just coincidence since they were each attempting to convey a similar message, but for different reasons. Anyway, Fallon was watching your house and saw the whole thing done by Jim. It pissed him off so much that he chased him down in the barn, beat him to a pulp getting answers out of him and broke his neck when he got what he wanted. Fallon didn't want anyone encroaching on his territory and *you* were his territory, according to him."

A baffled look covered Emma's face. "So, that explains that part, but what did Fallon have against us?"

"It ticked him off that David butted in at the bookstore incident and he just wanted to finish what he started, as he simply stated. Like it was some sort of art project he was attempting to complete. You weren't targeted personally to begin with, except the fact that you're a female and you were at the store, closing alone." He took a giant swig of his coffee.

David was concerned about Fallon still being a breathing member of the human race. "No way he's getting out this time, I hope?"

"No, they've got an extra special eye on him that sports all sorts of additional security measures. Try to put this in your past and leave it there. The only way he can hurt you now is if you let the experience take over your life. And I know that I'm sitting here and it's easy for me to say, but it's a very true statement and I would give it your all in the attempt. Anyway, I thought you'd want to know." Officer Stewart stood, holding out his hand to shake each of theirs.

Emma took his hand, his grip firm around hers, and shook. "Thank you. It does help to know. Not that it makes any sense, but not knowing would make it harder to put behind me." She turned to leave.

David stepped forward. "Thank you. Let us know if anything changes. We appreciate all your work in the matter." They shook hands and nodded their heads in respect for one another. "Bye."

"You two take care of one another."

Emma and David left in a contemplative state pondering the odd paths that life took them down.

* * * * *

The yellowish-green of early spring had now morphed to a solid green color—the color of summer. Full blooms covered the flowering plants, foliage was thick and full, the sky blue and the air warm on this day nearing summer. Emma loved the spring, with new life bursting forth across the countryside.

The horses, Duke and Daisy, carried Emma and David down the tractor path to the wide-open fields. With no particular place to go, they let the horses trot around, in any direction, after one another playfully.

Having their fill of riding, they dismounted and allowed the horses the run of the pasture. "Let's walk." David said.

"Sure." Heading toward the woods she couldn't help but smile. She was happier than she'd been in a very long time. She was convinced that it had everything to do with David.

He took her hand in his along the way. In the silence, a contentment and peace that could only be enjoyed shone through. Not far into the woods, he swung her around, catching her in his arms. He couldn't believe his luck in having Emma in his life. Some people search their whole life for someone special—he hadn't been looking at all. But he found it—love. He found her—Emma.

David ran his hands up her sides, to her upper arms, onto her neck, to the sides of her face. Her skin was warm and soft. Pausing there to stare into her deep, ocean-blue eyes he could see respect, loyalty and, most of all, love. His fingers dove into her thick mass of hair tousled by the riding, as he lowered his mouth, barely brushing her lips with his.

Emma's insides jerked, not outwardly, each time he planted a whispered kiss. Her hands roamed his arms of muscle—from more than poking keys on a keyboard—his taut back and neck and through his hair. As the intensity of his kissing increased, so did hers. Back at his waist, her hands slipped under his shirt, sliding fluidly across the ripples of muscle and flesh. She could feel those muscles flinch and tense.

David pressed her to him without ceasing the onslaught of kissing. The flaming trails her hands and fingers left blazed through his hazed brain. He reveled in the feel of her, of how she woke his body, how she responded to him. It took him and gripped like a vice.

Emma felt the movement of his lips and a vague sound like talking without the actual words making their way into her consciousness. She coaxed her mind to concentrate.

"Marry me."

"Huh?" Now she was focused. Their lips were separated.

"Marry me. Now. I don't want to wait. I want to start a life with you this minute." He kissed her again— deep, warm and with all the emotion he had within him.

Giving her system a second to catch up, she pointed out the obvious. "There's no clergy here."

His intensity didn't ease. "I mean 'now' in the relative sense. So, what will it be, my little smart aleck— my heart's desire or my heart in shards?"

"Yes. Yes, I will." Her heart was full. She'd known she'd say yes if he asked. It was a no-brainer.

David lifted her so they were eye to eye. His arms encompassed her tightly, as he kissed her like he'd never kissed her before, with the knowledge of Emma being wholly his. "I'm never letting you go."

"You had better not."

Called Home

About the Author

Gloria Schumann's love of reading romance novels brought her to a love of writing them. Keen observation of the human condition is her favorite pastime. A highly developed interest in relationships and what makes them work are central in her writing. Gloria resides in Austin, TX with her husband and three children.

http://gloriaschumann.yolasite.com.

Called Home

If you enjoyed *Called Home* consider
these other fine Books from
Savant Books and Publications:

A Whale's Tale by Daniel S. Janik
Tropic of California by R. Page Kaufman
The Village Curtain by Tony Tame
Dare to Love in Oz by William Maltese
The Bahrain Conspiracy by Bentley Gates

Scheduled for Release in 2010:
The Jumper Chronicles by W. C. Peever
Mythical Voyage by Robin Ymer

If you are an author or prospective author who would like
to be published contact Savant Books and Publications at

http://www.savantbooksandpublications.com